I0598745

Pulp Confidential

AIRSHIP 27 PRODUCTIONS

Pulp Confidential Volume One
"Scared Pretty" © 2016 Tim Bruckner
"The Missing Beauty" © 2016 by Derek Lantin

Published by Airship 27 Productions
www.airship27.com
www.airship27hangar.com

Interior illustrations © 2016 Rob Moran
Cover illustration © 2016 Rob Moran & Warren Montgomery
Editor: Ron Fortier
Associate Editor: Fred Adams Jr.
Marketing and Promotions Manager: Michael Vance
Production and design by Rob Davis.

ISBN-10: 0-9977868-2-5
ISBN-13: 978-0-9977868-2-8

Printed in the United States of America

10 9 8 7 6 5 4 3 2 1

VOLUME ONE
TABLE OF CONTENTS

SCARED PRETTY
BY TIM BRUCKNER

Wallace Wallerson had been in the business a long time. A *very* long time. His career began when his father, the well known comic actor Sam Wallerson, was appearing in an off Broadway play, *Baby Steps.* Just before Sam was to go onstage and deliver his famous *"So, what do you think, baby?"* monologue, the head of the prop baby broke off. As the curtain rose, Sam grabbed his son from his wife's arms who had been nursing her son in the wings, and walked on stage. Baby Wallace was in such a state of breast milk stupor, he barely moved. Sam, holding Wallace up to within a few inches of his face, began the monologue. The baby seemed fixated on his father's large red nose, trying several times to suckle it. The punch line was in sight. The audience saw it coming and started to chuckle in anticipation. Sam titled his head and scrunched one eye, looked at the audience and then back at his son and rolled it out.

"So, what do you think, baby?"

Wallace blew a spit bubble the size of a baseball and then turned to the audience, right on cue. The audience went wild. Wallace crapped his diaper. From the day on, Wallace was in show business.

As a boy Wally appeared in dozens of plays. His most notable, *The Brats of Broadway,* caught the attention of a talent scout for an up and coming moving picture company, Calliope Pictures. He began film work in New York in 1928 appearing in forty-three one-reelers. His most notable part as a child actor was that of Knuckles, the big boned bruiser in the Back Alley Boys. As Knuckles, Wally wore an oversized cap pulled down so far on his head, it made his ears stick out. The producers decided it would be a good gag if they glued fishing line to the back of his ears so when he looked into the camera and gave his signature sneer, a grip off camera would tug on the line making his ears flap. The audience loved it. It became such a popular bit in the Back Alley Boys movies, whenever he appeared on screen, all the kids in the audience would put their fingers behind their ears and flap them at each other. At the height of the craze, the jazz singer, Happy Mills recorded a song called, *Ears Today, Gone Tomorrow.*

As Wallace's career ascended, his father's career began to slide. Sam had an insatiable appetite for all things bad for him. The worse they were for him, the more he liked them, which in part, may explain his family's sudden move to California. Things got better. Sam found work. Wallace found work. Sam got less work. Wallace got more work. After four years in Tinsel Town, Sam, a serial philanderer, contracted syphilis and died. Wallace contracted to Mammoth pictures.

Wallace had been under contract to Mammoth Films for twelve years. In that time he'd appeared in thirty-one films. He was the comic, good natured sidekick. Playing against his tough guy appearance made him successful and famous. Now, at the ripe old age of forty-nine, he sat across the mammoth desk of the president of Mammoth Pictures, the one and only Joe Templeman. Wallace had been summoned to Joe's office for a face to face with the big boss. In his dozen years, Wally had met the man twice, casually, at publicity functions. At their first meeting, Joe called him Warren.

Wallace was ushered into Joe's office by a very pretty young woman with the longest eyelashes he'd ever seen. They looked like miniature harem fans whenever she blinked. Joe was on the phone and motioned Wally to sit, he wouldn't be on long. For fifteen minutes, Wallace watched and listened to Joe talk to a well known actress's agent whose appeal had more to do with her cleavage than her acting abilities.

"She'll do it," Joe said into the receiver that looked like a fire hydrant in Joe's small hand.

Wallace heard the muffled voice of the agent through the ear piece.

"Listen to me, you little cocksucker," Joe said. Wallace was stunned at how unnerving, if not downright frightening, it was to hear this little man threaten in his often mocked, high pitched rasping whisper. "She'll do it, or she don't work. Yeah, I know she's got three more years on her contract, and she can wait that out in her little love nest in Brentwood, eating pussy. Yeah?! Listen to me. The only ones that don't know are her adoring fans. It wouldn't take much for *someone* to leak it to the press. The hell I wouldn't. Don't forget what happened to that German bitch."

The agent was yelling so loudly into the phone, it sounded like he was at the other end of the room. As Joe listened, he looked up at Wallace, winked, shrugged and held up a hand to indicate the call was just about over. Wallace smiled back and felt his bowels loosen a little. Joe smiled and looked as if he'd just eaten his rival's baby.

Joe's expression changed as the tone of the agent softened. "Okay. Okay," Joe said in reply. "See, it's always better to talk these things out like gentlemen. Sure. Are you kidding? Can't wait. I'll see you at mom's. Okay. Bye-bye."

Joe put the receiver back in its cradle and looked over at Wallace. "Wally? I ain't much of a small talk guy, so I'll get right to the point. How's the wife, by the way?"

Wallace smiled and nodded.

"Good, Good. That's good to hear," Joe continued. "I got a picture I want you to star in."

"What?" Wallace said, stunned.

"I read the script last night," Joe said. "At first I thought of using Roy Hardgrove. But then I thought, hey, wait a minute, putting him the picture would be telling the whole story before the folks even walked into the theater. I mean, Roy's a nice guy and all, but he's got the range of a washtub bass. If you know what I mean."

Wallace nodding with uncertainty.

"Here's the beauty of it. Genius, if I do say so myself," Joe said, obviously pleased with himself. "You are the wrongest guy for the part. Completely wrong. Its genius."

"Genius?" Wallace said

"Fucking genius!" Joe said, beaming. Smiling broadly, "You want I should tell you what the picture's about?"

"Yes, Mr. Templeman, I'm very curious," Wallace said trying not to sound as panicked as he was.

"Enough with the Mister," Joe said, "Call me Joe. So it goes like this…"

For the next forty-seven minuets, Joe Templeman acted out the script of "Scared Pretty." Wallace was surprised at how good his new buddy Joe was at laying out the story. He did various voices that kind of sounded like the same person with varying degrees of a cold. When he did Wallace's part, he hoped to God he sounded nothing like the little man's impression of him, a cross between tough guy Hunter Steel and everybody's favorite aunt, Bessie Walters.

"So, what do you think?" Joe said, wrapping up. "Genius, right?"

"Well, I sure wouldn't think of me for the role, Joe," Wallace said tentatively. "I am a little worried about going so far from my type of characters. I've built a career by playing certain kind of roles and I'd worry if playing a character so far from what the public knows me as, might be a mistake. And diminish your investment in me." He added, trying to find a way for this guy to see what a really dumbass idea it was to cast him as a psychotic killer.

"You let me worry about that stuff, Wally," Joe said, brushing Wallace's concerns aside. "You just let me worry about that. You're going to be great. And guess who's directing?"

"Who?"

"No, guess," Joe said. "Go on and guess."

Wallace heard the question turn into a command and guessed. "Randal Hughes?"

"Hughes? Hell no. There ain't a horse or an Indian within a thousand miles of this script. I want someone who understands, you know, *art*. I want this picture to be more than a movie. I want this picture to be *art*. Know what I mean?"

Wallace knew exactly what Joe meant. A disaster. A career ending disaster. The end of a forty-nine year career.

"John Drexler!" Joe announced as if he'd just revealed the mystery of the Holy Trinity.

"But he's English," Wallace said, "He does all those swash buckling, damsel in distress pictures. I don't think he's done one that's supposed to have happened in this century. In his movies, everybody communicates through carrier pigeon. I don't think he's ever used a telephone in a movie. Has he?"

"That don't matter, Wally." Joe pressed on. "In fact its better that way. You ain't never played a bad guy and he ain't never done a story since there was electricity. It's perfect."

"Genius," Wallace said, trying to force a little enthusiasm in his voice.

"Absa-fucking-lootly!" Joe said.

Wallace slumped back in his chair and saw that he'd rolled the brim of his hat into soda straw.

"Did I mention you'd be starring?" Joe dangled the carrot. "You never starred in a picture before. Am I right? And with a starring role comes a star's salary."

"What are we talking? Wallace asked, finding the enthusiasm he lacked moments before.

"Your last picture. You worked with David Masters. Know what he got?"

Wallace knew exactly what Masters had been paid. He knew because Masters told him every other minute. Once, he told him how much his salary converted to Pounds and Francs.

"Here's the script", Joe handed Wallace a script that must have been at least two inches thick. "Go. Read it. Talk it over with the wife. Get back to me. Tomorrow. Before ten. My home number is on the title page. Tomorrow by ten. Okay? I got a tee time at ten-forty."

Joe's corner office was huge. The walk from the desk to the elevator seemed to take twenty minutes. The elevator doors closed in Joe's private elevator, and Wallace stood there in a kind of daze, looking at the single down button and wondering if there was symbolism in the single button being the only direction he could go from here.

He took the long way home, down the beach and up Sunset Blvd. to Bel Air. He drove on auto pilot. If he turned down the part, his life at the studio would be over. His contract would run out in less than a year. He'd seen the writing on the wall; it was a wall only the most powerful or hopelessly blind could not see. The days of the all powerful studio system were numbered. Maybe not so soon he'd have to worry about it. But this business was as predictable and dependable as the weather. The famous fell, just a little farther and just a little harder, but fall they did. If he got on Joe's shit list, that would, for all intents and purposes, be the end of his career. He could move the family to Spain or Italy, where he'd be a big fish in a small foreign pond, but the idea of it made him queasy. Tony Broadstreet did it. Had to do it. Watching *Blood of the Martyrs* was as painful as a kick to the nuts. To add insult to injury, they had dubbed Tony's voice with an actor who must have read the script phonetically. There was Tony, up on screen in a wig that looked like it had once been the business end of a mop, speaking dreadful lines in stilted English, in a voice not his.

Of course, if he accepted, it would be virtually the same end but down a different path. He'd read the script and go from there.

•••

The Wallerson house was not ostentatious. It was big. Not lacking in land. But it was comfortable and welcoming. And he felt some of his angst and anxiety melt as he drove up the drive. His wife of twenty-one years was outside picking pears from one of the fruit trees she tended to as if they were her children. She heard him come up the drive, turned and waved. What did she ever see in him? He was a big, lumbering, clumsy man, not well educated, a man of very simple tastes with a face that, if the truth be told, even his own mother found difficult to love. They could not have been more opposite. She was beautiful, petite, cultured, sophisticated and smart as hell. He waved back and pulled into the garage. He got out of the car, script under his arm and a knot in his stomach to rival the Gordian.

"What did his Lord and master want?" she asked, examining a pear for potential picking.

When he didn't answer right away, she turned to study his face.

"What?" she said.

He bent down, kissed her forehead and handed her the script.

"It looks like a script. Smells like a script and reads like a script," he said. "But in actuality, there between those mimeographed pages is a rock with its own hard place. And I, my dear, am stuck right between them. I'm getting a drink. You want one?"

She did. She put the picked pears into a basket, left the one she examined on the tree and followed him into the house, reading the title page.

Their favorite room, the room they spent most of their time aside from the kitchen and the bedroom was the back study. It was small, over cluttered and cozy as a cardigan and a pair of slippers. He had two glasses of wine filled near the brim by the time she joined him.

"Spill," she said, thumbing to the script.

They sat down across from each other and he spilled. He was a marvelous mimic and did Joe to a tee. They laughed until tears ran down their cheeks and then her face pulled in on itself, like all the muscles conspired to freeze whatever emotion was about to display itself.

"So?" she said, looking him in the eyes.

"So, what?" he said. "I'm fucked if I do and fucked if I don't."

"Wallace," she scolded. "Language."

"Okay. Sorry." He said. "I'm fucked in the ass if I do, and screwed up the shoot if I don't."

"Thanks. That'd better," she said. "Let's read it and see."

"Naw," he said.

"Come on," she said. "It'll be like the old days. I'll make sandwiches and get you get another bottle from the pantry. I think its going to be a long night."

"But, Marla, its not me!" he said.

"You know what's not you?" she said. "A quitter."

"Oh my Lord, that is so original" he said sarcastically. "Did you get that out of *Cliché Digest*? *Screen Writer's Monthly*?"

"I made it up all by myself, smart ass," she said.

"The hell you say," he said.

"Are you going to let a little smart mouthed Jew send you into a panic?"

"Ain't that a little like the pot calling the kettle black?"

"It takes one to know one," she said.

"Okay. Okay. My Passover Princess," Wally said. "You get the bottle, and *I'll* make the sandwiches. And no. No mayo. Mayo is a food of the Devil, everyone knows that."

Their English mastiff, Sal, short for Saliva, loped into the room, gave Wallace a wag hello and followed Marla into the pantry. Sandwiches consumed and half the second bottle of wine down, they cuddled on the couch and started on the script.

Ten pages in Marla bookmarked their place, closed the script and looked at Wallace. "Dammit, Wally, it's good," she said. "Who's the writer?"

"Don't know," Wally said. "Never heard of him."

"But its not just cause I'm half in the bag, is it?" she asked. "I mean, it's really good."

"It's good," he agreed. "Just not good for me."

They'd reached the part in the story where the psychotic killer has his victim strapped to a table in his basement. He delivers a monologue in which he describes what he plans to do to her. They read the dialogue together, in silence.

"Read it," she said. "Read it out. You know, act it."

"I'm too drunk and the shit is too weird," he said. "It gives me the creeps, truth be told."

"Truth Smuth," she said. "Scare me. Go over there," she said pointing to a high back arm chair near the fireplace, "and scare the crap out of me."

"Don't be dumb," he said.

She started making clucking noises. Soon the clucks sounded less like a chicken and more like a chicken saying the word "chicken."

"Don't be so juvenile," he admonished.

"Don't be such a chicken," she said. "Go on, Mr. Chicken, sir."

He got up, taking the script from her a little more forcefully than he meant to. She gave him a look. He looked back with a "sorry" in his eyes and went to the arm chair and settled.

"Go on," she encouraged.

He read the first few lines silently. Looking around, he found a nub of a pencil on the end table near the chair and made a few hasty notes.

"I can't, Marla," he said. "I feel stupid."

"But you felt smart making love to a seal in *Alaska Bound*?"

"I was supposed to be drunk in that scene."

"You're drunk in real life now. Come on, Wally. Do it for Marla."

"I'll only do it for first person Marla. I refuse to perform for third person Marla."

"Deal," she said.

He sat back, took a deep breath and a deeper drink of wine and began.

Somewhere around the eighth or ninth line something changed. Something in his voice? The set of his shoulders? His eyes? Something in his eyes had changed. And for the first time in their life together she was afraid of him. Not afraid. That wasn't it. She realized that he was gone from her. Her husband of twenty-one years was no longer in the body that occupied the chair across from her. Someone else was. A mad man, crazed with the need to murder, inhabited his body. And the stranger that looked like her husband, sounded like her husband, but was not her husband, frightened her.

"Don't, Wally," she said. "Stop. Please."

"The drug I've given you will… yes, there it is, I see it. The drug I've given you paralyzes. You won't be able to move." He said. His voice darker, deeper, devoid of feeling. No. Not devoid of feeling. There was a kind of joy, a kind of delight in it, which made the words themselves all the more unnerving. "You'll be able to blink. Yes, that's good. And your heart will continue to beat, you'll continue to breathe. That's because I've given you just the right amount. A little less, and I'd have my hands full, wouldn't I? A little more, and you'd be dead… before I was ready for you to be dead. But, this paralytic condition does nothing to minimize pain. It might, I think it even heighten it."

"Wally, come on," she said, hugging her knees. "It's not funny. Come on, now honey. Stop."

"Do you see this?" he said, gesturing as if there was something in his hand. "I get them from a supplier in Switzerland. The very best. It takes the body a full thirty seconds to feel the pain after the cut. You have to admire the Swiss."

"Wally!"

"Half your skin will be gone before you feel it"

"Wally! Stop! Wally!"

"You know, I've been told that when the air hits an exposed muscle, the pain is indescribable. You pass out from pain like that, you know. I mean you would. But I can't have that…"

"Wally, goddamn it! I'm leaving. I'm not going to… You are such a… such a…"

"Damned good actor? Brilliant, really. Oscar, here I come."

There was a long moment of silence. He raised his head ever so slightly and looked at her through the fringe of his bushy steel-grey eyebrows… and smiled his lopsided signature smile.

"Fuck you!" she screamed. "Fuck you, you fuck, you."

He gave her his best *aw shucks* smile.

"You are such a dick!" she yelled. "Such a dick. I mean, I asked you… I asked you to stop, honey. You were scaring me. I was scared. You fuck head. Godamnit! "

"You know," he said, with a Cheshire grin, "I think I could do this. I really do."

He started to get up and come to her, but she was on her feet and launched herself at him, landing in his lap, with the precision gained of two decades of target practice.

"You are such a dick," she said, kissing him.

At ten the next morning, on the dot, Wallace called Joe at his home. Marla was on the other line, in the library. Watching each other across the hall, they heard someone on the other end say, "Templeman residence."

"Hi, this is Wallace Wallerson, is Mr. Templeman available?"

"Just a moment, I'll see."

A couple of minutes later and Joe was on the phone. "Hello," his tone was brusque and he was clearly irritated. Wallace shrugged is shoulder in answer to Marla's "What the fuck?" expression. "How did you get this number?" Joe barked.

"You gave it to me, Joe," Wallace said.

"Who the fuck is this?" Joe growled.

"It's Wallace Wallerson, Joe," We met yesterday about Sacred Pretty?"

"Wallace?" Joe said, softening.

They heard Joe yelling to someone if not in another room, then certainly in another time zone. "It's Wallace Wallerson, you dumb bitch. Wallerson! Not waffle-sun! What were all those English lessons for?! Goddamn it!"

"Sorry, Wally," Joe said, apologetically. "That's what I get for marrying a Spic. So, you read it?"

"Yep,"

"And?"

"That character is so different from what I usually play…"

"I know! I know! That's why you doing it is so genius."

Marla looked at Wallace cross-eyed and let her tongue dangle out of the corner of her mouth like the village idiot he played in, *One Road Home.* Wallace frowned at her, trying not to laugh.

"Yep," Wallace said.

"Yep, what?" Joe said.

"Yep, you're right, Joe. It is so genius. I'll do it."

"Great! That's great!" Joe said excitedly. "Come to the office tomorrow. I'll have Drexler there. I want you guys to meet and get started. Great, Wally. This is going to be great." They heard someone saying something to him in the background. "I got to go, Wally, the current Missus is threatening to shop herself to death. But it never works, she always survives. See yah."

As soon they heard the click, Marla ran to him. She went airborne. He caught her and they hugged. "My leading man," she said, nuzzling his neck.

"My leading woman," he said, kissing her neck.

She leaned back in his arms and looked at him, "God, that was awful."

"My leading man was better?" he said.

"Take me to bed, handsome, and I'll help you with your delivery."

And she did.

•••

Wallace was escorted into Joe's office by the same young girl for his first meeting with Joe. There was something different about her. She still had those languidly lush lashes but her eyebrows seemed to have gotten darker and longer, the ends almost touching the corner of her eyes. Wally smelled fresh baked blintzes as soon as he stepped off the elevator. In the far corner of Joe's vast office was a sitting area. Wallace approached. Two high-backed leather chairs had their backs to him. Joe's chair sat across from them against the wall, a portrait of him hung directly above him. In the painting, he looked like Napoleon's Jewish Uncle. The table in front of him was laid out with coffee and pastries and a teapot and cup.

"Wally," Joe said cheerily, "meet John Drexler."

A immaculately dressed man got up from one of the chairs, stood and extended his hand. "Mr. Wallerson, I'm a big fan." His accent could not have been more upper crust. Each word seemed to have been molded to perfection by the hand of the Queen Mother.

"Me too," Wallace said, taking the man's slender hand in his own.

They shared a polite laugh and Wallace took his chair as Drexler sat in his. Wallace had him pegged as a fairy. He was the most delicate man he'd ever met, and he'd met some. It was impossible not to, in Hollywood.

They made small talk for a few minutes, commenting on each other's work with Joe chiming in with box office figures, letting each know, in his club fisted way, that both of them, the actor and director were equals.

"I'm ever so pleased you've decided to do this, Mr. Wallerson. I really am. Just delighted," Drexler said.

Wallace didn't know what to say. He smiled and gave his best, *aw shucks*, head tilt.

"I got to go take a dump," Joe said. "You guys get to know each other. If I'm not back in a half an hour, call my wife and tell her she's right. I am full of shit." With that, he got up and jogged to a door across the room. They heard the lock engaged and a sound from inside the small private bathroom most often heard in a barnyard rather than a Hollywood executive's personal commode.

They sat there, in an uncomfortable silence, Wallace sipping his coffee, looking into it as if he expected to find something swimming in it.

"We'd best be honest with each other, Wallace." Drexler said. Gone was the clipped precession of his Lord of the Manor accent. In its place was the rough edged cobble of working class London.

The surprise on Wallace's face was as obvious as a second nose or a third eye.

"I know," Drexler said. "But a bloke's got to do what a bloke's got to do. It's a long story, mate. But I just want to say before Joe gets back. I didn't want to do this movie. And I didn't want to do it with you. But then I read it. Me and the wife read it last night."

Wallace scrunched up his face in consternation.

"Yes, I'm married. Three kids. Again, long story," Drexler said. "As I was saying, but then me and the wife read it through. And it changed my mind. Honestly, mate, I can't see anyone else pulling it off. Joe, for once, is right."

"Marla and I did the same thing last night," Wallace said. "I really think I can do this. I think I can."

"Me, too," Drexler said. "But I want you to know something,"

"Okay," Wallace said.

"I've done so much swash-buckling shit, this is about the only way I think I might have a chance to get out from under it," Drexler said. "And I think I can do this too. But not alone. I don't know how you've worked with other directors, but I'm suggesting we try something different."

"Like," Wallace said warily.

"Like, a collaboration," Drexler said. "We're both heading into uncharted waters, mate. We're either going to sink or swim, together. So, in the spirit of covering my scrawny limey ass, I intend to share the glory or the ignominy with you, Wally. Yeah?"

"Yeah," Wallace said in his note-perfect Londoner's accent," I don't fancy moving to Spain and have myself dubbed by some the producer's boyfriend."

The shared a restrained laugh and shook hands.

"So, what's with the get up?" Wallace asked, gesturing to Drexler's attire

"Who do you think has a better chance of directing a Hollywood movie?" Drexler asked, "A retired jockey, gone stage actor, gone burlesque comedian, or… a tight assed British fag".

"Gotcha," Wallace said.

They heard the bathroom door lock disengage. Joe came ambling out, "You do not want to go in there," he said, thumbing over his shoulder. "You guys have a good sit-down?"

Drexler gave him a cheery thumbs up.

"A very interesting pairing, Joe," Wallace said. "It's genius."

Joe beamed. "Wally," Joe said, "Let me be candid, if I may?"

"Candid away, Joe," Wallace said.

"No offense, Johnny, but you're not exactly the kind of director Wally here is used to working with," Joe said.

"I assumed as much, Mr. Templeman," Drexler said in a crisp, Oxford accent.

"Okay," Joe said. "You might be a little light in the loafers, as far as Wallace is concerned. For me? I say live and let live. But I just hope that ain't going to be a problem. Is it boys?"

"None whatsoever, Joe," Wallace said.

"Ditto," Drexler said,

"Good. Very good," Joe said. "So, I want that you guys should get the fuck outta here and do a little brain storming. I did the hard part, putting you two together. The rest of it, it's gonna be up to you. Mind you, it's my picture. Get it? Mine. So, you don't do nothing that's gonna make me look stupid, or nothing. But I'm a generous guy."

Drexler and Wallace looked at each other.

"I saw that, you fucks," Joe said. "But look, I want this picture to kick ass. So that's what I want. Do what you have to do to make that happen. I got Lois Gibson casting. You guys work with her. She's the best. But no one gets in this movie you don't want in this movie. That's my promise. Now, get out of here. I got a studio to run."

The two men rose, shook hands with Joe. Thanked him and headed for the door and the private elevator. Just as Wallace's hand grabbed the knob, Joe called out to him. "Wally, hang a minute, will ya?"

"Shall I hold the lift, Wallace?" Drexler asked.

Wallace looked to Joe.

"Hold away, my good man," Joe said in a painfully poor English accent. "This *shan't* take long."

Drexler left, closing the door behind him.

"You okay with all this, Wally?" Joe said, eyeing the door.

"You mean because he's light in the loafers?" Wallace asked.

"He's about as light in the loafers as you are," Joe said, "You think I'd leave you guys alone and me not being able to hear everything? I trust you Wallace, but there's a lot at stake. And I don't trust nobody that much."

"You got the place miced?" Wallace asked.

"Of course, you numb nut," Joe said. "I'm asking if you're okay with letting that two faced limey bastard direct you in this picture. You ask me,

"…that ain't going to be a problem. Is it boys?"

he's a little twisted. But he's good, better than the shit I give him to direct. So, all that secret identity stuff's okay with you?"

"You knew?" Wallace asked. "I mean, you knew before?"

"What do you think?" Joe said.

"I don't know what to think," Wallace answered.

"Good," Joe said. "Just the way I like it. You tell anyone about any of this?"

"Marla," Wallace said.

"Anyone else?" Joe asked.

"Nope."

"Good," Joe said, "Don't.

"Why?"

"You want the part?" Joe said.

"I thought I had the part," Wallace said.

"Big tits sink ships," Joe said.

"It's, loose lips sink ships," Wallace corrected.

"That don't make no sense," Joe said "Just don't say nothing to nobody that don't need to be told. You know what this town is like. It's the Capital of Cannibals. We'd eat our young if we didn't need some poor sap to take care of us when we're too old to give a shit. Just keep it to yourself. Okay?"

"Sure," Wallace said.

"For me, that limey flamer is the right guy for the job. For you?"

"A bloke's got to do, what a bloke's got to do," Wallace said in a near perfect impression of Drexler, the London tough.

•••

Roy Hardgrove was a star. What he lacked in range and skill as a actor he made up for with presence, good looks and a body builder's physique. If a war needed winning, a nation needed saving, Roy Hardgrove was your man.

Roy sat in his *star chair*. For all intents and purposes, it was a throne. Its back was high and grew wider as it ascended. The arm rests were broad and blunt ended. Intricate carved molding accented its outline in dark, richly rubbed walnut. The most striking feature of the chair was its four large lion's feet legs. In contrast to the chair's formality, Roy demeanor was the epitome of casual. His legs crossed at the knee, an elbow propped up on the arm rest. It was a look he perfected when he played Richard the Lion Heart in *The Prince of Mystery*. At the sound of approaching footsteps, he turned his head slightly to present his famous profile.

"You heard?" Roy's long time agent, Paul Davis, said, easing the door closed behind him as we entered Roy's vaulted ceilinged study.

"It's a small town, Paul," Roy said. "An actor farts on Sunset and his agent smells it while he's having lunch on Beverly. Of course I heard."

"Not to change the subject, but where is she?" Davis asked.

"Where she's been since four-thirty," Roy said. "Passed out on the couch in the sun room."

"On her own?" Davis asked.

"She started out on her own," Roy said. "I just pushed her across the finish line."

"You're going to kill her one of these days," Davis said.

She was a young actress by the name of Peggy Monrose. The latest in a long line of aspiring actresses who believed that Roy Hardgrove was her staircase to stardom instead her spiral to oblivion. Not all of his consorts had been so willing to indulge his predilection for narcotics. But Peggy was more than willing, which was starting to put Roy off a bit. Where's the fun of corrupting innocence if it could be offered up so cheaply? It wouldn't be long, Paul knew, when he'd have to arrange for the young lady's exit. Usually, a check and a bus ticket were enough to get them gone. Sometimes, however more was needed. That *more*, was never discussed but mutually understood.

Roy smiled and shrugged. "Is Joe serious about Wallerson?"

"Seems to be," Davis said. "He's got Drexler directing and they've gone to Gibson to cast. Not sure who's producing, but knowing Joe, probably Atmont or Ellis."

"Correct me if I'm wrong, Paul," Roy said, "but wasn't that part supposed to be mine?"

Paul Davis turned to look out the picture window at the traffic snaking its way down Sunset Blvd. Dusk streaked the sky with flamboyant bands of hot pink and blaze orange. A red MG caught his attention and he followed it with his eyes. The top was down. The driver, a woman, had a bright yellow scarf tied around her head. Davis thought she looked like some kind of flower.

"Paul?" Roy said, watching the man's back as he rolled the ice around in his drink.

"It was supposed to be," Davis said softly.

"How did Joe even find *Sacred Pretty*?" Roy said.

"I'm not sure," Davis said, turning back to Roy.

"So, what are you going to do about it?" Roy said. The look in his eyes made Davis shiver. Sure, he'd seen that look before. Millions of people had seen that look before. It was that very look, that penetrating, slightly crazed stare that had made him famous. But that was acting. This was not. Davis knew the difference and knew to take it as it was meant. A threat.

"I don't see what I can do," Davis said, apologetically. "He is the head of the studio, after all. I can't very well say, *hey, Joe, you know, Wallace is the wrong guy for that part. But you know who would be great? Roy Hardgrove.*"

"A guy like Joe," Roy said, "you have got to have some leverage."

"He doesn't give a shit about that," Davis said bluntly. "He takes a perverse joy in bad publicity. He writes a big check, donates it to crippled kids or some army cause and all, and I mean, *all* is forgiven. And really, Roy, who cares about what Joe does? The public hardly knows who he is."

"What about Wallerson?"

"What about him?" Davis said. "He's just what he seems to be. There ain't nothing there."

"I want that part, Paul," Roy said. "I want it. And you're going to get it for me."

"But..." Davis started.

"I... want...that...part."

Roy Hardgrove got to his feet. Reflexively, Paul Davis took a step back. At six foot–four, two hundred and fifty pounds, Roy was an imposing figure. His barrel chest and broad shoulders had been the hook on which most impressionists hung their routines. For a man of Davis's stature, it was a little like having a tank amble toward you whose intentions are unclear, at best.

Davis took another step back.

Roy matched it with another step forward. Not more than a foot apart, he clenched his fist and extended his index finger, firmly pressing it into the middle of Davis's chest.

"Get me that part," Roy said in a low, threatening rumble.

Davis swallowed the bile working its way up his throat and said, "I'll do what I can."

"I know you will," Roy said. The smile that curled the corners of his mouth made the hardness in his eyes all the more terrible. "I mean, you kind of have to," he said in a light friendly tone. "Don't you?"

•••

"Lois Gibson," Lois said picking up the receiver on the third ring.

"Hey, Lois, This is Paul Davis," Paul said.

"Hello, Paul," Lois said. The friendliness in her voice was replaced with a cool professionalism. "What can I do you for?

"I hear you're casting *Sacred Pretty*," Paul said,

There was an awkward pause. "Yes," she said. "I am."

"Sounds like its going to be a hell of a movie," Paul said. "Drexler directing and Wallerson starring."

Another pause. "Yes, Paul," she said. "I'm a little surprised you know about this project. It's been kept under pretty tight wraps."

"You know this town," Paul said. "There's no secret too expensive to share."

"So, what can I do for you, Paul?" she said. "Since the lead has already been cast, I don't know how I can help you. And even if it weren't, I don't think your boy is right for the part, anyway. He's a little too larger than life to play your average sadistic killer."

This was a swipe at Roy Hardgrove's penchant for playing great men of history, biblical and secular. And the few times he ventured afield of those roles, the effect was the same. In what was supposed to be a light romantic comedy, Roy played a house painter who had fallen desperately in love with an Italian countess played by Lola Bardilino. One reviewer summed up his performance this way; *Roy Hardgrove's latest film shows another dimension of the actor. Unfortunately for the film and audiences, it's one dimension. All the comedic turns arise from Lola Barilino's sublime performance and, inadvertently, from Roy's stumbling.*

There was no love lost between Lois Gibson and Roy Hardgrove. Roy was an up-and-coming actor and Lois had just been promoted to assistant casting director. He wooed her. He screwed her. And got a co-starring role in a film he really shouldn't have even read for. He made the most of that part and it put him on the map. And then, for all intents and purposes, he forgot who Lois Gibson was.

Then, it was onto Lois's boss, a man by the name of Jersey Osborn. Osborn, a married man with four children, had also been wooed and screwed by Roy Hardgrove. That raison d'être resulted in Roy's first starring role. It also led to Osborn's suicide. Osborn was Lois's mentor from her first days in the business. She took the loss very hard. Harder and more bitter still when she discovered it was Paul Davis, Hardgrove's agent, who put the screws of revelation to Osborn to induce him to give Roy the converted leading role of Pontius Pilat in the film, *The Crucible and the Cross.* Paul had the conveniently short memory of those who enjoy power, money and success. Lois had the elephantine memory of the righteously wronged.

"To be honest, Lois," Paul said. "I agree. I don't think Roy is the right actor for this role. Audiences would have a hard time believing John the Baptist was a sadistic killer."

The role of the Baptist for which Roy received an Academy Award nomination.

"I was calling about the part of Katia," Paul continued. "Have you cast that part yet? I was thinking that maybe May Harrold would be perfect for the part."

"No, Paul, not yet," Lois said. "We're looking at a lot of girls. But to be honest, Paul, she's not even on the long list."

Another pause. This time on Paul's end.

"What would it take to get her on the short list?" Paul said at last.

"A miracle," Lois said. There was a lightness; a very faint humorous note in her voice.

Another pause. A longer pause.

"Paul?" Lois said, wondering if he's hung up the phone.

"You know, Lois," Paul said, forcing a matching lightness into his own voice. "I think I just might have one. In fact, I'm sure I do. Thanks for your time. I'm sure we'll be talking again real soon." He hung up.

Despite her years in the movie business and having a personal detestation for scenes where a telephone conversation had ended and one of the participants looks at the receiver after the line had gone dead, Lois did just that. Caught herself doing it and laughed to herself. It was a short laugh.

May Harrold was a young, very pretty, very sexy, very one-role actress, managed by her mother as if her mother were managing herself. She'd appeared in four films and made an impact in each. When she was on screen, you could not take your eyes off her, which was why a select number of major stars, veterans, to be kind, refused to work with her. She had *presence,* as one critic reported, but not much talent. But she was almost more famous for the dress she wore at a SAG awards dinner. It was low cut and loose fitting. At a table with Beth Banyon and Cyril Jacobs, she reached across the table to pick up her wine glass exposing her right breast and revealing a very pink and very erect nipple. The maneuver was caught on film... *accidentally.*

•••

Wallace and John Drexler where in the elevator after their meeting with Joe. Wallace filled Drexler in on his private chat with the studio head.

"Doesn't surprise me in the least," John said. "Not in the least."

"It's been nothing but surprises for me," Wallace said. "You'd think I'd be savvier, after all these years."

"You'd think you would," John said.

They decided to leave the building by different exits. Joe seemed more concerned about keeping the business under wraps after today's meeting than he had when he first pitched it to Wallace, and they reasoned if Joe was concerned, they'd be wise to share that concern with him.

"Call me later," John said. "We'll come up with a workplace where we can brainstorm, away from the prying eyes of the press."

"I get the feeling it's not the press we have to worry about," Wallace said.

They shook hands and agreed to touch base later that day.

Wallace's favorite place to get some thinking done was in his car. No one would ever expect to find Wallace Wallerson, star of stage, screen and radio, to be behind the wheel of what his wife called, the Clunker. He'd had it since his early days in Hollywood. When he was feeling a little full of himself, or when Marla thought he was getting close to the brim of being THE Wallace Wallerson, he'd go for a drive in the Clunker, and just the smell of its interior, a mix of cigar smoke, stale beer and petrified pastries would bring him right down to earth.

He stopped at Limelight Liquor, off Gower, and bought a bottle of Carlo's Premium Chianti, a buck and a half. Twenty minutes later he was out of the Clunker and sitting on a park bench. Warendale Park, two blocks off of Sunset, was a place of sanctuary for Wallace Wallerson. He hadn't been there more than ten minutes when he heard a greeting that warmed his heart and tugged at the stings that gave it music.

"Walrus!" a raspy, whiskey soaked voice called.

"Moose!" Wallace answered, and turned to see a thin small, grey figure of a man amble toward him.

They'd worked together as extras in silents. Because of their dichotomy, they were often hired together. Frank Moze was a year younger that Wallace and twice the actor, as Wallace told it. Moze came from a long and venerable line of stage actors. His kin had worked with the Barrymores and Moze's father helped Lon Chaney Sr. construct the brace he wore in The Hunchback of Notre Dame. Moze was that rare breed of actor who could make you cry while you were laughing, and laugh amid a stream of tears. If you asked him, how he did it, he'd say, "You just got to put yourself in the other guy's shoes, and lace them up a little tighter." That was Moze.

Moze had two enemies; alcohol and women. He liked them both equally. Only the alcohol reciprocated in kind. Wallace went on to work in talkies. Moze went on to live in the park. Moze became Moose. Wallace became Walrus. Despite the hundreds of dollars Wallace spent in trying help Moze move from sleeping under the stars to sleeping with the stars, this park is what Moze preferred. It took a long time for Wallace to accept it. And a little longer still for it to be okay. But now that he was, seeing Moose was like being home, in an odd sort of way.

Wallace handed Moose the paper bag with the bottle of Carlo's Premium Chianti in it and mimed a toast.

"Ah," Moose said. "The good stuff. You know, Walrus, you keep this up and you're going to spoil me."

"Nothing is too good for you, honey," Walrus said.

"Thanks, dear," Moose said. "So, I hear your doing *Sacred Pretty*."

Walrus looked at Moose as if someone had just introduced him to Jesus, and his band The Second Coming.

"How the FUCK, do you know that?" Walrus said, gobsmacked.

"Come on," Moose said. "This town? I know which way Roy Hardgrove hangs. Come on, don't be dumb."

"Holy Christ," Walrus said. "News travels fast."

"News travels slow, my friend," Moose said. "That script has been around when I was in the biz. I read it. Fuck, I auditioned for it. I read for Oscar Heinrich. I was going to play Alphonse."

"You would have been a great Alphonse," Walrus said.

"Hell yes, I would have killed that role".

"What happened?" Walrus asked.

"Everyone wanted to do it," Moose said. "Wanted to make that movie. But then, nobody wanted to make that movie. They liked the idea of making 'art', but they didn't want the red in the debt that making art would cost them. I knew the writer. I actually helped write some of the dialogue."

Moose quoted. *"I don't like what you do. I don't like what you make me do. I like it even less that you make me want to do what I don't want to do. But I love it when I do it. I'd kill you if I could. But then, it might be easier to kill myself."*

"Well, fuck me," Walrus said, in admiration.

"Don't you wish," Moose said. "But you'll be great, Walrus. You really will be great."

Moose took a long pull from the paper bag wrapped bottle. It was like watching a drowning man breathe again. Time had worked on Moose. Time seemed to work overtime on him. He was a year younger than Wallace but looked, easily, a decade beyond him. The Grim Reaper had marked him.

"So, tell me about the writer," Walrus asked. "Leo Chapman? What was Chapman like?"

"What the hell are you talking about?" Moose said, wiping his mouth with the back of his sleeve. "Leo Chapman had about as much to do with writing *Sacred Pretty* as I do writing the Declaration of Independence. That script was written by Ethel Rosen. Start to finish, it was hers."

"Who the hell is Ethel Rosen?" Walrus said. "Never heard of her."

"Good God," Moose said. "You are, without a doubt, the dumbest man I have ever met."

Walrus gave him a look which only compounded Moose's evaluation.

"Ethel Rosen?" Moose said, as if talking to a two year old. "Ethel Rosen is Rita North. Ever heard of her?"

Asking Wallace if he'd ever heard of Rita North was like asking a baseball fan if he'd ever heard of Babe Ruth. Without a doubt, Rita North was the most famous actress Hollywood had ever known. She had made ten films; five silent and five talkies. And then, she walked away. Why, was an endless source of gossip, speculation and debate. The more outrageous the supposed reason, the more credible it became.

Rita North left the movie business because:

She had fallen in love with the wife of a prominent Hollywood executive. The wife in question wouldn't leave her husband and so Rita, broken hearted, went into seclusion.

She had fallen desperately in love with the husband of a famous Hollywood actress. The husband in question, fearing he'd be separated from the lifestyle to which he'd become accustomed, refused to leave his wife. Rita, broken hearted, went into seclusion.

She had undergone a risky plastic surgery in a desperate effort to hold onto her beauty. The surgery was an abysmal failure, and so, deformed, she went into seclusion.

She'd had a stroke

She'd become a drug addict.

She'd gone crazy.

She was living as man.

She was a man, living with a man who lived as a woman.

She was working for the government as a spy.

She was a spy for another government and had been arrested.

She has been kidnapped by spacemen to breed.

She had been kidnapped by spacemen to become their queen.

She had had herself frozen so she could be thawed if ever a decent script could be written for her.

She was sick to death of the shallowness of Hollywood and the constant invasion of her privacy. But more importantly, the need to invest her time, her life, in the pursuit of creative outlet that she could be proud of. The soul saving pursuit of art. She gave up the fame, the glamour, the notoriety, to become a writer.

Under her real name, Ethel Rosen, she had written four screenplays, three of which were made into fairly successful movies. Two plays, one of which did a run of twenty-three weeks on Broadway. And two books, one of which had become a play, adapted by Leo Chapman, who adapted the play for a movie.

It was assumed, when *Sacred Pretty*, made its way through the various corridors of script considerations for the major studios, that the author was Leo Chapman. And who was there to contradict it? Chapman knew Ethel Rosen would never risk being found out, and so, he let the lie lie. A decade or so later, the script made its way to Joe Templeman's desk. He contacted Chapman's agent, bought the script and the rest, as is sometimes said, was history.

"That can't be true", Walrus said.

"Only too true," Moose said, going for another pull on the bottle.

"Does she know?" Walrus asked.

"Does who know?" Moose said.

"Ethel Rosen, Rita North?"

"She knows," Moose said.

Walrus looked hard at Moose. "You know she knows, *for a fact*," he said.

"For a fact," Moose said, returning the look, steady and unwavering.

Walrus had been leaning forward, his hands on his knees. He took a breath and sat back, watching the clumps of clouds shred to wisps in the summer sky. Neither man said anything. Moose had seen his friend deep think many times. Off to his right he watched a couple of boys play catch as he thumbed the lip of the bottle making little popping sounds.

"She going to do anything about it?" Walrus asked at last.

"Beats the fuck out of me," Moose said. "But if I know Ethel, and I do, she'll do something. She's a little crazy that way."

"You know where she is?"

"Why?"

"Do you know where she is?" Walrus asked a little more forcefully.

"Why?" Moose said, with equal force.

"Why do you think?" Walrus said.

"Yes, I know where she is," Moose said wearily. "I see her couple of times a month. She's gets an ear and a shoulder and I get a damn fine meal.

And wine that isn't a buck and a half a bottle. And no, she won't see you. Period."

Walrus went back into deep thinking mode and Moose returned to his bottle. The two men sat in silence for a good half an hour. Faint tints of pink and orange began to merge into the white ripped blue.

"That phone work?" Walrus said, pointing to a pay phone at the edge of the park.

"How the hell would I know," Moose said. "Why?"

"I got to call Marla," Walrus said. "Tell her I'm going to be late."

Moose's eyes drifted to his friend, dragging his head with them. "No," he said flatly.

Forty minutes later Moose and Walrus were in the Clunker, snaking their way up Laurel Canyon Blvd.

Moose was on his second bottle of Carlo's Premium Chianti. At the end of the first bottle he was a little less resistant to introducing Wallace Wallerson to Ethel Rosen, a.k.a, Rita North. By the middle of the second bottle he was congratulating himself on his brilliant idea.

"You guys," Moose said, "You guys are just going to hit it off like gangbusters. Like mother fucking gangbusters."

"You think so?" Walrus said.

"If I didn't think so, would I have suggested it?" Moose said. "You got a couple of bucks on you?"

"Yep."

"There's that little market coming up on the right."

Did Wallace feel guilty about using his friend's vulnerability to further his own agenda? Probably. A little. But not enough not to do it. And he knew, deep down, that Moose wanted to. He just needed a reason. Part of Moose's problem was his uncompromising sense of justice. No one fought harder for the little guy, than *this little* guy. And it's those kinds of little guys who care too much, often receive the least amount of care. But this was going to be tricky. No one, no one, had seen Rita North for more than decade. Their strategy was simple, they weren't going to see Rita North, they we going to see Ethel Rosen. The fact that Wallace Wallerson had done ten of the twenty-three weeks in her play, *Out on a Limb and Back*, didn't hurt things. Unless she thought he stunk. And Wallace couldn't remember if he had or not.

It was a new moon. The stars filled the sky to distraction. The Clunker was driving half blind, with its passenger side headlamp burnt out. It was only after they hit the crest that they knew they'd gone too far and missed the turn off. They turned around and headed back down the hill.

Shalimar Road came up on their right. If it hadn't been for a cat running into the road, they wouldn't have slowed to miss the cat, and would have missed the road. They made the turn and wound their way up the twisting low shouldered road until they came to a dead end. 13308 Shalimar Road. The house looked like a set piece for the Count of Monte Cristo. It was dark, aside from a faint flickering light in the turret. As soon as they stopped and Walrus engaged the parking brake, Moose was out of the car, trying to find his feet at the end of his ankles.

"Let me go first," he said. "I'll give you the high sign if it's copacetic."

Wallace sat in the car, watching his friend maneuver up the walk way, up the dozen or so carved stone steps to the front door. Moose knocked. A coded knock that brought the flickering turret light down past several Gothic widows to the first floor. The door opened. A shape with more curves than Mulholland stood with an oil lamp held high. She was dressed in white satin. Her hair was long, dark and wavy. Her face was veiled in shadow. The woman and Moose talked for awhile. Wallace knew body language, and by hers, she was not happy. Moose's' body language was pretty slurred. After some back and forth, she turned and disappeared into the darkness. Moose turned to where he assumed Wallace was and gave him the thumbs up and then followed the woman into the house.

•••

Each step closer to the front door eroded Wallace's confidence like high tide on a sandcastle. Had his impetuousness gotten him into more trouble than it was worth? This was a stupid idea. What did he hope to accomplish? Of course, he was intrigued and for sure, he wanted to have a look at Rita North. But then what? Leo Chapman's deceit had nothing to do with him. And Moose said she'd more than likely take care of it in her own way. This was none of his business. And on top of it all, he was feeling damn guilty for using Moose. He knew Moose well enough, when Moose and alcohol teamed up; drink was dynamite and Moose the fuse. He paused at the door and looked in. He could just make out the glow of light beyond the room. He could leave now, and the worst of it would be, Moose pissed and stuck without a ride and Walrus's integrity still intact.

"What are you doing?" Moose said, coming toward him. "She's waiting."

Moose saw the look in Walrus's eyes. "You get cold feet on me now, I will murder you," he said. "Besides," he whispered, "she remembered your performance in *Out on a Limb* and thought you were good. Come on." He motioned for Walrus to follow him as he headed down the hall. Wallace reluctantly followed.

Her face was veiled in shadows.

The room was white and everything in it was white. Coming from the darkness of night and the cave-like darkness of the living room, into the white room was like having the sun popped in behind your eyeballs. It actually made him stagger a little. Moose guided him into a chair. Sitting in a high backed white satin wing chair was Rita North. The contrast of the absolute whiteness of the room with her long dark and her penetrating dark eyes was unnerving.

Her real name may have been Ethel Rosen. She may have tried to put as much distance between her two personas as was humanly possible. But there was nothing she could do to shadow or shade the extraordinary beauty of Rita North. She actually looked younger, somehow, than her last appearances a decade or so ago. Her large, dark eyes seemed brighter and more dangerous. Her hair, although decorated with a delicate filigree of silver, was even more lush and full. Full lips that had kissed the most famous men and most likely women too, in Hollywood, were just as ripe and seductive as ever they were. She wore not a hint of makeup and was all the more stunning because of it. Wallace was speechless.

He knew he should say something, but his mind was a blank. He knew he was starring and knew, absolutely, he should stop, but he just could not make himself look away. Thank God for Moose.

"Wallace Wallerson let me introduce my friend, Ethel North," Moose said.

She looked at him. Was she scowling? He'd seen that look before. Half of the English speaking world has seen it just before she ran Drake Montgomery through with a sword. He watched her hand slowly close into a fist.

Wallace went white, as white as the satin chair in which he sat. He looked at Moose with incredulity and not a little dismay. Moose was oblivious and sat there beaming as if he had not only introduced them but was just about to marry them.

Wallace tried to appear nonchalant. But a cold drop of sweat snaked its way down his side, which made him even more nervous. By the look of her, he wouldn't have at all been surprised if she pulled out a revolver and shot him and Moose on the spot. She shot Lindsay Summer for selling pictures of her to the Hollywood Reporter. The pictures were innocent enough. Rita North in a bathing suit on Santa Monica beach. What had upset Rita was that the pictures were of Ethel Rosen. She knew her private life was part of the sale for her celebrity, but on that day, romping with her niece and nephew in the waves and building sandcastles, she was Aunt Ethel, and Ethel hadn't been part of the deal. She was a good shot. She did just what she wanted to do. The bullet passed through his calf. No serious damage. Rita settled out of court. Lindsay moved to New York and took a job with *Harper's Bazaar*. And not one picture of either Rita North or Ethel Rosen even appeared in a publication that she did not authorize.

Another bead of sweat ran from his Wallace's arm pit, down his side, to his belt line. He suddenly found is difficult to breathe.

Moose looked over at Walrus and saw the color had drained out of his friend's face. "Wallace, you okay?" he asked.

In the movie, *Shipwreck Shenanigans*, Wallace's character was in a similar situation, well, similar enough. His character, not being able to think of a way out of his dilemma, pretended to faint. He was just about to reprise the role, when he caught something in Rita/Ethel's eyes. They were smiling. Soon, her lips joined her eyes and then she laughed. A deep, smoky, throaty laugh, just as she had in her last film, The *Duchess of Brooklyn*.

"Please relax, Mr. Wallerson. You don't think I would have invited you here if I thought you would not keep my little secret a secret?" she said, the faint accent of her homeland, making music on the consonants. "I thought you were very good in *Out on a Limb*. You gave the character something human. A kind of Lenny, if you'll allow the comparison. All Craig ever played were the words. You played the man who spoke them. I saw you eight times in that role. A writer could not ask for more than for an actor to bring breath to the text and heart to the dialogue. So, I thank you."

She bowed her head as a kind of salute and Wallace felt himself lift a little out of his chair.

"You should have seen your face," Moose said, grinning from ear to ear. "For a minute there I thought you were going to go for *Shipwreck Shenanigans*."

"You are, without s doubt, the biggest shit head I have ever known," Walrus said. "Pardon my language, ma'am," to Ethel.

"I must correct you, Mr. Wallerson," she said. "That right, of the biggest shit head, belongs to me. I asked Mr. Moze to help me get you here. And he did a wonderful job. But the idea was mine."

"I've been had?" Wallace asked, looking between Ethel and Moose.

"In spades, my friend." Moose said, suddenly sounding uncharacteristically sober.

"I'm sorry, Walrus," Moose said. "I'm afraid The Clunker will smell a good deal like Carlo's Premium Chianti for a while. It's just a good thing that wreck smells like crap already otherwise you might have got wise.

Most of what you thought was going down my gullet wound up on the floor."

For some reason Wallace didn't understand, he was starting to get pissed. He'd been played and didn't like it. "So, what the fuck, Moose?"

"The fuck is this, Mr. Wallerton," she said, "I need your help."

A white cat the size of a foot stool stuck its head around the door jamb and meowed.

"Otto, meet Wallace. Wallace, this is Otto," Ethel said as way of introduction.

Otto looked at Wallace, and sniffed, decided the stranger wasn't worth the effort and ambled back from where he came.

"That is what the fuck this is about," Ethel repeated.

Wallace had never liked to hear a woman curse, partly, because they did it so poorly, but Rita or Ethel or whoever the hell she was, sounded like she'd helped invent it and he liked her all the more for it. She got up and walked to a white lacquered cabinet just to the side of her chair. She withdrew a milk glass bottle of Johnnie Walker and three milk glass tumblers, poured three fingers in each, with a little thumb on the back end, put everything back in its place and handed them out. Wallace tried, tried like hell not to notice the curves and dimples of her ass, bathed as it was in the sheer white satin. He tried. He failed. But he tried. Sitting back in her chair, she lifted her glass in a toast.

"To art. To truth," she said, "Let them never be strangers."

Moose and Walrus lifted their glasses and drank.

"You'd like an explanation," she said to Wallace. "Do you want to call your wife? This will take awhile."

Moose led Walrus to the phone. "I'm going to be late, honey," he said. "Don't wait up. You won't believe it. I'm in the middle of it and *I* don't. I'll tell you all about it when I get home. Yeah, me too. Bye-bye."

When he got back to his chair, his drink had been topped off. She waited a few minutes until the two men were clearly settled, and then began.

"*Scared Pretty*," she said," is not fiction. It happened. It happened to me."

•••

Paul Davis was waiting. It was something he did poorly. He folded his cocktail straw into a microscopic accordion. Every time the door opened, he sat up expectantly. And each time, not seeing the person he hoped to see, went back to work on his straw. He'd had a few more drinks than he really should have had. But he was okay. He was relaxed. And being relaxed helped him to assume a more human, buddy-buddy like character which he'd never really gotten the hang of. When he was a fresh faced budding actor, the only part he seemed to nab was the brainy, awkward, socially inept high school student. He was often paired with the handsome homecoming king or star athlete. The leading man was often in danger of flunking out and it was only due to Paul's character's friendship and mentoring that he got his grades up, passed, snagged the most beautiful girl in school and went on to play professional football. Or a variation thereof. He was once up for a part in a low budget horror movie. Aliens from outer space had infiltrated a small town, infecting the youth with a kind of mind-control virus. The director told him he'd be perfect for the part because he was the most unnatural human being he'd ever seen.

"You're perfect," he said."You act like you're learning how humans behave from a book or something. Did you grow up in an orphanage?"

A few cocktails helped. He didn't actually become more human, buddy-buddy like, but it made him feel as though he had. And in Hollywood, especially, perception was reality.

He was just about to hail the waitress when his waiting was over. A man about the size and shape of an industrial meat locker came in through the door. Paul was going to wave and then thought better of it. The man saw him, nodded and made his way over to Paul's table.

He sat down opposite Paul and took off his hat. It fit snuggly. Very snuggly and he almost had to pry it off his head with his thumbs. The impression of a hat band ran across his forehead, making him look like an extra in a cowboys and Indians movie. Hat removed, he looked Paul up and down and then focused on the near empty cocktail glass in front of him.

"What are you having?" the man asked. He had a strong east coast accent, New Jersey, Paul thought.

"Whiskey, soda and a splash of bitters," Paul said, looking at his glass and then looking for the waitress "You want anything?"

"Naw," the man said. "I don't like to mix business and pleasure."

Paul caught the waitress's eye ordered himself another drink, and waited. The silence, although short, was thick; a hack saw would have trouble making its way through it. The man's eyes never wavered. They sat, still and dead in his fat, flat face, fixed on Paul. Finally, the man spoke. "So, why am I here?"

Paul leaned in and began to whisper.

"Don't do that," the man said, a little annoyed, a little amused. "We're just two guys, at the bar, talking. So, talk."

"What did Murray tell you?" Paul said.

"It don't matter what Murray told me. He ain't my client. It's what you tell me that matters. So…?"

"There's a woman, Lois Gibson," Paul said. He felt the heat of his nervousness flush his face. "She works at…"

"I know who she is and where she works," the man said. "What I don't know is *why I'm here*." He said the last three words as if he were talking to a toddler.

"Okay," Paul said. He waited until the waitress put his drink down and left before he continued. "I want her to cast May Harrold in the part of Katia in *Sacred Pretty. That's* why you're here." He regretted his sarcasm as soon as the words left his mouth and took a sip of his drink.

"And how do you want me to convince her to do such a thing?" the man asked.

"I don't care how you do it," Paul said. "I just want it done." He slurred a couple of consonants and hoped the man hadn't noticed. "She's got some skeletons."

"Who don't?" the man said. And Paul suddenly felt a great uneasiness, as if this Jersey thug not only knew Paul's skeletons but knew where they were buried and had a shovel at the ready.

"Yes," Paul said. "*Who don't?*"

The man looked around the bar and then back at Paul. "Half now, half when its done."

Paul reflexively, moved his hand to his inside jacket pocket and then stopped.

"No," the man said, "I ain't going to give you a receipt. And yes, there's no way to verify I got the money or that you gave me the money or, and if you did give me the money, what's the money for."

"So, I just have to trust you," Paul said and wished he didn't sound so much like his mother at that very moment.

"Yeah," the man said, "You just got to trust me."

Paul was going to say something but the man said, "Or don't. Your call."

Paul was used to being squeezed. And he hated it. He paused for a moment, for what he thought was a face saving interlude, then reached into his breast pocket and withdrew an envelope and slid it across the table to the man. The man picked it up and shoved it into his breast pocket. His expression did not change a millimeter.

Paul was about to say something and was caught up short. "Please don't ask me if I'm going to count it," the man said. "It's not that I trust you. I don't. But I'm sure you know better than to fuck with someone in my particular line of business. Don't ask me how I'll get in touch with you, either. And don't ask me when. You'll know the answers to your questions as soon as you get your undies out of your ass crack and give yourself a chance to climb down off of that high horse. I'm leaving. You stay put. Have another drink. *Like you need it.* And then leave."

He got up, walked through the bar and out the front door. Paul felt such relief, he about collapsed into the booth. Skeletons? Did Paul have them? Did John Ford make westerns? You don't work for a guy like Roy Hardgrove and not frequent the bone yard. How many girls had he extricated from Hardgrove's life? How many directors, producers, actors, writers, boyfriends, girlfriends, wives, husbands had he pushed, prodded, cajoled, squeezed, threatened, blackmailed in the services of his one and only client? Did it bother him, the man he'd become? It used to. But power and money have a way of dulling one's conscience.

Anita Pangenelli. She was a very pretty olive skinned actress. She could dance. Sing. And, she could act. Her exotic looks, exotic by Hollywood standards, locked her into westerns, playing a verity of squaws; the chief's daughter. The chief's bride. The Indian girl who fell in love with the white solider. Or, she played the Mexican girl doing much the same things that the Indian girl did but with a different accent. Roy saw her in *Hurricane Plains* and had Paul set up a meeting. Anita was smart and ambitious. Her ambition dulled her smarts. Paul remembered their last conversation. Remembered it? It haunted him.

"When Roy gets tired of me, what happens to me?" she asked.

They were sitting in a booth at little coffee shop in Silver Lake.

"What do you mean?" Paul asked, trying to sound a little taken aback by the question.

"You think what Roy Hardgrove does is a secret in this town?" she said. "You better than anyone else know what they say about him. I want to get out before he wants me out. I won't make any trouble. I won't say anything about anything. I just want to keep working, make some movies; help my family. That's all I want. Okay?"

Paul sat back, looked at her, sipping his coffee. This meeting? This was supposed to be the, *here's a check, take a hike* meeting. Roy was done with Anita and Paul's job was to get her gone. He knew she meant what she said. He knew she meant it now, as she was saying it. But later, when the parts stop coming and she couldn't get a job hawking dish soap at trade shows, she'd be back. Hand out, willing to trade her silence for some dough. The funny thing was, as many times as he'd been through it before, he was surprised at how little they asked for. A couple months rent. Money for groceries. Money for clothes. Maybe new eight by tens so they could go out on calls again.

But Anita was smart. Smarter than most. If she came back? She wouldn't go away with rent money in her purse. She's need a big chunk of the Hardgrove bank before she'd fade off into the sunset.

He reached into his inside jacket pocket, removed an envelope and handed it to her. The expression in her eyes told him she knew what it was. There was sadness in it. For a couple of seconds replaced by anger. She took the envelope, smiling and tore it in half and tossed it at him.

"You and Roy?" she said. "You can go fuck yourselves. I don't want anything from you except to be left alone."

"Or?" Paul said, picking up the torn pieces and putting them in his pocket.

"Why does there have to be an *or*?" she asked.

"Because there always is," he said flatly.

She looked at him and then looked around the café. It was practically empty. An old man in the corner booth reading a newspaper. The waitress behind the counter trying to look like she gave a shit.

Anita leaned in. "Okay," she said. "You want my *or*? He leaves me alone *or*, I go to the papers."

"And?" Paul said trying to work up a smile but having a hard time making happen, knowing what was coming.

"And I tell all about Catalina," she said, with a genuine smile on her full red lips. "All of it."

It was late summer. Roy hired a boat to take a select group of friends to the island. He'd rented a house on the west side with staff. Roy promised everyone a weekend they'd never forget. He was right about that. The trip took a little over an hour once they got underway. It was an odd mix of people even by Hardgrove standards. Anita saw a young girl she assumed was the daughter of one of the guests. She had the look of a deer caught in headlights. Anita made of point half way across to find the girl but she was nowhere to be found. By the time the boat docked Anita was ready to head back to the mainland. She felt uneasy, she told Paul. He told her she was just being silly. Relax, he told her. Try and enjoy herself. He pointed out several of Roy's guests it would be smart for Anita to get to know.

There were a couple of casting agents, a writer and a couple of up and coming directors, a bald man with an accent named Oscar Promengala, who was going to direct Roy's next picture. The house looked as if it belonged on the beach in Hawaii. It was a large two story structure with a with a full wrap-around balcony. Beach chairs were set up in little groups under palm trees and pines.

"Let the party begin!" Roy announced.

There were two full bars, one near the main entrance and another on the second story around the back that overlooked a panoramic landscape. Someone had the radio on. Smooth, lazy swing eddied like a beckoning tide. By nightfall, everyone was pretty well lit. The smell of reefer competed with the scent of magnolia and the salt infused breeze. Before long, most of the women had gone native. Anita had never seen that many bare breasts in her entire life and such variety. Large, small, medium. High water. Low hangers. Nipples the side of dinner plates. Nipples no bigger than blouse buttons.

Paul wandered over, clearly loaded to his gills, if he had them, and suggested she might want to join the rest of the ladies in going *au nautrale*.

"Maybe later," she told him.

He left her to meander to a woman with breasts the size of beach balls who was swaying rhythmically to nothing in particular. There was no moon that night. She's never seen stars like that. They lit up the sky in luminous swaths of sparkle. It took her breath away. Someone had lit the torches, dotting the landscape with islands of light.

Then things got weird. People started pairing off. A couple of men with a woman. Three women together. A couple of men together, joined by a couple more men with their lady friends. Groups changed and shifted like copulating shadows. Anita and another girl, Joyce something, hung back. Watching. Uneasy. Considering their options.

Appluase erupted as Roy Hardgrove staggered into the center of the gathering of guests. He said something Anita couldn't make out. He stood there, hands on hips, surveying the crowd like a conquering Roman Emperor. He clapped his hands and the crowd parted as Paul led in a young girl. If she was more than sixteen, it wasn't by much. The girl from the boat Anita had seen earlier. She was naked except for a lei of white flowers around her neck. She could barely stand. Paul presented her to Roy. She bowed. Paul caught her before she fell to the ground. Roy took her by her shoulders, kissed her hard on the lips and turned her around. He tore off the cloth he wore around his waist. He was fully erect. For a man as handsome as Roy Hardgrove he had a disturbingly ugly penis.

He bent the girl over until she had to keep herself upright by supporting herself, hands on knees. The crowd hooped and hollered. Anita thought of the Christians in the Coliseum watching Caesar's thumb turn down. Roy stepped up behind the girl, lasciviously positioned himself and rammed himself into her so brutally she screamed in pain. The crowd loved it.

He rammed her. Hard. A hand on her back. His hands on her hips. A slap to her ass. His hands high over his head in a kind of victory salute. It seemed to go on forever. Anita saw she was bleeding. Blood ran down the inside of her thighs. The girl reached behind herself, putting her hand up to try and buffer Roy's thrusts and then she went limp. And then she went to her knees. Her face flat in the dirt. And then she stopped moving.

Paul rushed in, picked up the girl and carried her away. The woman with the beach ball breasts took her place. On the boat ride home, the young girl, Roy's sacrificial lamb was not on board.

Paul emerged from his memory warren to find Anita staring at him. She said something he didn't catch. She grabbed her purse off the seat of the vacant chair to her left and stood. Looking down on him she said, "You really are a loathsome man," and walked past him to the door. He turned to see her getting into her car. As she drove off, he got up and went to the pay phone located on a wall between the men's and lady's bathroom. He dropped a dime and dialed a number. When someone answered, he said, "She just left. Take care of it."

Anita Pangenelli disappeared that day and was never heard from again.

•••

She lived in the Franklin Arms. Second floor. In the back. Away from the noise of traffic. She lived alone. And for all intents and purposes, that was true. Her name was on the mailbox and the lease, just in her name. She liked her independence. It was a point of pride with her. Her mother had been little more than an extension of her father. A shadow. She was never going to be that. Never.

She was at the top of her game. True, most casting directors were women. "They had a feel for it." But few, in fact only one, wielded the power she did. So, Lois Gibson's relationship with Tom Millerson was awkward. Complicated. If she could work it out another way, she would. She tried. He left. And she abased herself to get him back. A white Jewish woman did not shack up with a Negro man. They had too much self respect, for Christ's sake. She used the phrase a lot. *Christ's sake.* She never lost sight of the irony. It made her smile. Tom was a smart man. Razor smart. He knew what he needed and knew how to get what he needed and was never afraid, never, of throwing it all away.

"Look," he said. "You want me; crave me, because I am the most forbidden fruit you can imagine. I want you too. But for very different reasons. But I want, I need my self respect more than I want or need anyone. So, if we're going to do this, we're going to do this my way. It's that simple"

And it was. At work, she was served, her needs anticipated. At home, with Tom, she served. She anticipated. And the truth? The terrible, bare faced truth? She needed to be that for Tom like she needed air. And the more servile she became, the better...the worse...the better she felt.

If he left the apartment, it was agreed he left at night, when few people were to see him. When he came back, night or early morning, for the same reason. Neither of them was stupid. If the landlord or fellow residents found out he lived in their building, with a white woman, no less? Well, it was too awful to think about. Too awful. And they'd pulled it off for two whole years. There was that one time, the old bat in 6B, had seen him leaving on a bright Saturday morning. She was going to raise holy hell. Was determined to bring hell down upon them. But it was the smell of several Ben Franklin's, and not fire and brimstone, that helped her see the wisdom of discretion and the folly of forthrightness.

The man with the New Jersey accent and a pocket full of Paul Davis's money, sat in his car, across from the Franklin Arms. He had enough coffee to float a battleship and more doughnuts and cigarettes to keep a platoon contented for the duration. He did not leave his car. He pissed in a corked jug and shit in a lidded bucket. He'd done it before. He didn't mind. Perversely, he kind of liked it. It was like being in the trenches. You put up with almost unbearable conditions, but when you got the job done, it was all the more sweet. It was the army or prison. That's what it was coming down to. He'd known guys in both and it didn't take a genius to know which door opened onto a future and which door locked you into a life that really wasn't no life at all. He didn't have to look far to see the reality of what prison life was like. Both his father and older brother were in the joint. His dad, a three time loser, was in for killing a guy during a robbery. He could have taken the guy's wallet and left with a total of ninety-six dollars. But the guy gave him lip and nobody gave Dutch Mulligan lip. Dutch shot him three times in the face. Convicted of aggravated murder, Dutch was in for life.

His brother was in for trying to steal a car with a baby in the back seat. When asked by the judge why he didn't stop when he discovered the presence of the baby, Anthony told the judge he thought it was a dog and was going to take it home after he sold the car. He liked dogs. Three years.

So, Frank went into the army and spent four years learning the one thing he would have never been able to learn out on the street. Discipline. He learned that no matter how bad things got, how much pressure he was under, how much stress and strain, he could deal with it, come out the other side of it. And go back for more. The most important lesson he got in serving Uncle Sam was control his anger instead of it controlling him. A doctor told him, while he was being patched up after a fight in the barracks, that there were two kinds of anger. The first kind was the emotional kind. You got pissed off. You yelled, harrumphed (he actually used the word *harrumphed,* Frank had to look it up), and then you settled out and walked away from it. But the second kind was the physical kind. It started of with being emotional but then the body got involved, adrenaline got involved. Made your heart beat faster. Made your muscles tighten and tense.

When it was just in your head, there was a way to back it off. But when it was in your body, chemistry made anger different. There was no backing off until you punched it out, beat it out.

"What was worse," he asked Frank. "Yelling at some guy and going home? Or beating the crap out of some guy and going to jail?"

So, the army taught him discipline and how to control his anger; both qualities made him excellent in his current profession.

The night of the third day, all the bullshit, all the stink, the sour stomach, the feeling as if there wasn't enough hot water and soap on the planet to get the grime off his body, paid off. Tom Millerson slid out of the subterranean parking garage, keeping close to the deep shadows, slid himself across the street and eased into a Pontiac. Frank waited until he saw the brake lights of the Pontiac. It was what you did. Brake, engage the clutch and then head out. As soon as the Pontiac left the curb, Frank was on him.

He would have bet real money he would end up tailing the guy to another woman's apartment. So, when the Pontiac pulled up into a parking spot at Allied Metals, he was, begrudgingly, a little surprised. He watched the guy get out, big ass thermos in tow, and head into the building. Allied Metals could not have been more average in its construction if it had tried. An industrial, cinder block slop-together like every other bundling in the complex. The fucker had a job. A real job. Son of a bitch! It was going to be a long night.

Dawn crept up on him like a purse snatcher. It was the light in his eyes reflected into the rear view mirror that woke him. Five-fifty-seven. Who, in their right mind, was up this goddamn early? Cars were backing out of driveways. Kids were lining up for a bus that wouldn't come for another forty-five minutes. Tom came out goofing around with a couple of other guys. Frank was not happy. Despite the cork and the lid, the car was starting to reek. He was not a man of infinite patience. Enough was enough. But he was a professional, he reminded himself. Later. Payback later. The Pontiac pulled out of the parking lot with Frank a couple of car lengths back. When Tom should have turned left, onto Sycamore, heading back to the Franklin Arms, he took the right. They were on La Brea, past Melrose, Beverly. A half an hour later, they were deep in Jig Town. Frank didn't have another name for it. He was sure this part of the sprawl that was Los Angeles had a name, but Jig Town was all it was ever called by people who didn't live there.

They wove through residentials until Tom turned purposefully onto Leland Ave. and into the driveway of a house in the middle of the block. Frank drove by, turned at the four corner stop and headed back, parking across the street a few houses down. Just as he killed the engine, he watched Tom getting out of the car. The front door of the house opened and two nappy headed kids ran down the walkway and pounced on the man. Tom put down his lunch pail and took them both up in his arms and hugged and kissed them as if he'd just rescued them from a well. A light skinned black woman sashayed down the walkway, stood a few feet from the man and children, smiling, taking in the scene as if she were getting ready to take a picture. Tom, his arms full of wiggling kids, walked to the woman and kissed her. He walked past her. She collected his lunch pail and followed him into the house. This spun things in a different direction. Jersey was pretty sure how this was going to play out but he had to be sure. He keyed the engine to life and headed out of the neighborhood. A few miles further out, he found a motel and got a room. He dumped the bottle and the bucket in the trash bin at the back of the motel and headed to his room. He took a long, hot shower. Wrapped in a towel, he lay on the bed and was asleep in less than ten minutes.

He woke a little before dark. He took another shower, got dressed and walked across the street to a sandwich shop, got a bag of food and a beer and got in his car. He stopped at a Sears and bought a pair of new underwear, socks and undershirt and changed into them in one of the dressing rooms. Pity the poor sucker that would find his dirty under clothes.

He was at Tom's by 9:00. The porch light was on, as porch lights lit up front doors all up and down the block. He saw the flickering light of a fireplace undulating across an expanse of drawn living room curtains. Frank never understood having a fireplace in Southern California. He caught a glimpse of Tom and his wife through a kitchen window and headed toward the Franklin Arms. He was in no big hurry. This was just a confirmation stop. When he got what he needed, and he knew he would, then he'd have to confer with his boss, and not that mealy mouthed Davis character. His real boss, as what to do next. All he knew for sure was, May Harrold as good as had the part. No way this Gibson woman wouldn't pony up. The way Frank saw it, she had to.

•••

The sun had been up for a couple of hours when Wallace drove into his driveway. He'd just dropped Moose off at the park. Moose had been chatty. He hadn't stopped talking all the way down Laurel to Sunset. Wasn't Ethel amazing? Horrific what she had gone through but she survived. She was a survivor. She turned her nightmare into art. That took courage. Facing all that, reliving all that. That took guts. And how was it possible, after all these years, she looked so damn fine. Fine! Did Walrus get a look at her ass? You wouldn't see a caboose like hers on women half her age. They said their goodbyes and made tentative plans to visit Ethel again and continue where they'd left off. All the way down Sunset toward home, Wallace's ears rang from his friend's constant jabber.

Wallace was as tired as he'd ever been. He was spent. Getting out of the car he thought, if this was a script, no one in the world would buy it. It was like Science Fiction, but without the science or the fiction. It was just too odd to be believed and yet too odd as to be anything other than the truth.

Marla opened the door as he stepped up on the stoop. She had his cup full to the brim with coffee.

"Well, Mr. Wallerson, I must say, I have seen shit, and right now, I can't tell the difference between you and it."

"Well, Mrs. Wallerson," he said, taking the cup from her, "Not to put too fine a point on it, but I feel like shit as well."

"I'm sorry," she said, "but all that will have to wait. Tell me. Everything. Leave nothing out."

"After a little sleep, honey. Please."

"Tell now," she said, ushering him into the house. "Sleep later."

She had a full breakfast ready and waiting. In between bites of pancakes, sausage and eggs, he told her, everything. He left nothing out.

Occasionally, she'd interrupt with a, "You're lying!" or "That's crazy."

When he got to the story, the real, the true story of what had happened to Ethel Rosen, tears filled her eyes.

'What are you going to do?" she asked when he'd finished.

"I don't know," he said, more serious than she'd seen him in a long time. "Marla? Honey? I really don't know."

•••

Reggie Fennel sat in a plush arm chair, a cup of coffee in a saucer in his lap, looking across the expanse of Lois Gibson's desk. She was running late, he was informed, and he should make himself comfortable. What would have made him comfortable were a pillow and a mattress. Actually, he didn't need either. He just needed a little shut-eye. He finished his cup of coffee poured himself another from the side table and wondered what on earth he was doing in Lois Gibson's office. He'd been in sixty-seven films. Not once had a casting director ever asked to meet him. Why would they? In his sixty-seven films, only two were not variations of his stock character. For one he played a blind man who was healed by a bogus faith healer. And the other, he played a one legged tap dancer. For sixty-five films, he played the same guy; sometimes a little younger, sometimes a little older. Sometimes Irish. Sometimes a European of indeterminate ethnic origins. But he was, always, the loveable rascal that amends his ways through the intervention of a daughter/son/best friend/mother/father/sibling/priest/pastor/old maid/ or an ill treated animal.

The door opened. Lois entered. She wasn't a bad looking woman. A little lean for his taste, but still surprisingly attractive, despite her best efforts, suited up in her broad shouldered professional armor. All she needed was a battle ship, Reggie thought, and she could pass for multi-ribboned military. But there was little she could do about her boobs. They saluted you before she'd ever get the chance.

"Good morning, Reggie," she said brightly.

"Good morning. Miss Gibson," he said.

"Do you know why I've asked to see you?" she said.

"I haven't a clue."

She fingered her intercom and told her secretary she was not to be disturbed.

"What do you know about *Scared Pretty*?" Lois asked.

"What should I know?" he asked cautiously.

"Nothing."

"Well, that works out grand, then," he said. "I don't have a clue what you're on about."

"How would you like to play a psychopathic killer's accomplice?"

"How would you like to quit pulling my leg?" he said, and wished he hadn't

She told him just enough. And it was enough.

"Well, Mrs. Wallerson...I feel like shit..."

"You know, Wally and I used to do the burlesque together."

"I know," a faint smile turned up the corners of her mouth. "He's why you're here."

"Well, I'll be fucked," he said, and really wished he hadn't said that either.

She laughed. "What you do on your own time, is your business, Reggie." They both laughed. "Drexler and Wallerson would like you to be part of this project. Do you need some time to think about it?"

He looked at his watch, tapped the crystal, held it up to his ear, looked at it again bringing it closer and pulling it away. "Okay," he said at last. "I'm in." His smile sent the wrinkles in his old Irish face up into his ears.

She told him he'd have to sign a *confidentiality agreement,* After she explained what it was, he signed his name, shook her hand and thanked her a few dozen times, each an improvisation on the *thank you* before it.

Lois felt pretty damn good. The best she'd felt all week. The best she'd felt in a month. How rare it was to be able to bring that kind of unabashed joy to someone in her job. He was just out the door, after a few more "thanks yous when her intercom buzzed.

"Miss Gibson," her secretary said, her voice sounding like it came from within a tin can. "There's a call for you on the inside studio line."

"Who is it?" Lois asked.

"He wouldn't say, Miss Gibson. But he sounded as if it were very urgent."

Lois paused, considering the possibilities. Only a few people had the number to that line. Tom had that number.

"Put it though, Becky."

The phone rang and Lois picked it up. "Hello?"

"Lois Gibson?"

"Yes."

"You don't know me." Lois thought. Where do I know that voice? "But we have a mutual acquaintance."

"Really?"

"Yeah," the voice said. "Tom Millerson?"

She felt cold and flushed at the same time, and panic pushed up her heartbeat.

"Who? she tried.

"Really?" He was amused. She could hear it in his voice. "Tom Millerson. The jig you've been shacking up with? The married jig with two kids? That Tom Millerson?"

Her hand began to shake. The receiver vibrated against her ear. She made a point to get herself under control, or at least sound as if she was. After a pause she said, "What do you want?"

"What makes you think I want anything?" he said. The smirk in his voice pissed her off.

"What makes you think I'm an idiot?" she shot back. "Tell me what you want or go fuck yourself."

He didn't like that and she could hear it, plain as day. "You want to know what I want?" He was right on the precipice of calling her a cunt. The way his voice worked around the question, she knew the word was hanging between them. "Here's what I want."

She thought, just say it, already. You know you want to. So do it. I've been called it and worse. And if you do, when you do, the balance of power shifts to me. So, do it. Do it.

"I want," he said in purposeful, measured tones, "you to cast... May Harrold in the part of Katia. That's what I want. And that is what you will do, jig lover."

She laughed. She couldn't help herself. "You are threatening me, willing to expose me, drag me through it, right down deep through it, so I cast that girl as Katia?" The way she said the word girl, could have just as easily been substituted for, whore, cheap ass bitch, no talent tease and... or...cunt.

"What's so fucking funny?" he said. She could hear uncertainty and vulnerability creep into his voice.

"I just want to get this straight," she said, the chuckle making her voice irritatingly musical. "All this. All this gangster, tough guy, George Raft bullshit. Threatening me. I don't know how you found out, but I'm guessing it was not easy. Stakeouts never are. All this, just so I'll cast that cunt in that part in Scared Pretty? Oh my God!" She could not hold back. She laughed until tears welled in her eyes. She got that wheezing inhale from not being able to catch her breath. It took her a good two minutes, a long two minutes, before she was able to get herself under control.

"Okay," she said. "Done."

There was a long silence.

"Okay, then," he said, trying to force the sound of victory into his voice. "Done."

"Oh, by the way," she said. Her tone had changed so dramatically, it unnerved him a little. "Tell, Paul Davis he's a dead man. He still may have a heartbeat. His lungs may still breathe in, breathe out, but in this town, with this studio, he's dead. I will personally make it my life's mission to bury him, you little runt. Now, fuck you and goodbye."

She hung up the phone and smiled to herself. Was this the first time some sleaze bag had tried to blackmail her into exchanging a part in a movie for silence? Hell no. Her first week on the job someone tried to muscle her into giving a part to a no talent kid who was sleeping with the director. Wisdom, they say, is born out of experience. Each and every rime she'd been pushed into a corner, she'd given them what they wanted. Why not? And each and every time, it was the last time that actor or actress appeared on screen. You can force opportunity but you can't force talent.

She thought about Sal Savino. Good looking, Italian boy. Eyes so dark and smoldering it was a wonder people didn't melt from his gaze. He had everything but talent. Nice boy. Very respectful, but could not act to save his life. His agent/boy friend put the squeeze on her. Not her personally, but on someone she cared about. She anguished over it. Spent many, *too* many sleepless nights trying to figure out what to do. She decided there was nothing to do but give in. Give the fucker what he wanted it. She cast Sal as the bullfighter who gets mortally wounded. What should have been an Oscar nominated death scene turned out to be comedic relief in a film that was already rife with unintended comedic turns. It was Sal's last movie. And as a bonus, it was the director's last movie as well. They, Sal and the director moved to Italy. Less than a year later, Sal was dead, shot by the director in a jealous rage.

The consequences of casting May Harrold may not be equal those of Sal Savino, but even if they were close, as they were bound to be, she'd be okay. More importantly, Katia was a minor character, she told herself. May could literally stink up the joint and not hurt the film, she told herself. Whether she believed it, she'd have to think on that.

•••

I used to see him at the park, every Friday. He might have been there other days but Friday is when I went and there he was. Reading a book. The same book. I know this because it had a very distinctive cover. I thought, he must really like this book or must be a very slow reader, I spoke to him only a few times. I think he was German. I don't know why. I was only a child. He had virtually no accent, to speak of. But it was something in his cadence, I think. He was not from Sweden, of this I was sure. He looked like somebody's uncle. You know adult men who seem out of place in amongst children, but he was not that. He was very at ease. Very relaxed. At home, so to speak. He was there so often, I stopped paying any attention to him. Oh, there's the man with the book. And then I'd go play with my cousin.

One day, he was there with a puppy. It was a mutt, to be sure. But so cute! Brown and white with a big brown circle around its eye, like Petey, from Little Rascals. We, all of us, went to see the puppy. He was so cute and playful. The other kids left, one after another, but I stayed. I was not allowed pets, and so, I was unusually eager to spend time with the puppy. Two Fridays in a row, he was there with the puppy. Fritz, I think, was the puppy's name. I became very fond of Fritz. One time, I went over to play with him, that's when he told me that Fritz was part of a litter he had and would I like to have one of Fritz's brothers or sisters? If I would like to have a puppy, I would have to select one that I liked the best. "I don't think I can have a puppy," I said. "I don't think Papa would approve."

"When he sees how cute the puppy is, he will not be able to say no." he said.

I was just thirteen. I wanted a puppy more than anything. I knew he was right.

I did not like to leave my nanny. I knew how much she would worry. I loved her very much and would not ever want to be the cause of her concern. But, I wanted the puppy more, so I followed him to his house. I was a very foolish girl. Pretty girls are often more foolish than plain girls. There is no pride in that. Contrary. When you are made to feel special, you believe, you know, that you are special. Even if there is, really, no reason for it. I was a pretty girl. But I was a foolish, vain girl. And, good God, how it would cost me.

It was a long walk to his house. Several times I wanted not to walk any farther. But he would let me hold the puppy and tell me it was not much farther and then I would get to pick a puppy to have all my own. At last, we got to his house. It was not very grand. I don't know why I thought it would be, but it was not. It was very plain, but very well kept. As we walked up the pathway to his front door, I began to feel uneasy. I think he knew this and handed me the puppy while he unlocked the door. He showed me into his parlor. It looked as if he had just cleaned it. Or, it looked as our house does after Margaret cleans. And there was that smell of vinegar and furniture polish. He showed me to a chair and put the puppy in my lap and asked if I would like some coco or lemonade. I asked for the lemonade. I was so excited about the idea of having a puppy of my own. I would be the very best momma my puppy could ever want. I would give him baths and take him for walks and teach him all kind of tricks.

He came back with the lemonade. I took a sip. It didn't taste like the lemonade my nanny makes. She makes it sweet. In my mind, I heard my father say how expensive sugar is and how lucky I was to have enough to make things sweet. So, I thought that maybe this man with the puppy did not have enough money to waste on sugar.

We sat and talked for a while. He asked me so many questions. Adults never ask children anything, so it was a strange thing to me.

"I'm sorry," I said, "but I should be going back. I think my nanny will be very worried about me. And would you be so kind to walk with me a ways, I don't think can find my way back on my own?"

"But you haven't seen the puppies," he said.

"Maybe I could have a quick look and then come back later with nanny to pick one," I said.

You know that little voice, the angel on your shoulder? That little voice was saying something to me. I couldn't make out what, but I felt her words and I knew I needed to go home. There were people on the street. If he did not want to walk back with me, I was sure someone would give me directions. I knew my address by heart.

"I'm sorry," I said again, "but I really do need to go home now."

I handed the puppy back to him. The puppy was wiggling and being naughty. The man took the puppy from me, but in a gruff manner which made me a little afraid for the puppy.

"Okay," he said. "Finish your lemonade and I will show you the puppies. Then I will walk you home and next time, you can pick out one. Yes? Okay?"

I drank the lemonade which was very bitter at the finish of it. He told me the puppies were in the basement. Walking down the stairs, my legs felt funny and I almost tripped a couple of times.

"They're over here," he said, taking my hand to lead me.

"I don't hear any puppies," I said. "Are they sleeping? Why don't I hear any puppies?"

He led me to a large cage that was draped over with a blanket.

"Are they puppies in there?" I asked. My voice didn't sound like it came from me and I was feeling a little sleepy. "Why don't I hear them?"

He held my hand very tightly. "You don't hear them," he said and pulled off the blanket. "Because they're dead."

There was so much blood. So much blood. He dragged me closer. I tried to pull back. He shoved me hard until I was pressed up against it, the metal rods digging into my chest. Eight little bodies piled in the corner of the cage, one atop the other, covered in blood and each other's entrails. Eight heads stacked in the center of the cage their eyes open, staring into nothing.. It made no sense to me. I could not understand what I was seeing.

"Pick any one you like," he said from a long way off. "This way, you can mix and match."

I felt my stomach clench and vomit was in my mouth. Tears stood in my eyes making everything look as if I were underwater. My legs dissolved under me. One of the last things I remember was the man throwing Fritz, with all his might, against the wall. The sound was terrible. I threw up as he dragged me by my hand into a darkness that seemed to be inside me and surround me. I remember hearing the heels of my shoes drag across the cement floor and thinking how upset my momma will be when she sees my ruined shoes.

•••

"It's done," Frank said.

"Really?" Davis said. "What did you have to do to her?" There was such expectation in his voice, Frank actually felt a little bad for the guy.

"Nothing," Frank said reluctantly.

"Nothing?" Davis's voice rose an octave.

"Nothing," Frank said. He was starting to get annoyed. "What's it matter what I did or didn't do, you little runt. The girl's got the part, that's what you wanted and that's what you got."

"Well, yes," Davis said. "But I was thinking maybe you might have to get tough with her or something.."

"You watch too many movies, pal," Frank said.

"But for that kind of money I thought you'd, you know, do something."

"If you want I should do something, I can start with you." Frank said. He was almost yelling now.

There was a pause. Davis said thanks. Meant no disrespect and hung up the phone. He called Roy Hardgrove the next minute.

"Its all done," Davis reported. "May's got the part."

"Good," Roy said. "I want her at my place tonight at ten."

"What are you going to do, Roy?" Davis said. "How does May getting the part get you in and Wallerson out?"

"Ten," Roy said, and hung up.

Davis went to the fridge and poured himself a cold glass of milk. It was about the only thing that settled his stomach. And his stomach needed a lot of settling lately.

•••

When Lois got home, Tom was waiting for her in the back bedroom. He was still in his dungarees and his lunch pail was open on the bed, a half eaten sandwich nestled in a clump of waxed paper. He gave her that smile. That special smile. Ordinarily, she'd walk to him, remove his shoes and socks, get him out of his T-shirt and take her time peeling off his dungarees. Ordinarily. But not this time.

"What's up, babe?" he said, patting the bed.

"Gee, Tom," she said, leaning up against the door frame, her hands jammed in her jacket pockets. "It's hard to know where to start."

His face grew grim. He didn't like her tone. Didn't like it one bit.

"You were followed," she said.

His eyebrows rose. Her eyes were expressionless.

"Followed," she said. "How are the wife and kids, by the way?" She was taunting him and the more she saw his dislike for it, the more she enjoyed it. "And what's worse, you were followed, here." There was an edge to the last word that cut. "That's not good. I had to cast a no talent cunt, in a movie I actually give a shit about. And if I hadn't I'd have lost my job, my *career*. And you, you would have been found dead in a dump somewhere with your cock shoved down your throat. That, Tom, is what's up."

He started to get up. She stood erect and put her hand up. "I'm going to the market. When I get back, you and your stuff will be gone. Don't worry about returning the key. The locks will be changed within the hour."

He stiffened and his eyes grew narrow. This was not how this worked. He put his hands on his knees. She knew what was next. He'd push himself up and launch himself at her. He'd only done it a, couple of times, but that's all it took. She'd back down. Back up and back down. She'd hang her head and look up at him, her eyebrows raised, looking at him through her eye lashes. And then, she'd say she was sorry. Afterward, he'd reward her. Let her give him a bath. Massage his shoulders. Or do that thing he liked that always made her feel dirty but did it anyway. But not this time.

"You move," she warned. "I scream rape."

She turned, picked her purse off the table by the door and walked to the parking garage, got in her car, brought the engine to life and drove out onto Franklin. She hadn't known she's been crying, until she glanced down at her lap when she was at a stoplight and saw the dark spots of her falling tears. Parking at the grocery store, she dried her eyes, checked her makeup, grabbed a cart and went in. Whenever she was upset, walking up and down the aisles at the market calmed her, soothed her. She did some of her best thinking while grocery shopping.

Over the course of an hour, she thought how she would, without a doubt, destroy Paul Davis. And putting the noose around Davis' neck would put a serious squeeze on Roy Hardgrove as well. That made her smile. When she found the man from the phone call and she would, she had no doubt that would lead back to Davis. She'd try and find a way to help Tom. Not that he needed her help and not that he'd accept it. But his wife and kids, they might. She'd been foolish and careless. That wasn't Tom's fault. He was a good man. A solid man. And she knew. She knew, he loved her. Just as he knew she loved him. But what could she do? Any other way would have led to his death. The death of a husband. The death of a father. She'd figure out something.

Her basket was half full of stuff she didn't need. Half of that was stuff she actually didn't even want. None the less, she got in line. She really wasn't paying much attention when the man in front of her, dressed in a sharp, caramel colored suit, which offset his dark features, smiled at her. She smiled back. She glanced down at his left hand. No rings. She showed teeth. He showed teeth. What a smile! As the clerk was bagging his groceries, she wondered how she could cast him in a movie. Heck, everybody wanted to be in the movies.

At first, Tom was angry. Heart pounding, pulse deafening angry. Then, a little remorse began to creep in. Just a little. But it was so colored with self-pity, it joined forces with anger and they collaborated with revenge. How to get back? How to get even? He went through the apartment and took anything and everything of value. It didn't take long. He knew where everything was. Hell, she showed him! A pillowcase stuffed with cash and jewelry still wasn't enough. He needed the hurt to go deeper. At least as deep as his hurt. He went into the kitchen, got the butcher knife, went into the living room and just started cutting, slashing. The couch, the chair. He carved *cunt* into the dining room table. He disemboweled the mattress He broke the bathroom mirror. He didn't even hear the sirens over the shattering glass.

Two officers, McCullen and Bower, stood on either side of the apartment door, listening to the rampage, their weapons drawn. It had been a shitty week. It was Friday night. The crazies were out. And there are no crazies like Hollywood crazies. Earlier, Bower had been pissed on by a drunk who was trying to get frisky with a lamp post at Hollywood and Highland. Hair-triggered by nature, Bower was ready to snap. Fuck, he *needed* to snap. McCullen tried the door. It was unlocked. He eased it open.

"Police," McCullen said.

"Police," Blower called out.

Tom was pulling stuff off the bathroom shelves. Bottles crashed and shattered on the white tile floor. When there was nothing left to destroy, and pulling up the toilet seemed just too much damn work, he leaned against the wall, near the bathtub, and felt the anger drain from him like so much soapy water after a bath. Tears filled his eyes and made bright ebony streaks down his cheeks. And then he felt something so unfamiliar, at first he didn't know what it was. It started in his gut, worked its way up into his throat and brought with it a choking feeling, like an undigested bite of Mexican food. Fresh tears began to flow. He thought of his kids, Daren, nine and Alicia, eleven. He thought of his father and remembered promising himself, as soon as he learned they were pregnant, he'd never be that to his kids. But that's what he'd become, a selfish, distant, dad of convenience. He worked. He paid the bills. He put food on the table. Put a roof over their heads. What more was he supposed to do? When he thought of his wife, what he had done to her and what it would do to her if she ever found out he'd cheated on her, again, bile rose up in the back of his throat. Lois wasn't the first. Not by a long shot. But at least she was a stranger. At least he wasn't cheating on his wife with her own sister. Mercifully, it didn't last long. But long enough for things to get ugly. So this was guilt? Regret? Whatever it was, it nearly brought him to his knees. It was over with Lois. He knew that. He looked around and saw what he had done. The damage. The brutality of it. And understood the pain it would cause. Not because he stole from her and busted a few things up. But because all of it was meant to do was cause her pain. And that's not what you did to someone you loved. And yet, that's exactly what he had done to everybody he gave a shit about; his wife, his kids, his mistress. He pulled himself together, took a deep shoulder shuddering breath and dried his eyes with his sleeve. Hunched from the weight of despair, he staggered into the living room, dragging the pillowcase behind him.

•••

After the market, she went to the liquor store and bought a bottle of gin and some tonic. Without thinking, she bought a bottle of Johnny Walker, Tom's favorite.

Really, what had actually happened? She'd been squeezed before and had caved before. Sal Savino, a perfect example. Whoever had wanted May Harrold in *Sacred Pretty* had gotten what they wanted, and it was over. She over reacted. She knew she had. She was pissed and she took it out on Tom. She'd been gone a little over an hour. Maybe he was still there. Most likely was. Tom was a strong man. A patient man. An understanding man. He'd wait until she got back and she'd apologize and things would go back to the way they were. A couple of blocks from her apartment, traffic was all but a crawl. At the corner of Grace and Franklin, a traffic cop was directing cars off Franklin, down to Hollywood Blvd. She slowed,

"What's the problem, Officer?" she asked.

"You'll need to take the detour, miss," he said, directing oncoming traffic to make the turn.

"Can I get to the Franklin Arms if I come up at it from Highland?" she asked.

He walked over to her while directing the traffic behind her to veer around her. "You live at the Franklin Arms?" he asked, putting his hands on the window frame.

"Yes. Why?" she said. She saw something in his eyes. "Say, what's this all about?" Her tone was sharp and confrontational.

"Stay here," he said, and walked back to his squad car. She could see him on his radio. He kept his eyes on her the entire time. Finally, he put the radio back in its cradle and came toward her.

"Lois Gibson?" he asked.

Her instinct told her to lie. She could lie a blue streak at the office, but in real life, she was God awful. "Yes," she said. "Why? What's this all about?"

"An officer will meet you at your apartment," he said and walked away.

It looked like a movie set when she pulled in front of her apartment building. Cop cars were parked at odd angles everywhere. An officer the approximate size of a city bus walked toward her shining a flashlight in her face. "Miss Gibson?" he asked.

"Yes," she said. She didn't like this guy. She didn't like the strut. She hated the condescending way he said, *Miss*. As if, just by her being female, he would have to take care not to use words with too many syllables.

"Please get out of the car, *miss,* and come with me."

He waited until she got out of the car and made a point, it seemed, to walk just a little behind her, in case she decided to make a break for it. But walking a pace behind made it almost impossible to follow him and she had to keep looking back to see if she was heading into the right direction. They got to the foot of the stairs that led to her apartment.

"Please wait here, miss," he said, trying not to look at her breasts, which through no fault of her own were large and very well situated.

From where she stood, she couldn't see her apartment, but it sounded like there was a small army upstairs. A series of flashes bounced around the surrounding walls like miniature lightening strikes. Mrs. Topeka, in the apartment across the courtyard from her, kept pinching back her drapes to look at the commotion across the way. During one peek-in-progress, she saw Lois standing, looking anxious. They made eye contact. Mrs. Topeka pulled her curtains closed and switched off her light. A few minutes later she ventured another look, saw that Lois was still looking at her window. Lois heard the faint click of Mrs. Topeka's security lock engaged. She was trying to process this, when she became aware of someone standing next to her. She turned to see a tall, rugged looking man dressed in a hopelessly wrinkled suit, looking down at her.

"Lois Gibson?" he asked. There was faded drawl in his voice.

She nodded.

"I'm Detective Philip Stanza ," he said. "I need to ask you a few questions. Would that be alright?"

She said it would. He gestured for her to join him on the bench that sat directly under her apartment balcony. He waited for her to sit, then he joined her. She felt like a kid sitting next to him. His eyes were dark slits of concentration. A sprig of white hair sprung from the left side of his forehead. It seemed to glow, nestled in the rest of his thick black hair. She noticed a scar that ran from it, down the side of his head and stopped at his cheekbone.

"Miss Gibson." he began. "There's been a robbery. Someone broke into your apartment just about an hour ago, we think. Officer's tried to arrest him but he resisted. He withdrew a firearm with the intent of shooting the officers and they were forced to shoot him in self defense. He did a fair amount of damage but was prevented from actually removing anything from the property."

"Someone broke into my apartment?" she asked, as if she hadn't heard anything else.

"Yes, ma'am."

"Why would anyone break into *my* apartment?" she said.

"Well, miss, a pillowcase in the procession of the burglar was filled with a quantity of valuables. It seems he knew the location of them. The damage to the apartment seems unconnected to the theft. Would you have any idea why anyone would target you personally?"

"I work for Mammoth Pictures, detective," she said. "In this town it's impossible not to make enemies."

"Does anyone specific come to mind?"

She was going to tell him to look at Paul Davis. She looked up at Mrs. Topeka's window, saw it close and then looked back at the detective. "Yes," she said. "Paul Davis."

"Is Paul Davis a Negro, ma'am?"

"A Negro?" she laughed. "No, detective. He's homo." And laughed again. 'Why?"

"The man that broke into your place was a negro," he said. "We have a tentative ID but we'll need to verify it."

She felt the blood drain from her face and she was suddenly very light headed.

"Miss Gibson?" the detective asked. "Are you alright?"

It took her a minute to run it through her mind. The dots connected quickly, but the picture they made was unclear. She put her hands in her lap and pressed the thumbnail of her right hand into the palm of her left. All of it hit her hard, like an emotional gut punch.

Tom. He was angry. He was hurt. He was a prideful man who would not let the injury go unpunished. She was sure he didn't have a gun. She didn't have one and he would have had to bring one with him if the account of the cops was right. Tom wasn't stupid. A Negro with a gun was a dead Negro with a gun. Because of their sensitive situation, Tom was committed to a low-key life. As invisible as a Negro man could be in this part of town, he tried very hard to disappear. All she knew for sure was, according the Detective Stanza, he was dead. And it was all, the break in, the burglary, the Negro killed in her apartment, it was all of it, news to her.

"Ma'am?" he said softly.

"Yes," she said. "It's all a bit much. A little overwhelming."

"Of course," he said and put his hand comfortingly on her knee. "I wonder, Miss Gibson, if you'd be up to going up to the apartment with me? I'd like you to take a look to see if anything is missing before we catalog the stolen items. We'll need to take them to the station but they'll be returned to you in a couple of days. I certainly will understand if you don't feel up to it.

She looked into his eyes and he understood the unspoken question.

"The body has been removed, Miss Gibson, its safe. I'll be with you."

She said she'd be fine. He got up, waited for her to rise and then offered his arm for support. She smiled and swallowed the tears that threatened to choke her from grief

"Thank you," she said, "but I'll be fine.

They started up the stairs, had to back down to allow a crew of men to pass laden with bags, satchels and boxes. Each looked at her as they passed her. It made her angry. There were two officers by the door as they approached. The men nodded as if to the detective and moved aside as he led Lois through the door.

"Oh my God!" she said, when she saw the devastation. Holes had been gouged into the walls. Pictures had been torn off the walls and smashed against broken and splintered furniture. The couch and chair had been gutted. Food had been smeared on the kitchen walls, the icebox door open, the icebox empty, and its contents strewn across the linoleum floor. The detective motioned for her to follow him into the bedroom. Not a piece

"Why would anyone break into my apartment?"

of furniture had been left intact. The mattress has been sliced to shreds. A white cloth, not hers, had been laid in the center of the mattress and in the center of that was one of her pillow cases stuffed with her valuables. He asked if she would look into the bathroom. He waited by the door. The light was on. All her perfume bottles lay smashed on the tile floor. The little room was heavy with the combined scents and it made her a little dizzy. Then she saw it, scrawled across the bathroom mirror, in her lipstick was the word, "Cunt".

She staggered back; the detective caught her by the shoulders. She turned into him and began to sob.

"I can't," she said between sobs. "I…I thought I could but I can't."

"That's all right," he said comfortingly, patting her back. "It's my fault. I shouldn't have asked. Do you have a place to stay?"

She shook her head.

"We can put you up at the Roosevelt for a couple of days or until you can make other arrangements," he said. He was going to suggest that she might want to pack a few things, but looking around the room, he was pretty sure the burglar hadn't left anything in any shape to be of use to her. He called to one of the officers.

"Radio the station. Tell them I'm taking Miss Gibson to the Roosevelt and have them assign her a room," he said. "She's going to need a few things," he said, motioning with his eyes at the destruction. The cop, a young man who'd been on the force eighteen months, looked a little uncertain. Detective Satanza gave him a stern look and again, called the young cop's attention to the ransacked dresser and the ripped and torn garments. The cop nodded and if the light bulb of understanding had just been switched on, saluted for no good reason, and left.

"Okay, Miss Gibson?" he said gently. "Will that be okay?"

She nodded, trying to bring herself under control. He turned her so she was now at his side. His arm around her shoulder, they walked toward the front door. Passing through the living room, trying to pick a path through the debris, something dark and shinny caught her eye. She turned. It looked as if someone has dropped a bucket of red paint on her carpet that had splattered against the wall and the hallway doorframe. She froze. The detective stopped and saw what she saw. He tightened his hold on her as her knees buckled and her head lulled limp against his shoulder. She said something. Too faint to hear. And she was out cold.

•••

Investigators determined that Tom Millerson, Negro male, thirty-nine years old, married to Catherine Millerson, father to Daren and Alicia Millerson, resident of Culver City, California, 256 Leland Ave, had broken into the apartment of Miss Lois Gibson, unmarried Caucasian female, thirty-four years old, Hollywood, California, who resided in the 1300 block of Franklin Ave. Millerson ransacked the dwelling, loading a pillow case with property belonging to Miss Gibson of cash and jewelry with an estimated total value of six-thousand-sixty- eight dollars. When confronted by officers McCullen and Bower, Millerson was directed by the officers to lie on the carpet, face down and place his hand hands behind his back to be subsequently secured with handcuffs. Millerson did not comply. He withdrew a forty-five caliber Smith and Wesson from the waist band of his dungarees and aimed the weapon at the officers with the intent of firing. Millerson verbally challenged the officers with threats and profanity. In self defense, both officers drew their weapons and discharged them, shooting the suspect eighteen times until he no longer remained a threat. McCullen and Bower, who had subsequent to the shooting, been on probationary leave, were reinstated with the full confidence of the department pursuant to the completion of the investigation.

•••

May Harrold, real name Fran Kielsler, was a very pretty girl with very little talent. She had a very ambitious mother. It's one of the oldest show business stories ever.

May's mother, Katherine, knew, in her heart, she was destined for greatness. Her second home was the Rialto Theater, two blocks from her apartment. She spent every Saturday, from the time the theater opened until closing, in the dark, in the balcony, watching one movie after another. She knew the actor's dialogue by heart. She could perform whole scenes from memory, adding sound effects and sometimes, humming parts of the score. The Theater manager, a nice older man with ill fitting dentures took a liking to the little girl and would often let her pick something from the concession counter for free.

"Where's your mom or you dad, little miss?" he'd ask.

"My mom works," she told him, "and I ain't got no dad."

She performed in every play her school put on. She played both Jo and Beth alternating performances of Little Women. She played Juliet in Romeo and Juliet and Ophelia in a much edited version of Hamlet. She was the president of the Theater Club two years running. Upon graduation she moved to New York to study with Olga Stranisginsky. She worked two jobs to pay for her lessons and even landed a small role in a small play in a miniature theater off, off-off Broadway. She ate, slept and breathed acting. But three things worked against her. Her talent as an actress was more workman like than inspired. She was told, more than once, that her performances were mechanical and passionless. She knew all her lines but didn't know what to do with them. She was very plain. Not that you had to be a beauty to work in the theater. There were lots of plain girls who were doing really well. It was that even her plainness lacked character. But her biggest problem was her over-reaching ambition and her arrogance. If she didn't get a role, it was due to jealously or short-sightedness. Other actors purposely worked against her in order to make themselves look better, to compensate for their lack of talent.

In a scene from *A Madman's Mercy*, she was supposed to slap an actress out of her hysterics. In rehearsal, the actress complained that Kate wasn't giving her what she needed. Kate's slap was more like a fleshy push than an awakening slap. How was the actress supposed to react to that? Opening night, Kate slapped the actress knocking out two teeth.

At her lowest, being fired from both her jobs for an attitude problem, broke and on the verge of losing her apartment, Kate met a young actor named Thor Thorensen, a.k.a. Bobby Gamble. He was tall, blonde and handsome. He was a little slow, Bobby was, but with the support of his family, a not too distant relation to the Gambles of Proctor and, he had appeared in several plays and was scheduled to head to Hollywood for an audition with J. S. Wurley, the acclaimed agent who handled some of the biggest B-list actors in Tinsel Town.

That Bobby wasn't very bright worked extremely well for Kate. That he was painfully naive was suprising given the sophistication of his family, but incredibly useful. Their relationship began as two actors running lines together. They'd meet as his apartment in the evening and work on scenes. Bobby would have laid out a tray a snacks and a bottle or two of moderately priced wine. They'd rehearse well into the night. The work was gratifying and productive. A comfortable companionship developed over the weeks they honed their craft. The structure was loose. One session Bobby would have a scene he wanted to work on and the next time Kate would bring one she was anxious to develop. There were occasions when, having rehearsed for several hours and having consumed a little too much wine, Kate would stay over in the extra bedroom that doubled as Bobby's office. The mornings were a little awkward to start, but it wasn't long before that awkwardness became a natural progression of their relationship.

One evening, Kate brought in a scene she was eager to work on. It was from a play by an up and coming playwright Bobby had never heard of. Kate managed to get a couple of copies through a friend of a friend. She handed Bobby his copy, the scene earmarked with a paperclip. As she poured them each a glass of wine, Bobby read through it. She watched his reaction from the corner of her eye. She handed him his glass of wine and took her seat at the end of the couch.

"So?" she said.

"I don't know," he said. He was a little nervous, she could tell.

"I know," she said, taking a sip of wine, "I don't know what to make of it either. I mean, I know, as actors, our job is to connect emotionally with our audience. And there's nothing here," she said, tapping her finger on an open page of the script, "that doesn't happen every day in real life. I just," her she paused and looked out the window, "I just wonder if I'm a good enough, or brave enough actor to make the audience believe it."

Bobby looked down at his script and then up at her.

"It's okay," she said. "We don't have to do it. Let's work on that scene we did last week."

He took a drink of his wine and read a few pages of the scene. "It won't hurt to read it through," he said. "We can always go back to that other thing."

Reluctantly, she agreed. They both closed their eyes, focusing. A moment later, eyes open, giving each other a formal nod, they began. Bobby opened the scene.

"Why does it always have to be about love?" he read. "I don't love the ocean but it gives me pleasure to be near it. I don't love a summer breeze but it gives me pleasure to feel it caress my face. I don't love the blue bird that sings in the tree, but it gives me pleasure to lose myself in her song. I don't love you and you don't love me, but it would give me pleasure to touch your naked skin and feel you tremble under my finger tips."

The scene progressed, Bobby's character making the point that two people can find physical and emotional pleasure together without them being in love. Kate's character resists at first but eventually, agrees and to prove it, she bares her breasts for him to fondle. They struggled through the scene several times, Kate becoming more and more flustered with her performance.

"Ah, Bobby," she said dejectedly "Lets face it, I stink."

He tried to encourage her but nothing he said seemed to help. She tossed back the rest of her wine, lowered her head, took a deep breath and they started the scene one last time. They were at the last few lines of the scene.

Bobby's character says, " Do you mean it. Really. Mean. It?"

Kate laid her script in her lap and looked at Bobby in his eyes. Then started to undo the buttons of her blouse. With the last button undone, she slid the blouse off her shoulders. Looking directly into his eyes, she reached behind her and undid her bra and slipped it off letting it fall in her lap.

Kate was a plain girl with a splendid pair of breasts. They were not large but they were perfectly shaped with nipples rose tinted and excruciatingly erect.

Bobby confessed the next morning, as she cooked them breakfast, that he had been a virgin. She was his first, you know...

"Me too," she lied.

When it came time for Bobby to go to California, over his parents' objections, Kate went with him. They had planned to get married right after his meeting with Wurley. They found a little studio apartment off Santa Monica. Kate went on auditions and was cast as an understudy in a murder mystery as "the dead body." Bobby, now officially Thor Thorensen, got work as an extra in a costume picture. Things were actually looking up for the young couple until Kate got pregnant. It was one thing for the Gamble's son to shack up with this *woman* but quite a different thing for him to marry her and be saddled with her baby. Pressures were brought to bear. It took a leading role on a Broadway musical to lure Thor back to New York and a guarantee of generous finical support to prevent Kate from going with him.

The baby was born. The money stopped coming. The baby had just celebrated her first birthday when Kate learned of Bobby's death at the hand of a jealous lover. Rather than collapse under the weight of dire circumstances, Kate formed a plan.

When it became apparent, at a painfully young age, that her daughter, Fran was going to be an exceptionally pretty girl with an exceptional body, Katherine "Kate" Kiesler knew where her fortune lay. There were the requisite beauty contests and talent contests. To compensate for Fran's lack of ability, she would let certain judges peek into Fran's dressing room, as her mother stood guard, so the judge could watch the girl undress. It was a game that Fran enjoyed.

The game: Katherine would pick a place in the dressing room where Fran could pretend it was where a movie camera was set up. Then they would pick a song. And Fran, who had, from a very early age, talked of her desire to marry and have children, would pretend, would "act", as if she were doing a very special dance for her husband. How did Fran know what kind of dance her husband to-be would enjoy? Well, what's a mother for?

Fran developed early. Her mother thought there was a decided advantage to have Fran lose a few years to make her more of a stand out among girls who were still, very much, little girls. Fran took after her father in respect to her hair. He was a blond near the point of being platinum. So was Fran. And he was furry as a woodland creature. And so was Fran. Nearly every morning, Fran's mother lovingly, tenderly wielded the razor. Fran's mother could have had a career in any salon or barber shop in some of the most ritzy establishments, such was her skill. But her talents were employed exclusively for her daughter. Even now, at the age of twenty-three, May Harrold's mother denuded the actress several times a week. Because, after all, what's a mother for?

Fran, a.k.a. May Harrold, was on her way home from meeting one of the most powerful, biggest, most successful actors in Hollywood, the one and only Roy Hardgrove. They'd discussed her part in *Sacred Pretty*. They discussed her future. The discussed how he could help her become a major star. He told her what he needed to do. It was kind of like the Game, she knew so well, but with a few new twists, but nothing she couldn't handle. He also told her it was time she got a proper manager. Someone who knew the business side of Hollywood. Someone who could open doors for her, her mother could not. She saw the truth in it almost before the words were out of his mouth. It was time for her mother to go back to New Jersey and for May Harrold, movie star, to take her rightful place in the celebrity firmament that was her due. She was excited. She was over the moon. He even intimated that they, Roy Hardgrove and May Harrold might have a future, if things worked out, if she did her job right.

She'd heard of Wallace Wallerson, of course. She'd seen his movies and thought he was pretty good. She was a little encouraged, every time she saw him on screen. If a guy that dumb could be a movie star, then there was nothing stopping her. She would meet Mr. Wallerson tomorrow, him and that director, John Drexler. Drexler had directed some big movies. She was pretty sure, after *Sacred Pretty*, if she worked on her English accent, she could be in one of his films. She sure did like the costumes a whole bunch. She knew men Wallerson's age. They seemed more than willing to be *cooperative*, as her mother put it. She didn't think Wallerson was going to be any different. When she got home, it would be hard not to tell her mother about her meeting with Roy. But Roy counseled her, if her mother knew, she'd kill the thing. Better to keep mum and wait until everything was in place. Besides, who would give her that baby smooth shave if her mom took off now? She couldn't do it. She tried once and damn near cut off one of her labia. She pulled into the driveway of the house the studio rented for her, imagining what it would be like to have her hands and feet immortalized in cement.

•••

Wallerson had always been an early riser. The meeting was called for eight a.m. The first time that Drexler would meet some of the other members of the cast; Reggie Fennel and May Harrold. This was the official beginning of pre-production meetings. And rare as such meeting were; pre-filming meetings were as rare as a college graduated boxer. But Joe insisted they go through the extra work and paid for it separately, pulling from another picture's budget. There'd be many more such meetings before film rolled.

Wallerson and Drexler arrived within minutes of each other. Drexler was wearing a pale lime green suit with an apricot ascot. Wallerson took one look and said, "You're kidding."

"Appearances," Drexler said. "One must keep them up."

"You look like the fucking inside out watermelon," Wallerson said.

"Maybe," Drexler said. "But a very well dressed watermelon, my good sir."

Wallerson punched Drexler in the arm, good naturedly, and they entered the meeting room together. Reggie was already there. The other half of the bag he was in was most likely waiting to close the deal in his inside jacket pocket.

"Gentlemen!" Reggie said. "What a morning. What a blessed morning!"

He strode toward Wallerson and hugged the much larger man as if he was trying to squeeze juice from a tomato.

"Good to see you, Reg," Wallerson said, returning the embrace. "This is…"

"Oh, good God in heaven, I know this man," Reggie said, hugging Drexler. "We worked together on *The Pilgrim and the Pirate*. Lovely to see you, John. Just lovely,"

The two men embraced. Drexler gave Wallerson a knowing look over the shorter man's shoulder, and Wallerson smiled.

"All right then," Drexler said. "Let's take our places."

They each took a chair at which a script, two inches thick, awaited them.

They'd just settled in, picked up their scripts and were thumbing through them, when May Harrold sauntered in. She was wearing a pastel peach dress so sheer; you could see the lace trim of her bra and the little embroidered hearts on her panties. Introductions were made. Hands were extended and shaken. But the eyes of the three men were focused, despite their best efforts on May's peek-a-boo undergarments.

"Sorry I'm late," she said. "Mother and I had some business to attend to."

May would not bleach. She hated the smell and it hurt like hell and left her red and raw. Shaving was quick, easy and relatively painless. Today, she was meant to impress. When they were done, her mother would slide a finger over a freshly shaved place and say, "smooth as a baby's butt." For some reason, May always found this funny. Even now, after all these years, she laughed like a little girl.

The reading began. Drexler read the parts of the characters not yet cast. He wanted to get a sense, a feel, for how his primary cast would, could, work together. From the beginning, he sensed trouble. Reggie was actually better, the more in the bag he was. So, no worries there. But May... something was wrong. She wasn't there. Physically, she was more than present. But as an actor, she was someplace else entirely. She sat directly across from Wallerson. And all her attention, all of it, was focused on him. When she read her lines, she *read* her lines. It was an exercise in pronunciation. The mouth working. The voice saying. But there was nothing in there.

"Oh, I'm such a dunce," she said. "I don't know why I'm having such trouble. I'm so sorry, Mr. Drexler."

"That's all right, my dear," Drexler said. "That's what a read through is for. A process of discovery. The more comfortable you are with the material, the easier it will become. Shall we go again?"

She blushed. She actually blushed and looked sheepishly at Drexler and Wallerson. She straightened her pages, smiled, made eye contact with everyone, but saved her eyelashes for Wallerson.

There was a scene where Wallerson's character tries to convince May's character to leave the restaurant and accompany him to his lodgings. He's new in town, has an important meeting in the morning, and could use her help refining his pitch to his new, potential boss. Just as she's about to go with him, her boyfriend shows up. The scene ends with her looking longingly back at him as she leaves, her boyfriend leading her through the door.

They did several read-throughs. It was bloody awful. He knew she was not a competent actress, but Drexler had no idea she was this pitiably bad. Halfway through the fourth read, she stopped, looked up at Wallerson, and broke into tears. Tears. Real tears cascaded down her cheeks onto her open script. She put her face in her hands, sobbed, and then bolted toward the door, overturning her chair. She was out the door in seconds.

Her heart wrenching sobs could be heard echoing throughout the hallway. Drexler looked at Wallerson. Reggie looked at them both with a look of utter confusion and patted his jacket pocket. They sat there for a few moments in stunned silence; May's sobs ebbed and flowed like an ocean tide of grief and shame.

"Go to her," Drexler said to Wallerson.

"You go to her," Wallerson said. "You're the director."

"Yes I am," Drexler said. "But I'm a homo, remember?"

Reggie found Drexler's remark hilarious and doubled over in fit of laughter. In doubling over he was able to free his flask and increase his sense of purpose.

"What the fuck does that have to do with anything?" Wallerson countered.

"Look, Wallace," Drexler said. "Her problem, if you don't mind me saying, seems to be you. For whatever reason. If you can put her at ease, perhaps some of her nervousness could be settled and we can actually get something done. Eh?"

Reggie came up from his doubling over and agreed, whole heartedly. "Something done!" he said with the conviction of the ignorant.

Drexler and Wallerson looked at each other for a long moment. At last, Wallerson got up, giving Drexler a venomous look and exited the room. She was crammed into a corner, her face in her hands. Her shoulders shook in deep silent sobs. Wallerson walked up behind her and gently put his hand on her shoulder.

"May?" he said softy.

She continued in her wretched sadness.

"May?" he tried again. "It's going to be all right."

He was just about to pat her lightly on the back and go back to the reading when she turned suddenly and launched herself into his arms. Awkwardly, he embraced her. She buried her face into his shoulder and wept. Wallace was jarred by the recollection that he'd actually done a scene frighteningly similar to this in a movie called, *The Desperate Mr. Dunne.* Life imitating art, he thought, and held her with a little conviction.

Between tear induced gasps, she said she was sorry. She didn't know what had come over her. It was just, just that, she was such a big fan. Admired him so much. So, very much. To have the opportunity to work with him. Act with him. And to have her admiration, her nervousness, rob her of her meager talent. Well… it was all too much for her to bear. She would go in there, right now. And tell Mr. Drexler, she could not go on. After that, there was a litany of "sorry's" and a waterfall of tears. She held him tight. He felt her breasts, her nipples, through his vest, to his skin as if they were hot spots of punctuation. And, in spite of himself, his body responded. He ended the hug. She was reluctant to let him go. He disengaged himself with some difficulty, put her at arm's length and looked into her unnervingly blue eyes.

"Look, May," he said gently, "This is my first starring role, and I'm going to need all the help and support I can get. Believe me, kid, I'm not worried about you. You'll do swell. If there's anyone to be worrying about, it's me."

She looked at him as if he'd just quoted the bible in a Baptist church.

"But…" she ventured.

"Listen, you need help, I'm here," he said. "I know Lois. We go back a long time. She's the best there is. If she cast you in this part, then she knows you're right for it. So, let's go back in there and give them a reading old Twinkle Toes Drexler will never forget. What do you say?"

She was quick. Like greased lightening, as the saying goes. Her lips were on his while his arms were still outstretched holding shoulders that were no longer there. His instinct was to shove away. He was not only not used to such behavior but the liberty pissed him off. And yet, it wasn't altogether terrible. She smelled great. She felt great. He let the kiss go a fraction of a second too long. Then he moved her back from him, holding her shoulders and giving a light, but firm push.

"Oh gosh," she said, her eyes wide, her cheeks flush with color. "Oh, Mr. Wallerson, I'm… I'm so sorry. I just… well, gosh, thanks. Really, thanks so much."

He told her not to worry. Everything was fine. He turned to go back into the room when she stopped him, withdrew a handkerchief from her sleeve and purposefully wiped his lips. She held it up for him to see when she was finished. A bright red smear stained the white cotton cloth.

"Thanks," he said, chagrined.

They went back to the reading together. Later, both Drexler and Wallerson commented on how surprisingly good May was.

"You know, Wallace," Drexler said. "I was fully ready for her to stink. But she was not bad. I don't know what you two talked about out there in the hall, but whatever it was seemed to have done the trick."

"Twern't nothing, partner," Wallerson drawled.

"You know," Drexler said. "My dream. My absolute, dream would be to direct a western. I've been working on a screenplay for the past few years. *A Handful of Silver*. Good Lord, it's bloody. Someone gets shot, slashed or done in some horrible way, almost every other page."

"Can I read it sometime?"

"My good man," Drexler said. "I wrote it with you in mind. Can you read it? It would be an honor. And there's not a swash nor a buckle within a Texas mile."

Wallerson laughed, gave Drexler a good natured punch in the arm and they went their separate ways. May watched them go from an upstairs office. She thought about Roy Hardgrove. He was old. At least he was to her. There was something a little spooky about the guy. But he had power. And a shitload of it. And she was going to get as much as she could from him before giving him the brush off. He wasn't so special. He was a man. He might be one of the switch hitters. She was pretty sure he was. But he had a dick. And that's all she needed him to have. The poor dumb fuck thought he was using her. By the time he figured out it was the other way around, it would be too late. She blew a kiss to Wallace Wallerson as she watched his car leave the parking lot. Men were all the same. Simple. She knew men. Women? She just didn't get them at all.

•••

Marla was waiting for him when he drove up the drive. He waved when he saw her. She didn't wave back. Guilt crowded around him like a football huddle. But there was no way she could know anything. No way. Still, he felt shamed and dishonest as he smiled broadly, parking the car near the front door.

She didn't wait for him to get out of the car. She almost ran to the driver's side and opened it just as he killed the engine.

"Wally!" she said excitedly. She pulled an envelope from her skirt pocket and shoved it at him. He took it and read the return address.

He read," Saint Anne's Orphanage."

She was all energy. Lightening in a bottle. She practically bounded from one foot to the other. He opened the letter and read. He read it again and then looked into her eyes. Tears made her dark eyes shimmer. He felt his own eyes fill.

"Oh, Wally," she said. And squeezed herself onto his lap, the steering wheel pressing into her hip. "Oh, Wally," she said again, buried her face into his shoulder and wept.

They'd pretty much given up hope of ever having children. After the third miscarriage and a long bout of guilt and depression Marla and Wally faced the painful reality that they were not going to have kids of their own. Both of them wanted them desperately.

They were looking through the house for the first time. The real estate agent was walking Wallace through the downstairs, explaining the value of certain features, like the keyhole fireplace and the secret sliding bookcase that lead to a small room big enough for a chair. They found Marla upstairs in a room across the hall from the master bedroom. When the agent and Wallace entered, she turned to look at them; her eyes were moist with tears.

"The nursery," she said.

He walked to her; put his arm around her as her head rested on his chest. After they closed on the house and got things moved in and arranged for daily living, more or less, Marla began work on the nursery. Not knowing if it would be a boy or a girl, she settled on a *sea foam green*, the decorator called it. She painted it herself, added a wallpaper border of white and peach rocking horses, soft finished porcelain sconces and a carpet so thick and plush it was like a bathrobe for the floor.

For the past year, the door to the nursery was not opened. As much as was possible, with it being right accross from their bedroom, it wasn't even looked at. They'd talked about redoing the room, transforming it into a sewing room or a studio of an office for Wallace to write his long talked about memoir. But Marla couldn't bring herself to do it. Not that she hadn't tried. When it came right down to it, she couldn't go through with it.

They began exploring possibility of adoption as someone might explore the temperature of a lake; a toe at a time. They both had reservations for different reasons. Until they went to Saint Anne's.

It was the most depressing place Marla had ever been in. It broke her heart to see all those children, no mother, no father, sad eyed, suspicious, scared. They were ready to leave. Wallace was already in the foyer waiting for his wife and Sister Agnes to join him. He would have brought the car around, but thought that might look rude.

He waited. And waited. He was just about to go look for them when he heard them coming down the hall. Sister Agnes was carrying Marla's purse. Marla was carrying a baby in her arms.

Joy was ten weeks old. Her mother, a fifteen year old girl who currently lived in Utah with her aunt, had given her baby up as easily as if she were returning a library book. Joy had Marla's coloring, olive skin, midnight black hair and large dark eyes. And a deformed right foot that, the sisters believed, was not so at birth.

They began adoption processing that afternoon. They'd been interviewed and re- interviewed. Their family histories explored, their finances reviewed. Of course, the child would need to be raised Catholic. And there was the slightly troubling issue of Wallace being an *actor*. But, when all the formalities were done, it was now a waiting game. Would they be approved or not. Marla greeted the mailman everyday at the mailbox.

Doug knew what she was looking for after the first week. She'd be at the mailbox and could tell by his expression there was nothing from St. Anne's in his bundle of letters and magazines. Until today. He was smiling so broadly, she could see his molars. She took the letter from him, hugged him and ran up the driveway. She set the letter on the dining room table and stood, looking at it.

"Its not going to open itself," she said to herself, and with trembling hands, slid the letter opener under the flap and cut.

She read it once. She read it twice. She called St. Anne's just to make sure, double sure. Then she ran upstairs to the nursery, opened the door, walked inside and knelt by the crib and cried tears of absolute joy for Joy. For her baby. For her baby daughter, Joy.

•••

She came into the station in a yellow slicker. There was so much blood, it looked orange. She walked cane-legged to the desk sergeant, a thirty year vet named Norquist. He didn't see her at first. He saw her, but didn't *see* her. When she registered, he came from around the desk, took her by an arm and sat her down on the bench. There was blood in her eyes. He couldn't tell if was blood from somewhere else or her eyes were bleeding. At first, she stiffened at his touch, a moment later; she dissolved, trying to disappear. After several attempts, she said her name was Marlene. She didn't know where she was or how she got there. She'd been dropped off, curbside by the man that had done this to her. He wanted to make sure that she told. The man told her, kept saying, over and over, how beautiful she looked when she was frightened. The more frightened she was, the more beautiful she became. Norquist noticed she held something tightly in her white-knuckled fist. Slowly, she let him pry it from her fingers. It was written in blue ink with a fountain pen. The penmanship was so precise it had the look of calligraphy.

"I'm pretty when I'm scared." It read.

Norquist looked across the room hoping to make eye contact with anyone. Marge Franklin, the chief detective's secretary caught his gaze. A nod brought her over. She wanted to be anywhere else but there. Bile rose in her throat at the sight of the girl. Norquist motioned for her to take his place. The girl made the transition difficult, unwilling to let Norquist go. After some gentle maneuvering, they made the switch. She took the

"The nursery," she said.

girl's hand held, feeling her trembling subside. The girl, her eyes focused nowhere said, softly, "I'm pretty when I'm scared." She said it several times before she stopped breathing.

Karen Doe's cause of death was loss of blood. Her body was a landscape of fine incisions. There were hundreds of them. All close to the same depth and length. There was virtually no part of her that had not been cut. There were even slices in her scalp, the inside of her rectum and vagina. There were clean ligature marks on her wrists and ankles. Cleaned of blood and grime, she was a pretty girl, somewhere between fourteen and sixteen.

•••

Burt Stone: *Los Angeles Examiner.* May 17.

"I'm pretty when I'm scared." Those were the last words of a pretty young girl who died last night in Hollywood Police Station, in the arms of Marjorie Franklin, secretary to Division Chief Detective, Oscar Fromann. It is believed the girl was dropped off in front of the station by her killer. "There was lot of blood," Mrs. Franklin said, "So much blood. The poor thing."

She was reportedly covered in hundreds of small surgical-like cuts. She had no identification and wore only a yellow, knee length raincoat. A witness, who wished to remain anonymous, said she had a hand written note clutched in her lifeless hand. The contents of the note were not available at the time of this writing. The public is urged to contact the police with any information that may have a bearing on this case. This reporter recalls a case identical to this case over twenty years ago. The first victim, Rose Marshal, sixteen at the time of her death, was found on a bus stop bench by Officer Rud Percospy, while on patrol. The victim too wore a rain coat. She too had been covered in small, precise cuts. She too died from loss of blood. Were her last words,"I'm pretty when I'm scared?" Did she too clutch a note her in bloody hand? We'll never know. The records of Miss Marshal and those of a second victim, Bethany Winsor, have been lost, misplaced or buried in the bowels of the basement of the LAPD headquarters. When asked to about the older cases or upon the current murder, Chief Detective Oscar Fromann had no comment. To serve and protect or to be silent and neglect?

Burt Stone: *Los Angeles Examiner.* May 19

The victim of the Sacred Pretty murder has been identified as Marlene Ester Frome. She had just celebrated her seventeenth birthday. Like so many in this town of tinsel and heartbreak, she came to Hollywood to pursue her dream of being an actress. She had done some modeling in her hometown, Marble Ridge, Illinois and participated in some high school plays. Her drama teacher, Mr. Roland DeMartini encouraged her to follow her dream… in Chicago. Marlene's mother was sure her beautiful and talented daughter had the goods to make it in Hollywood Land. Pictures were taken, bus fare purchased and a room at the YWCA were reserved. What set Marlene apart was her passion and her professionalism, all the more impressive for her age. She auditioned for anything and everything. She was never late for an appointment. She was always polite and took criticism well. She was last seen leaving Mammoth Studios after auditioning for the role of a peasant girl in the next Vladimir Romansky thriller. The famed director had confirmed that Marlene had gotten the part and was to be fitted for her costume the following day. The one appointment Miss Frome did not and could not make. Still no comment from our esteemed Chief Detective.

Burt Stone: *Los Angeles Examiner.* June 1.

Crossroads of the World, that hub of hope, that emporium of wished for distant lands was last night transformed to a morgue. The second Sacred Pretty murder took place sometime after midnight. The victim, as yet to be identified, was discovered by Morgan Silberstein, on his way to work. He told police he had passed that location at 12:10 AM, leaving the bar, The Night Crawler, to get ready for work. He passed that same location at 1:15, where he saw a girl sitting on the sidewalk, her back against the iron gate. Her bare legs were stretched out in front of her. They appeared to be covered in something dark and wet. She was wearing a raincoat which appeared to be liberally splattered with the same dark liquid. Mr. Silberstein drew close and asked the girl if she was alright. She turned her head at the sound of his voice. He thought she said something but there was so much blood in her mouth, it was impossible to make out what she said. Mr. Silberstein noticed she had something clutched tightly in her hand. Not wanting to leave the girl, he flagged down a taxi and told the driver to contact the police immediately, which he did. By the time officers arrived on the scene, the girl was dead. Mr. Silberstein witnessed one of the officers open, with difficulty, the girl's hand and remove a crumpled piece of paper. The officer did not open or unfold it, but put it in his shirt jacket pocket. A body wagon was radioed. Mr. Silberstein was thanked by the officer and was told he would contact him if there was a need for additional information. As of the writing of this article, Mr. Silberstein has not been contacted by authorities. Not surprisingly, there has been no comment from Chief Fromann. How many girls have to die before our Chief Detective decides its time to speak up? I guess we'll see, eh detective?

•••

A confluence of events occurred that are only too typical in movies and as rare as an honest politician in real life. Wallace Wallerson was reading the newspaper, which he did religiously, every morning, when the phone rang. Marla answered. She listened for a moment. She caught Wallace's eye, put her hand over the receiver and mouthed, "Joe". He shook his head.

"Just a minute, Joe," she said. "He just walked in."

She held out the receiver to him. He gave her a venomous look, got out of his chair, newspaper in hand, and took the phone from her.

"You reading the paper?" Joe Templeman said.

"Yeah," Wallace said.

"You read Burt Stone's piece?" Joe asked.

"I never read Stone," Wallace said. "He's an asshole."

"Maybe," Joe said. "But you'll read him today. Call me after you've read it."

"Why?" Wallace asked.

"Just do it," Joe said, and hung up.

As soon as he put the handset in the cradle, the phone rang.

He was just about to tell Joe to go fuck himself, sure it was him when he heard a female voice say hello. He recognized it immediately.

"Wallace?" the voice said.

"Yes," he said.

"It's Ethel. Ethel Rosen"

"I knew who you were the instant I heard your voice," he said and felt foolish for having said it.

"Have you been reading the paper?" she asked.

"Every morning," he said

"Burt Stone?" she asked.

"Say, what is this? I just got off the phone with Joe Templeman asking me the same exact thing. What gives?"

"Its happening again, Wallace," she said. There was something in her tone, something that felt like worry.

"What's happening again, Ethel?" he said. "I don't understand."

"Him," she said. "He's…"

Wallace knelt down on the floor and spread out the paper, turning the pages until he came to Burt Stone's column.

"Wallace?" she said.

He was silent while he read. "Oh my God," he said softly. "Oh my dear God." Rereading the article, he said, "But it can't be him. That was twenty years ago. He was an old man when he… when you knew him. He's got to be in his nineties by now, or dead."

Ethel read from the newspaper, "She was reportedly covered in hundreds of small surgical-like cuts. She had no identification and wore only a yellow, knee length raincoat. A witness, who wished to remain anonymous, said she had a hand written note clutched in her lifeless hand."

"What's that from?" Wallace said.

"From Stone's article," Ethel said.

"I don't have that," he said. He was surprised at the panic in his voice. "I don't have that."

"It's from the seventeenth. May." she said. "There's one after that and then today's."

Marla, who had been in the kitchen came into the living room to find her husband on his knees, newspaper spread out in front of him and a curious look on his face. She mouthed, "What?"

He pointed to the article. She knelt next to him and read while he continued talking with Ethel.

"This is no coincidence, "he said, watching Marla read, seeing it hit her, seeing the fear, the dread widen her eyes as she looked up at him. "It can't be." He continued, "We're making a movie about this and it starts up again?"

Marla pressed her face close to his, to the receiver, as Wallace tilted it out so they both could hear.

"I don't know what to think," Ethel said. "I don't know what to do."

"You don't think, whoever it is, you don't think he'd come after you. After all this time?"

She was silent. He could hear her breathing, but she said nothing.

"Ethel? He said softly.

"Yes," she said. 'Yes, I do. I'm the one that got away." She said it with a half laugh and the sound of it made him uneasy.

"No one knows where you are, Ethel," he said. "Most everyone thinks you're in Switzerland or France. Even if he wanted to, do something, he can't know where you are. Nobody does."

"Forgive me for saying so, Wallace," she said, "But I think that's a little naive. Mr. Moze knows where I am."

"Moose would never, in a million years, say anything to anyone," he said. "Never."

"You're right, Wallace," she said. "Mr. Moze would never betray me. But Mr. Moze, under the influence, may not even know he's done it."

She was right, of course. Moose would never knowingly give her up. But there were times, many times, when Moose didn't knowingly know much. And these days, with little or nothing to do but drink in the park, it was more his state than not. Wallace was thinking of a way to respond when Marla took the phone from him.

"Miss Rosen?" Marla said. "This is Marla Wallerson, Wallace's wife. Forgive me for butting in, but I think that, with everything that's going on, if it might be better for you to come here. We've got plenty of room and you'd be more than welcome."

She couldn't read her husband's expression, but she was prepared to deal with whatever his objections.

"Mrs. Wallerson?" Ethel said. "I don't know. I appreciate your offer. It's really very kind but…"

"Ethel," Wallace said, taking the phone from his wife. "Marla's right. You should come here. You'll be safe here. We…we want you to come."

He could almost hear Ethel thinking. After a long, tense silence, she said, "You're very kind. Ordinarily, I'm not such a coward. But, I think, I'd feel better not being a sitting duck. Thank you. Thank you both, so much."

Wallace put Marla back on the phone and let the two women sort out the logistics while he pulled the car around. She was waiting for him as he pulled up to the front.

"I'm coming with you," she said, leaving no room for argument. She had a blanket folded under her arm as she reached for the door handle. "You'll see," she said to answer the question in his look. "It was Ethel's idea."

•••

Zander Wilde, homicide detective for the Hollywood division had interviewed Lois Gibson, at her office at Mammoth Pictures, twice. She asked that he not to go to her apartment, nor let anyone else enter her residence without her. There were several scripts there, property of the studio, for which she was responsible and could not risk her security and that of the studio by those scripts inadvertently falling into the wrong hands. It sounded like bullshit, but he agreed to her wishes. He lied. He'd gone back to the crime scene on his own, twice, trying to piece together what might have actually happened. The way her placed had been trashed? It was personal. A burglar was not going to take the time to carve "cunt" into the dining room table. This was an act of rage. The stealing was secondary and could mean lots of things. But there was no getting away from the fact that this man, Tom Millerson, wanted to cause Lois pain. There was no explaining the dresser drawers with a man's clothes neatly folded. Why were they not disturbed during his rampage unless they were his? Her side of the closet looked like a bomb had gone off. The other side containing several men's suits, trousers and work shirts were left untouched. Zander was sure he knew why Lois lied; all he had to do was get her to trust him enough to tell him the truth.

Zander got the Gibson case handed off to him by Detective Philip Stanza, who was there on the scene. Stanza was a good cop but he'd been at it awhile and didn't really have the endurance for an investigation like the Millerson case. He generally worked domestic violence cases which ended up being mostly desk work. So, it got dumped in Zander's lap.

But the Millerson case would have to wait. Two girls had been murdered in exactly the same manner, both bleeding to death, both with a note clutched in the hands. This was one of those career making cases. Given everything he knew, he was going to have to careful. There was just too much at stake.

•••

They drove in silence until they were about a mile up on Laurel Canyon Drive. It was a beautiful day. The sky could have been a matte painting for a romantic country movie. A menagerie of clouds moved across the blue canvas sky in every altering modulation. And, like the sudden shifts in scene in cinema, the sky changed. With a suddenness that dislodged their silence. The blue changed to grey. The clouds became black restless beasts. Rain spilled down like a rip in a sack of wheat. Lightening had always frightened Marla. By the time they turned onto Ethel's road, Marla had the trembles. There was a crack of thunder was so close, the car swayed on its suspension. They saw the lights of Ethel's house in steaks of glowing yellow run down the face of their windshield. Pulling up onto the steep slant of the driveway, Wallace said, "I'll go get her. You wait here."

"Okay," Marla said.

Wallace smiled to hear her sound so cherry. He got out of the car and ran to the front porch. By the time he reached the cover of the overhang, he was soaking wet. His shoes squeaked as he walked onto the mat and rang the bell. He looked back at Marla, smiled and waved. He couldn't see her and he was sure she couldn't see him, but it made him feel good to do it. After a few minutes and no answer, he rang again. Still no answer and no movement, as far as he could make out through the pebbled glass. He tried the door. It was unlocked.

"Oh, come on," he said to himself. How many times had he done this very thing on a sound stage. If life were an imitation of art, the lights should go out as soon as he set foot on the threshold.

He opened the door and called Ethel's name. No reply. He walked in wiping his feet on the doormat and the lights went out.

"Oh, come on! Really!" he said. "All I need now is a big ass, motherfucking bolt of lightning."

The tree the lightening hit, shattered like a tower of drinking straws. The thunder was deafening, literally, plunging him to a sonic cocoon. He looked back, the stump of the tree smoldered dragon-eye red. He saw movement out of the corner of his eye. He turned to see Marla running toward him, her arms flailing like apron ties on a laundry line. She didn't see him in the dark, standing just beyond the doormat, and slammed into him, sending them both, hard, to the oak floor.

"What?" Wallace yelled, not being able to make out what she was saying over the rumble of thunder and his gimpy ears

"Fuck!" she said. "Fuck, fuck, fuck fuck"

"What?" Wallace said.

"How are you doing?" she said as if they were old school mates meeting after many years.

"Doing?" Wallace said. "I'm lying on the floor, hoping my wife will get to her feet soon. You?"

She eased herself off of him and stood, extending her hand. He couldn't see her in the dark. He got up on his knees to get to his feet and discovered Marla's outstretched hand as her index finger poked him in the eye.

"Shit!" he cried.

"What?" she said nervously.

"You poked me in the eye," he said, standing.

"You poked yourself in the eye, yah' big boob. Where's Ethel?"

"Beats me," he said, finding the rest of her, "No answer to the bell. Tried the door…"

"And it was unlocked," she said flatly.

"And it was unlocked," he said. His tone added, "No shit. I swear to God."

"Oh come on."

"I walked in, maybe two steps…"

"And the lights went out," she followed.

"They did!"

"Oh, please."

"See any lights on?"

"You walk ahead of me," she said. "The next scene is where we trip over the body. And I'd rather it be you doing the tripping."

He took her hand and they walked cautiously into the room calling Ethel's name. Somehow, Marla had managed to keep hold of his hand and walk almost directly behind him.

"Ethel!? Eth-el!?"

•••

Oh, the smell! I woke with a start because I thought the inside of my nose was on fire. I went to rub it but couldn't. My hands were tied. My feet were tied. I jerked my head up. Oh God! Sharp pains radiated from the inside of my head and felt as if they shot out through my eyes. I was lying on a table. The room was dark. Basement dark. There was a light above me. Not far, dim. I was ringed with a pale light, like moonlight. Cold light. My eyes started to water. I was not crying. It was the stink. I was not crying. I never cried. I heard footsteps coming toward me. They stopped near. I could just make out the figure of a man. It was him.

"Good evening," he said.

My expression must have prompted him.

"Yes, its evening," he said. "Nearly ten o'clock. You've been asleep a long time."

"My momma," I managed.

"She's probably in a panic by now," he said. "I'm sure they've called the police. She must be worried sick. Don't you think?"

I said nothing.

"Oh, and your father must be so angry. He must be threatening all manner of punishment… if… you return. But you won't. And then, all his threats and schemes to make you pay for your willful behavior, they will haunt him for the rest of his life."

Still, I said nothing.

"They'll have to let your beloved nanny go. With no child to look after."

And still, I said nothing.

"You're quite a strong little girl, aren't you," he said. "But you won't be for long."

He took a step forward and leaned over me. The fringe of curly silver hair that circled his head was backlit by the overhead light to form a grotesque halo. The light reflecting off my white satin dress sent light into his eyes. His pupils were as large as dinner plates and darker than night.

"But… you… won't…be…for…long," he said.

I peed myself. A little. I squeezed my legs together as tightly as I could. Oddly, the more I squeezed, the more I felt in control. I vowed, I would not scream. And I would not let him see me afraid.

He leaned in closer, studying me as one would study a butterfly under glass. I remember his breath smelled like lavender. Funny, the things one remembers.

He straightened up suddenly and spun on his heels and left, his foot-steps becoming more faint with each stride. The light slowly faded from dim to dark within several minutes. And there I was, strapped to a blood stained table, the stench so strong and acidic my eyes stung. Alone. In the blackest isolation. I knew if I let myself think about what was happening to me, I'd be lost. Fear would speed me to victim. So, I went with Alice.

Whenever I was afraid, or sad or frustrated or feeling alone, I went into the Looking Glass with Alice to a world I knew better than my own. And I stayed there until he woke me. I heard the whimper of a small animal amid his echoing footsteps.

•••

Wallace knew the white room was just down the hall from the living room, a quirky right turn, and even quirkier, left and there it was. The peculiar layout out made the eccentricities of the twists and turns to the white room particularly difficult in the dark. There was a distinct advantage to not being the front man in such a situation. More than once, Wallace made a turn he thought would lead him to his destination only to discover an unforgiving wall, that led to nowhere, being the nature of walls.

"Where are we trying to get to?" Marla asked.

"The white room," Wallace whispered.

"Why are you whispering?"

"The white room," he said, full voiced.

She knew the white room from his recounting his evening with Ethel and Moose. A moment later, Wallace stopped dead in his tracks.

"What the fu...?" Marla said slamming into Wallace's back.

He shushed her and pointed. A faint light flickered ahead of them, emanating from a room to their right, sending undulating light patterns against the facing wall.

Wallace let go of her hand and motioned for her to stay where she was. There was just enough reflected light for her to read his gesture and stay put. She watched him step as lightly as a man of his size could manage. His bulk of a silhouette disappeared around a corner. There was an interminable claustrophobic silence that seemed to her to last an endless stream of extenuated minuets.

"Moose!"

She heard the distress in his voice and ran to him. Even in the subdued light of a solitary candle, the sheer whiteness of the room set her back on her heels. Gripping the door frame, Wallace seemed to overwhelm the space. He blocked the candle's light, sending his shadow out, behind him, like the light at the end of a tunnel, making the small things huge by the light's proximity.

A shudder went through Wallace's body that sent him to his knees. Just over the top of his shoulder, she saw what he saw. As he shrunk into jagged sobs, his hand thrust out in a gesture of reclamation, she saw Moose, sunken into the high-backed white chair, blood cascading from the gash in his neck. His face was turned to the ceiling at a right angle. She could see the faint, pink stained lightness of his neck bone in the gap of the wound that all but separated his head from his body.

'Moose," Wallace sobbed.

Marla tried to speak. Trying to comfort him. But her voice was stuck somewhere in the fear that clogged her throat. She reached out a tentative hand and lightly touched his shoulder. He tensed, brought his hand back from beseeching the dead man, intertwined his fingers with hers and wept. Suddenly, his body was too heavy to support him under the crushing weight of grief, and he went to the floor as if he were trying to sink into it.

There was a lot of blood. It didn't look real. She'd seen floods of it on the various sets she'd visited when Wallace was shooting a movie. Gallons of red-dyed sugar syrup poured or pumped, splashed or dripped to amplify the gore, to crank up the horror of a scene. But this was real. The front of Moose, from his neck to his lap, was soaked in glistening red. The pool that flooded the cushion between his splayed legs had soaked through to the chair skirt in an almost perfect oval that spread into the white carpet like a Daliesque soft watch. Then the smell hit her. A stomach churning stench of blood and feces, top noted with the floral scent of the candle. She wretched and swallowed. She knelt down beside Wallace and purred sounds of comfort. She didn't know what she was saying, if she was saying anything. She stroked his forehead and watched him uncurl from the knot of desolation. She'd only seen him cry a handful of times; once when his mother died and then when she'd miscarried. Now, he sobbed. Deep shuddering sobs.

She wanted to focus, try to on focus on easing his pain, but the needling fear that the killer still might be in the house wouldn't let her.

She spoke only when she was sure she had control of her voice. "Wally," she said softly, "Moose in gone. Maybe we should… you know, try and get some help, or, something."

He turned and looked up at her. She saw him return to her. There was purpose in his eyes. He only needed to see the fear in her eyes to put his grief aside and take care of her. More times than she'd like to admit, his compulsion to solve her problems and make things right, infuriated her. But now, she welcomed it.

He got to his knees, reached a hand out and rested it on Moose's knee. He said something she couldn't hear and then stood up. He seemed like a conquering hero to her, at that moment. Bigger than life.

It sounded like the blade of a knife pinged against the lip of a crystal wine glass. The tone was pure but faint and made them both look back toward the open door. Instinctively, Wallace moved in front of Marla, and she, instinctively, shielded herself behind him. The sound grew louder. It was a bell. A small brass bell. She felt him relax just a bit. A white, fury head eased around the door jamb and the tinkling stopped.

"It's Ethel's cat," he whispered.

"It's huge," Marla said.

"Twenty-seven pounds of pure feline lard."

"This isn't a good sign, is it?" Marla asked.

"No," Wallace said. "She'd never leave that cat behind."

The cat eased itself into the room. Once over the threshold, it sat, its considerable bulk spreading out like thirty pounds of sand in a ten pound bag. It sniffed the air which was ripe with the smell of meat. It looked at Marla and then at Wallace.

"I'm a cat magnet," Marla said over Wallace's shoulder. "They love me, for some reason. But if it starts to go for Moose, you need to do something. I'm not going to sit here and watch that thing dine on him."

The cat's lazy gaze rolled over to Moose. It actually licked its lips. Later, Marla would recall how the cat smiled in anticipation. It labored up to its feet, its belly dragging on the carpet. It took its time. It had all the time in the world. It waddled up to Marla, who shot Wallace's back a smug grin. She was just about to say something to confirm in way of a "told you so", when the cat turned up its nose, sneezed and took a few steps back to run itself up against Wallace's pant leg. Despite their desperate situation, Marla couldn't help her indignation.

"What the hell?" she said. "Animals hate you."

"All but this one," Wallace said, and leaned down to stroke its back. "We're pals."

"The fuck you say," Marla said.

She watched him go to one knee as the cat rolled onto its back for a belly rub. She saw what Wallace saw a second after he spotted the small roll of paper wedged between the clasp of the cat's collar. He continued to rub the expanse of the cat's belly while lightly removing the paper. Without changing his petting rhythm, he handed Marla the paper over his shoulder.

"What's it say?" he asked.

She unrolled it and read, "me 2 U."

"What?" he said, still petting the cat, which had slipped into the bliss of a deep rolling purr.

She read it again.

"Let me see."

"You either think I've gone blind or don't know who to read," she said testily. "I'm telling you what is written."

"But what does it mean?" he said, getting to his feet with a cat sprawled over this shoes clearly unhappy.

"Me to you," Marla said again. "We need to go home."

Uh? was all over his expression titling his head from the weight of it.

"Come on, numb nuts," she said. "Catch up."

If he looked anymore blank, he'd have had to be in a coma.

"Come on, Sherlock, grab the cat and let's go," Marla said, taking his hand and leading him to the front door. "She's waiting for us at our house."

He bent to pick up the cat. She held out her hand for the keys. "I'm driving. You and Lardass are in the back seat."

"But what about Moose?" he said, settling into the back seat.

"He ain't going anywhere," Marla said, starting the car.

The rain had let up a little, but the downpour had turned Ethel's slopping driveway into a mudslide. Just as she got the car headed in the right direction, it started to skid downhill, heading for a knoll of pine trees.

"Turn! Turn! Turn!" Wallace yelled from the backseat.

She eased her foot off the brake and waited until she felt traction and pulled the car back onto the driveway shearing off a sizeable number of evergreen branches. After a few more slides and slips, they finally made it to Laurel Canyon Blvd. Feeling the tires grip the blacktop made Marla laugh out loud with relief.

"You sure about this?" Wallace asked from the backseat.

"No," she answered over her shoulder. "But getting the hell out of that house? That I was sure of."

•••

Traffic was a mess, as it always was after a rain storm in Hollywood. Granted, it was an unusually potent storm, but for some reason, people seemed to drive through the rain as if they expected the road to open up and swallow them and their car whole. What would have ordinarily taken them half an hour to get home, took them almost three times longer. The house was dark when they pulled up the drive.

He said something…then stood up.

"I thought you…" Wallace began.

"I did," Marla said.

Marla had a habit of leaving the lights on throughout the house when they weren't home to discourage burglars. Wallace used to kid her that a burglar would know when to rob them when the house was ablaze with light and stay clear when the house was dimly lit. There was not a light on anywhere. Even the porch light, which they left on day and night, had been switched off. Neither of them moved. The cat in Wallace's lap began to snore.

Finally Marla said, "Unless you plan to sleep in the car, I think you'd better go see what's up."

"Maybe there's been a power failure," he said hopefully.

Marla pointed across the street to the Limegolds, whose house was brightly lit from top to bottom. Wallace hefted the cat off his lap and laid it on the seat next to him. The cat gave him a dirty look and went back to sleep. He eased out of the backseat on the driver's side and crouching, crept along the side of the house to the front porch. In any other circumstance, especially if Marla was involved, Wallace was fearless and ready jump into the breach as the protector. But Moose's death had hit him hard. He'd never known anyone more brave to the point of foolhardy, than Moose. He knew how to take care of himself and those close to him. When faced with threat of danger, he seemed to forget he was a scrawny mutt in a world of Bulldogs and Dobermans. If that could happen to Moose, it could happen to him. As he stepped onto the porch, he looked back at Marla. The hoot of an owl raised goosebumps on Wallace's arms. He eased his house key into the lock, turned it, removed the key and gave the door a slight push, He cursed himself as the hinges squeaked and vowed he would finally grease them up, instead of avoiding the job as he had for the past three years. He stepped in. Heard the ticking of the grandfather clock in the foray, took another step in and listened.

"Don't move," he heard a low voice say.

He didn't. Not a muscle. He heard the car door open. Panic gripped him. He couldn't risk Marla walking into this. He heard her footsteps on the walkway. She stopped. He took a step forward.

"I said, don't move," More force behind it. A warning.

Marla started up the walk way. Up onto the first step to the porch. She stopped. Wallace put effort into relaxing his upper body. He learned it from a stunt man he knew. Push all the tension from you upper body into your legs. Your torso will be more supple and responsive while your legs will be piston ready for action.

Marla was at the top step. She stopped. He could see her in his mind's eye peering into the darkness. She took a step up, felt her weight on the floorboards.

"No!" he yelled.

A shaft of white light burst behind him. His shadow loomed into the room overlaying the figure in front of him. The figure, a man, slender, blonde hair, mustache, workman's cap, jerked to the left and raised a gun. He saw the man's arm go rigid, his stance set and ready. Wallace threw himself forward. Marla let the flashlight drop. The lens shattered when it hit the floor. It rolled, skittering light at odd angles. Wallace rolled into the man's legs sending him backwards. The man screamed.

"Get the light!" Wallace said.

Marla chased it down, retrieved the flashlight and pointed it at Wallace, who had the man pinned to the floor, his knee shoved into the man's back. Nobody moved. Marla made a sound Wallace couldn't read. She walked over, bent down, put one hand on her husband's shoulder, and with the other reached to the man's face and peeled off his mustache.

"Get up, Wally, you're hurting her."

•••

They sat at the kitchen table, a candle at its center making them look like a painting by Georges de La Tour. Ethel reached for her glass of wine and winced from the pain in her back. She had removed the cap and wig but still wore her workman's costume. Even dressed as a man she was undeniably sexy, maybe more so because of the get-up.

"I was upstairs when I heard voices coming from the white room," she said. "I recognized Mr. Moze's voice, of course, but the other, a man's, I did not know. Mr. Moze was speaking loudly. He sounded angry. I caught a word or two but nothing that meant anything to me. It was his tone. The louder Mr. Moze became the softer the other man became until I could not hear him at all. And then everything went quiet. I waited I listened. I heard Otto's bell. He was coming up the stairs. I am ashamed to say, I was frightened. I hid. I hid like a little girl. I thought the stranger would follow Otto to me and I hid. Then I heard a car engine, tires on the gravel and the car drive down the hill. It took me some little while but I went downstairs to the white room. And I saw him."

She brought her hands to her face and wept. Marla got up and put an arm around her. After a few moments, she collected herself. "I have many costumes for when I want to go out. I put this on. I knew you had given Mr. Moze a key. I took it, I got my car out of the garage and drove over the hill to Ventura and then around. Traffic can be terrible on the hill when the weather turns. I parked two blocks down, walked to your home and let myself in. I turned off all the lights and waited."

"The note you left on Otto?" Marla asked.

"Otto seemed to take a fancy to your husband," Ethel said. "I hoped you would find it and understand."

Marla gave Wallace a look.

"The gun?" Wallace asked.

"It's a prop from *Brave Angel*." Ethel said. "It's come in handy now and then." She took a sip of her wine and grimaced.

"What were you able to make out?" Wallace asked.

"Really, very little, "Ethel said. "Mr. Moze kept saying, 'You? You?'"

"Did he say a name? Anything that would help us figure out who the other man was?"

"No," Ethel said. "He just kept repeating '*You?*' as if he could not believe who it was."

"We need to call the cops," Marla said.

"We need to call them anonymously," Wallace said. "And we need to keep her," gesturing to Ethel, "out of sight until we can figure out what the hell is going. You can't go back there."

Ethel nodded slowly and then her eyes went wide with panic, "Otto! I have to get Otto!"

"He's safe," Marla said. "He's in the car."

Ethel wept with relief.

•••

"Homicide. Detective Zander Wilde. How can I help you?"

"There's been a murder," Wallce said, disguising his voice. He was a master mimic. For reasons he'd never understand, he was doing Joe Templeman.

"A murder?"

"Yeah. You know, when someone gets dead and they don't want to be?" Wallace as Joe gave him the address.

"Who's calling?" the detective asked.

"A concerned citizen."

"Anything else you can tell me?"

Wallace hung up.

The sun was an orange thread strung between banners of receding storm clouds. On the way up the hill, Zander was surprised to see how much damage had been done. Tree limbs dangled by strips of sodden wood. Debris littered the road. A car had slid sideways into someone's mailbox. He'd almost missed the turn off. The house belonged to an Ethel Rosen. Up the driveway, the house was impressive. Ethel must have had some dough to be able to buy it. He parked. The gravel had been rutted by several cars but the rain made it impossible to read any tire tracks.

On the porch, he studied the door and the landing. Might have been a couple of footprints but they'd been turned to vague shoe sole shapes. The door was unlocked. He went in, revolver drawn. In the white room, a man sat in a white, high-backed chair, his throat cut, deep enough to almost sever his head from his body. There was a lot of blood which had begun to darken, dry and congeal. One of the things he noted in his report as he examined the room and later, as he went through the house, there was not one photograph. Art decorated the walls; paintings, drawings, etchings, a few African masks, but not one photo in the entire place.

The victim had the distinctive look of the homeless; scrawny, unshaven, ill-fitting clothes. A general unkempt quality but not typical. There was something different about this homeless man. Zander noted it in his report. Near the body, there was a partial footprint. A big foot. Likely a big man; the right foot. From the position of it next to the body, the pressure of the toe to the heel, the man had knelt, one kneed. When he got up, he must have seen his print, took a step back and wiped the blood off the sole of his shoe on the carpet resulting in a long rust-red smear.

Zander was no stranger to death. He witnessed, first hand, the depth of mindless cruelty one human can inflict on another. But as a detective, he'd never come across anything like this. Not that it was any more brutal than any other murder scene he'd observed. There was something strangely elegant about this set up. As if it'd been arranged, staged. The absolute whiteness of the room and everything in it, juxtaposed against the savagery of the act and the contrast of the flood of blood.

He went back to the car and radioed for back up and the M.E.

•••

Wallace and Marla owned a small cabin in Arrowhead, a mountain community in the San Bernadino Mountains, seventy some miles from Los Angeles. It was agreed that Marla and Ethel would head up there for a few days until things settled out. The cabin had been in Marla's family and couldn't be traced back to Wallace unless someone knew Marla's maiden name. It was business as usual for Wallace. Things needed to look absolutely normal. No variation. No reason to for suspicion.

There was a scheduled read-through at the studio later that afternoon and he'd be there. With Marla and Ethel in costume, on their way to the cabin, Wallace spent the morning getting ready for the day. He made a point not to think of Moose. As soon as he felt himself drift to thoughts of his murdered friend, he tamped them down. There'd be plenty of time to grieve. And he would. But not now.

Just as he was heading out the door, the phone rang. "Mr. Wallerson?" He recognized May's voice. Everyone with two working ears would recognize May's voice. Its soft, whispered sing-song.

"Hi, May," he said, forcing casual cheer into his voice. "What can I do for you?"

"I was hoping you might be willing to work with me a little on today's scene," she said. "Just the two of us? I still feel pretty unsure about what I'm doing and I so want to be good in this part. This could movie could make me a real actress instead of a film star with great tits. Please?"

Her frankness struck him. Just her honest, unflinching assessment of how Hollywood and the public saw her moved him and made her respect her in a way he hadn't before.

"When did you have in mind?" he asked. "The read-through is at three."

"Its almost eleven now," she said. "Noon? Could we meet at noon?"

Wallace thought about it. He could run his errands after the reading and help the kid out before.

"Okay," he said. "Where?"

"You wanna come here?" she asked. "My mom's going to be out all day, so we'd have the place to ourselves."

Thinking back to their encounter in the hall, he felt uneasy about meeting her in such a private place. She was a very attractive and sexy young girl and he did not want to be tempted or even near a situation where temptation could lead him to do something stupid. Not that he would. He adored his wife and would never do anything to hurt her or threaten their life together. But there was something about May Harrold that he knew he needed to be mindful of.

"I'll meet you at the studio," he said. "There's a rehearsal space next to makeup. I'll meet you there at 12:30. Okay?"

"Oh, okay," she said. She couldn't have sounded more disappointed. It was as if she were a five year old and he just told her there was no Santa Claus.

The car smelled like wet cat. He drove into Hollywood with the windows down hoping to exchange the cat smell with the comforting odor of car exhaust. Clouds still hung in the sky but it looked it was shaping up to be a nice day. The turn off to Warendale Park was coming up. He almost pulled off. The image of Moose sitting in the blood soaked chair, his half closed lifeless eyes staring into the deep nowhere made it hard for him to swallow.

"You died because of her, you know," Wallace said. "Wrong place. Wrong time."

If it hadn't been for this damned movie, Moose would still be alive. It was that simple. He knew there was nothing he could have done about it but it didn't stop him from feeling guilty.

He pulled onto the lot at a quarter after twelve. May's car was already there. He greeted friends and co-workers on his way to the rehearsal space. It was a good sized room, devoid of any decoration. A long table surrounded by chairs that looked liked they'd come over on the Mayflower. The only concession to creature comfort was a water cooler and a window. There was a peculiar greenish tinge to the water and the window had been painted shut decades ago. Despite the bleakness of the room, fond memories made the space one of welcome familiarity. He'd rehearsed here with Randolph Masters and the great director, William Carl Sokall, for the movie *The Last Hero*. Later he'd recall in an interview for the Hollywood reporter for a piece about Sokall after the director's death, he learned more about acting in those few short weeks than he had in all his years in the business.

"He taught me how to listen," Wallace was quoted as saying. "Not an easy thing to do when you're waiting to say your lines. The trick is, stop waiting. Just respond as if it's the first time you're hearing it. He was a great man and a good friend."

He'd just taken a seat at the far end of the table when May walked in. He almost said what he was thinking. Instead, he commented on the potential for a sunny day. She was wearing a powder blue V neck sweater. It wasn't any tighter or form fitting than any of the tops she wore. But if the V would have been any lower, he'd have been able to see her belly button.

She took the seat across from him. When she bent over to retrieve the script from her bag on the floor, Wallace knew two things; she was not wearing a bra and it was it must have felt colder to her then to him. She came up quickly and caught him looking. He felt the tips of his ears warm with embarrassment.

"Can we start from page forty-five?" she asked looking directly into his eyes, which unnerved him. "I don't get what I'm supposed to do."

He flipped to the page and read the scene to himself. When he was done, he looked at her. She was leaning forward with her chin hearted in her hands. He made a point to look into her eyes. He'd be damned if he'd let himself be played again. And that's what it was. He knew it. She was playing him and had from that scene in the hallway outside of their first reading.

"The scene is about manipulation," he began. "My character is trying to persuade you to something you don't want to do."

She looked confused. "I thought he was trying to get me not to spy on the guy, you know, the doctor."

"Don't pay too much attention to what he's saying to you," Wallace said. "Pay attention to what he's *not* saying."

She scrunched up her face and titled her head. "I don't get it."

"Let's say that I have a big bowl of candy," he said. "What's you favorite kind?"

"Chocolate raspberry bon-bons," she said and all but licked her lips.

"Okay. Let's say I have a bowl of chocolate raspberry bon-bons. They're right there in front of you. And I'm going to tell you how awful they are. How they're not going to taste sweet and creamy. How the chocolate is not going to be smooth and delicious. I'm going to tell you how much you don't want one. Instead, what you really want to a tuna fish sandwich. You certainly don't want one of these fresh, delicious, smooth, creamy sweet bon-bons. No, you don't"

"Here's the crazy thing," she said. "The more you told me I didn't want one, the more I wanted one."

"That's it, May," he said enthusiastically. "That's exactly it!"

She sat up, leaned back a little and looked at the ceiling. And he saw the light bulb go on. She lowered her gaze and looked into his eyes. Gone was the coy, flirtatious girl with the great tits. Here was a young woman who had just experienced an epiphany. A young woman who had just experienced an epiphany who also had great tits.

"Acting isn't only what's on the page," he said. "In fact, it very rarely is. Nobody says anything with nothing behind it. You job is to find out what's behind the things you're supposed to say. And listen to the other actors to hear what's behind what they're saying. Or *not* saying."

"You're a pretty smart guy, Mr. Wallerson," she said. "Nobody ever told me any of that."

They read through the pages a half dozen times. With each read she got better. At the end of the last read, there were tears in her eyes.

"What's wrong?" he asked, a little confused. "You're doing great."

"For the first time in my life, I feel like a real actress. I feel like I actually might have talent… some talent." She took her script up in both hands and pressed it against her chest, concealing her cleavage. "I'm real sorry," Mr.

Wallerson. Thank you. Really, thank you so much." With the script still held close, she got her bag off the floor and headed to the door. "See you at rehearsal," she called over her shoulder.

"May?" Wallace called.

She stopped to look at him.

"Call me Wally."

She smiled. Nodded and left. Sunlight streaming through the opened door.

Rehearsal went really well. Everyone was getting much more comfortable in their character's skin and more than once Wallace and Drexler shared a conspiratorial glance at how well the work was going.

"Same time tomorrow everyone," Drexler said.

Alone, Wallace and Drexler commented on May's much improved performance.

"We did a little work together before the read-through," Wallace admitted.

Drexler gave him the raised eyebrow.

"The scene at the first table read?" Wallace began. "That was a play. I'm not sure what was behind it, but she played me. And I got to admit, if I were a lesser man, married to a lesser woman, it might have got some traction. Same thing today."

"And?" Drexler asked.

"She said something to me on the phone as we were setting up the meet. I think it was the first honest thing she'd ever said about her career, about her acting. And about how people see her. So, when we got together, I treated her like a fellow actor."

"A fellow actor with a remarkable bosom," Drexler added.

"A fellow actor," Wallace continued. "I told her a version of what Sokall told me. And she got it."

"The single most important thing an actor can do is to learn to listen," Drexler said. "Anyone can deliver dialogue. Very few actors know how to listen."

"Exactly."

"You know who I thought of the other day?" Drexler said.

"No. Who?"

"Frank Moze," Drexler said. "He was a terrific actor. He would have been great in this picture. Too bad about the drink. What a waste."

It took everything Wallace had not to tell Drexler about Moose, about Ethel about the truth behind *Scared Pretty*. He was starting to trust this guy and felt sure the director could keep his mouth shut. And Wallace would have loved to just get some of the grief and misery off his shoulders, even if it meant relocating a little of it on the slightly sloped shoulders of his comrade in arms. But he decided against it, punched Drexler playfully on the arm and said goodbye. Passing Limelight Liquor, he let himself shed a few tears. A few. Anymore than a few and he was afraid he wouldn't be able to stop.

Detective Zander Wilde was waiting on Wallace's porch when the actor drove up. As Wallace exited his car, the detective, walked to him, introducing himself with a show of his badge.

"Got a minute?" Zander asked.

Wallace walked him around to the back of the house. Two redwood patio chairs flanked a small table. Wallace sat in one and offered the detective the other. Ordinarily, someone seeing the Wallerson's back yard for the first time commented on the landscaping which was spectacular or the large cement statue of their dog, Sal, that was, if truth be told, was hideous. Zander mentioned neither.

"Ever hear of a guy named Moze? Frank Moze?"

"Sure," Wallace said, making sure to keep his tone casual. "We worked together years ago."

"Seen him lately?"

"No one has seen Frank lately," Wallace said.

"Well, turns out he got himself killed night before last."

"Really?" Wallace said, holding the detective's gaze. "How?"

"What size shoe do you wear?"

"A twelve," Wallace said. "What's this all about?"

"Where were you Wednesday night?"

"Here," Wallace said, "With my wife. There was a hell of a storm and we decided to stay in."

"She here, your wife?" Zander asked.

"She's out of town visiting friends," Wallace said, letting irritation tighten his voice. "If you've got something to say, detective, you ought to come out and say it. Or you should leave. I've got a shit load of things to do and I don't have time for this crap."

Zander got up, thanked Wallace for his time and headed to the gate that led to the front of the house. He stopped with his hand on the latch and turned, "Sorry about Moose," he said. "Hard to lose friend, even if you've lost touch."

"Thanks," Wallace said and watched the detective leave.

•••

He had been waiting in his car since 3:30. In the week and a half since he'd been watching her, he was surprised to discover how punctual the metro system bus line was. Before, he'd thought the public transit ran on a schedule similar to the appearance of the Northern Lights. But buses arrived, on average, not more than eight minutes either side of its posted time. Not that he would ever take a public bus, but there was some kind of comfort in the metro line working so well.

Her bus pulled up, stopped for four minutes and then drove away. There she was, waiting on the bench for her transfer. It was rare to see a girl in a school uniform these days; the deep blue skirt and sweater. The bright white starched blouse. And those sexy little ankle socks. She had a book open on her lap as he approached. She didn't notice him until he sat down next to her. He gave her his card. Her eyes widened as she read.

"No, no. Everything's fine," he said. He explained. She listened. Looked at the card. Looked at him. He was a good looking guy. He had kind eyes. He reminded her of someone. Someone on TV. A detective? Maybe someone in a western. He had that kind of face. He pointed to his car across the street. She was hesitant. She didn't want to miss her bus. She didn't want to worry her mom if she was late. After she helped him with his business, he said, he'd drive her home. Did he know where she lived? Well, no. North Hollywood over the Cahuenga pass. No problem. He had friends in Ventura. She'd actually being doing him a favor. It would give him a reason to go visit them. Hadn't seen them in awhile. This would work out prefect.

A moments more hesitation and she agreed. He had such kind eyes. They jogged across the street to his car together. She was on the plump side and he enjoyed watching her bounce and jiggle and she trotted next to him. She had the cutest little dimples. He'd always had a thing for girls with dimples. She climbed into the car, pulling her skirt down to cover her knees.

He asked about her. Did she have any hobbies? What did she want to be when she grew up? She wanted to be a vet or an actress. She loved dogs and wanted be able to help them. He loved dogs too. She had a dachshund named Trixie. She was kidding, right? When he was growing up, they had a pair of dachshunds, brother and sister. Arnie and Anna. He wished he could have a dog again but he lived in an apartment where you couldn't have animals. You could have a fish, but who wants a fish? You can't pet a fish. And if you do, you just get all wet. She laughed at that. There were those dimples.

Traffic was running slow. He said he needed to make a phone call to tell them they were running late. He pulled into the first gas station on their right. Did she want something to drink? A Coke? He was going to get one for himself. Yes, she did. That would be nice. A few minutes later he came to the car with two Cokes and handed one to her. Back in traffic, they headed toward the pass. Did she want to listen to the radio? Did she have any favorite singers? She loved Judy Garland. She'd seen the Wizard of Oz six times. Had he seen it? That was one of his favorite movies. But he'd only seen it three times. Too much work, not enough time. She recited dialogue from the movie. The last scene where Dorothy wakes up in her bed surrounded by the people she loves. She was good, he thought. If she lost a little weight, she could maybe pass for Judy. Maybe. He turned on the radio. Glen Miller's Moonlight Serenade was playing. They were silent for a while. He looked at her and her eyes were half closed. He'd learned that Coke, for some reason, was the only pop that real masked the taste of the drug.

At the corner of Wilcox and Hollywood, he turned right and maneuvered his way down to Sunset, another right to Laurel Canyon Drive and another right. This was his favorite time to drive the canyon road. The sun had just dipped behind the hills, turning the sky a rose tinted peach. He had to pass a car making a left and the go-around made her head bounce against her window. She had a thin silver thread of drool from the corner of her mouth to her chin. She moaned softly but didn't move.

He felt his excitement build. He knew it was connected to street signs he passed. Each block bringing him closer. At times like these, he was amazed at how well he was able to compartmentalize. Any other time of the day, in any other circumstance, he'd be appalled by what he was doing. Wrong? It was well past being wrong. Of course, it was criminal, but even that wasn't the full extent of it. In rare moments he thought that maybe it was time to get some help or stop. Stop altogether. Just not do it anymore. It's not like he didn't have a choice. But if he stopped, there'd be consequences. He was a smart guy. He knew right from wrong better than most. But at times like these with his newest victim right there with him. Inches away. So close he could smell her. Well, none of that mattered. Soon, he'd have to carry her from the car. And then there was no going back. His turn was just up ahead. His hands began to sweat in anticipation.

By nine o'clock her mom was frantic. She's called everyone she knew and everyone she knew her daughter knew. No one had heard anything. Her daughter's friend, Dorothy Pender saw April get on the bus. They'd arranged to talk later on the phone to go over a homework assignment.

When she didn't call, she just figured April had sorted it out on her own or forgot. April was like that sometimes.

At nine-thirty April's mom, Janey, called her sister who lived in Studio City. Janey didn't have a car. And even if she had, she didn't know how to drive. Janey told June about April not coming from after school. Maybe she was with a friend. No, Janey called all the friends she knew April had. Maybe she was with a boy. No. April didn't have a boyfriend. And besides, even if she had, she'd never been this late without calling. It took June a little longer to get to her sister's house. Traffic. Looked like a stall. When she did, Janey was waiting for her on the front porch. They spent the next two hours driving around town starting with the bus stop. Up and down block after block of residential neighborhoods. After the first half an hour June knew it was a waste of time but her sister was so worried, so frightened, she didn't have the heart to mention the obvious. April had gone missing. When June dropped her sister back at her house, Janey ran to the front door calling April's name. June parked and went into the house to find Janey on the phone.

"April Adams," June heard her sister say into the receiver. "She's sixteen. Five-four, about a hundred and thirty pounds. Brown hair and eyes. St. Michaels. Yeah. That's the one. She was supposed to be home by four-thirty. She takes the bus from school to the Colfax bus stop and then catches the transfer to the Riverside stop. No. Not a word. I called everyone I know. No one had heard from her. What! That's crazy! She's missing. Goddamnit! She's going to be missing just as much in twenty-four hours as she will now. I can come down to the station." She said this looking at June who still had her car keys in her hand. June nodded.

"No! Now!" Janey yelled. She listened for a another minute and then slammed the receiver down.

"She has to be missing for twenty-four hours before I can file a missing person report," Janey said, pacing.

June settled her sister into a chair, called her husband to tell him what was happening. No, she didn't need him to come over. She made her sister a strong vodka martini, made her drink it and then made them each one. Janey started to calm down, a little. She hadn't stopped crying since she walked in the door and her eyes were puffy and bloodshot. A little after three, Janey finally fell asleep in the easy chair near the phone. A call at 9:00 am woke them both. It was the school. April had not been to her classes and the vice principal wanted to know if she was excused that day as she hadn't brought a note the day before. No, Janey explained and told

They jogged across the street…together.

the VP April had not come home all night. The VP said she'd ask some of the other girls if they knew anything. She'd get back to her.

Jane Adams did not sleep or eat for three days. She did file a police report but was told that most likely the girl had run away and that she'd probably get in touch in a few days, maybe a month. That's how these things often played out. She spent most of the second day on the phone to relatives. If April showed up, all she asked is that they call her and let her know. No, she didn't want to make a big fuss if April had run away. All she wanted to know was that her daughter was safe. That's all. They'd sort all the other stuff out later.

The morning of the forth day, she got on the bus to the Colfax bus stop. The last place April had been seen, according to the bus driver who dropped her off. She sat there in a daze. Watching the traffic. Watching buses come and go. Her eyes weren't right. They didn't seem to want to focus. And she felt awfully weak and so tired. She closed her eyes just for a second and when she opened them she thought she saw April on a bench across the street. She rubbed her eyes to help clear them.

"April!" she called. "April, honey!"

She managed to get to her feet and took a few steps forward.

"She just came out of nowhere," the man told the cop. "I mean, she just stepped right in front of me. There wasn't anything I could do."

Jane Adams died at the scene.

•••

Burt Stone, *Los Angeles Examiner.* June 25.

Her name was April Adams, 16, originally from Cincinnati, Ohio. All she ever wanted to be was an actress. She'd put on plays for her stuffed animals. She knew "a rose by any other name" from Romeo and Juliet by heart at the age of eleven and could perform whole scenes of The Wizard of Oz, her favorite movie. She was kind, sweet natured and beautiful. Her future was golden bright and full of promise. And then it wasn't. The night of June 24th, her blood soaked body was found propped up in the doorway of Limelight Liquor. She was wearing a knee length white raincoat covered in her own blood. She was found by Louis Sandalinsky, a taxi driver for the Yellow Cab Company. He'd just dropped off a fair at the corner of Grace Ave. and Hollywood Blvd. at 1:36 a.m. She was still alive when he knelt beside her. She looked at him with tear filled eyes and tried to lift her hand to him but was too weak to raise it but a few inches. There was something clutched in her mutilated hand. A note.

"I'm pretty when I'm scared," she whispered.

It was the last thing she ever said.

She was reported missing June 21st by her mother Jane Adams. She'd not been heard from for twenty-four hours. Her mother tried to file a report earlier but was told the girl had probably run away and would most likely show up in a day or two. She showed up all right. Dead. Four days after her daughter's disappearance June Adams was killed by being hit by a car steps from the bus stop at which her daughter was last seen. Maybe, if the police had taken the girl's disappearance more seriously, she and her mother would both be alive today.

Do we have a police department? If we do, and there have been rumors to that effect, what are they doing? Three brutal murders and still…still no word from our esteemed Chief of Police. Oh, wait, that's not entirely true. Apparently, according to the official press report, the department cannot comment on an ongoing investigation. Well, this reporter can. And will! Come on, Mayor. What will it take to put some muscle behind protecting our little girls? How many more must die before the police department is at the service of the law rather than the service of politicians?

•••

In the middle of a dinner Paul Davis was having with Jeremy Regal, he was summoned to Roy Hardgrove's estate. Summoned. Traffic was a snarl down Sunset to Laurel Canyon Blvd. He pulled to the gate forty-five minutes later and spent another ten waiting for the gate to be opened. Not a good sign.

Roy was in his study which looked out over the canyon. He sat in a throne-like leather chair. He was wearing his trademark purple ascot, a long sleeved white shirt and grey trousers with a creases so sharp they could cut glass. His legs were crossed at the knee, calculated to appear casual. But the set of his jaw and the furrow at his brow belied that. Paul headed for the chair to the side of Roy's when he was stopped by an imperious hand. He'd been through this scene before. It was getting harder and harder to take. When all was said and done, this guy was just an actor. Powerful, yes. Wealthy, yes. But times were changing and his bigger-then-life persona would not survive the trend to a more interior and natural kind of performance. Unbeknownst to Hardgrove, Paul had been working on building a roster of younger, more modern actors and writers. When the time was right, he'd tell this ego-bloated camera hog to go fuck himself. And enjoy the hell out of it. But, for now, he played the game with Machiavellian patience.

"You have a problem, Paul," Hardgrove said.

"I have a problem?" Davis said moving to the chair only to be halted again by the imperious hand.

"I just got a call from May," Hardgrove said. "She's a little uncomfortable following through with the plan. In fact, she's decided she'd rather not."

Ignoring the steely look, Paul went to the chair, sat and settled, making Hardgorve turn slightly to face him. Point for Davis.

"Seems Wallerson was nice to her. Helped her with her acting. Gave her an insight to her character. She just wouldn't feel right helping to remove him from the picture since he's been so nice to her."

"And that's my problem?" Davis said.

"We got her that damned part so she could work on Wallerson," Hardgrove said, his voice rising in irritation. "To compromise him. Publicly humiliate him so Drexler and Templeman would have to take him off the picture. Who else could they get to save that film with Wallerson gone? Me! They'd have to come to me. I want that part, Paul. And I'm not going to let some stupid cunt ruin my chances of getting it. So, your problem is to fix it. Get her back on track and get Waterston out!"

"I'll talk to her," Davis said.

Hardgrove uncrossed his legs and re-crossed. "You'll do more than talk to her, Paul," Hardgrove said. "If she doesn't play ball, she's off the picture."

"Do you have any idea what I had to do to get her on that project?" Davis said. "I can't just turn around and get her fired. I got nothing left to use on Lois. You know what happened?"

"I don't care what the fuck happened!" Hardgrove said, his voice rising. "Fix it, or you're out!"

Hardgrove had threatened before. Davis considered. Was now the time to tell this asshole to go fuck himself? Maybe in six months. Maybe a year. The kid he just signed, Darren Armstrong, had what it took; looks, talent and charisma. But it was going to take a couple of pictures to break him.

'I'll talk to her," David repeated.

•••

Its took Paul Davis twenty minutes of persuasion, pandering cajoling and to get May to agree to meet with him at Musso and Frank, on Hollywood Blvd at eight that evening.

"I don't want to be out late, she said, "I have script work to do"

Script work? Davis had a hard time keeping from laughing.

"And come alone," he said.

"You mean don't bring my mother," she said.

"I mean, come alone," he repeated.

If there can be a smirk in a laugh, she did it before she hung up.

She was seated at a back booth when he arrived. She was wearing an oversized plaid wool shirt and a dark red beret. He got rid of his smile before he joined her. She was working on a salad and a glass of wine. When the waiter came, he ordered an Old Fashioned and a plate of fries.

"What's all this about?" she asked.

"You made a deal with Roy," Davis said. "You need to keep to that deal."

She put her fork down, laced her fingers in front of her and looked at him in a way he didn't like.

"You know what I am in this town?" she began. She unclasped her hands, cupped a breast in each, pushed them up, giving each a playful jiggle.

He smiled, eyeing her tits as if they had just winked at him, caught himself and moved his gaze up to her eyes.

"You know what happens to an actress with tits like these who can't act?" she said, letting go of her breasts, her hands back on the table. "Of course you do." There was a bitterness in her voice he hadn't heard before.

"I have a chance to actually *act* in a movie," she said. "I have a chance to become an actress with this movie so when these things," she said looking down at her boobs, "are hanging somewhere near my knees, I'll still have a career. And you know why? Because the guy you wanted me to screw out of this movie helped me. Helped me discover what acting is. A guy who knew I was playing him and helped me anyway. So, you go tell Roy he can go fuck himself. He wants that part that bad; he's going to have to find another way to get it. But it won't be through me."

For a moment, Davis was so taken aback, he was speechless. He had to give it to her. In the course of a couple of days, this dim witted, vacant sex kitten and transformed herself into a woman with a sense of herself and was willing to fight for it, in her own way.

The waiter brought his drink and fries and left. Paul looked around to make sure no one was listening. He leaned in, making sure he had her attention. "You have no idea who you're fucking with," he said. "You make a deal with Roy Hardgrove, you'd better fucking keep it, or you won't work in this town again…ever."

"I don't know what you did to get me on this film, and I don't what to know," she said. "But I bet it's going to be a lot harder to get me off it then it was to get me on." She met his gaze and held it, in a kind of challenge.

They sat there in silence for some minuets. She put her fork down, fished a ten spot out of her pocket, laid it on the table and made to get up. He reached across, put his hand on hers and she sat back, appraising him.

"Look," he said. "Lets try this another way."

She crossed her arms.

"We both know the Hardgroves in this business are on their way out. Things are changing. Hollywood is changing. And I'm going to be part of that change. What Roy told you before about needing a real agent. He was right. Your mom can't do it but I can. You help me figure out how to handle Roy and when *Scared Pretty* is done, I'll get you the kind of movie you want. The kind that will show people you're a real actress and not just a pair of tits."

Her posture relaxed a little. He watched her thinking about it.

"How?" she asked.

Paul Davis was a hell of a tap dancer and he was dancing for all he was worth as he spun out a vision for May on how he was going to make her a star. He dropped names, potential projects, marketing strategies, long term career goals, and most importantly, how the industry and the public would see her in five years; as an accomplished Oscar nominated *actress*.

"I'll think about it," was all she said before she got up and left him alone in the booth.

He gave her a couple of minutes before he got up and followed her. She would think about it from now until doomsday; he knew what her answer would be. She'd found religion, so to speak, and she wasn't going to slip back in bed with the Devil and give up her Salvation. It was quite a transformation; he had to admit, from clueless starlet to serious actress. *Script work*. It made him smile as he watched her get into her car. She had just turned off La Brea. He was two cars behind her.

As he drove, he considered his options. May wasn't going to back down and Hardgrove had dug his heels in so deep, he was up to his knees in it. Was there any way back to Lois Gibson? With his new secret stable of talent, he was going to need someone in casting to get his clients parts. There were other studios besides Mammoth. Movies were a big business but the network of movers and shakers was small and incestuous. It only took a bad word at Mammoth to snow ball through the corridors of other studios to put the freeze on an up-and-comer. Paul thought of Tony Hunter. Good looking. Talented. Indiscrete. He was signed to a four picture deal over at Galaxy. Practically overnight his four picture deal dissolved to a no picture deal. He couldn't even get a reading places like Castile Entertainment or Silver Circle Pictures, purveyors of movies that might be considered C movies if they were done in color. If Lois dug in, trying to get his new actors work would be damn near impossible. He'd figure a way to rebuild that bridge. He could always blame Roy but he'd need to come up with a scenario where Roy put the screws to him that *made* him put the screws to her. He'd work on it. His big problem now was what to do with May and Roy. Maybe it *was* time to break with Roy. Maybe take May on now. He was still rolling it around when he watched May pull up into a driveway.

The house the studio rented for her was a small, well maintained stucco structure with an attached garage. He turned off his lights and watched from across the street as she exited her car and walked to the front door and knocked. She waited a few moments and knocked again. When there was no answer, he watched her bend down, lift the corner of the door mat, pick up a key, open the door, reach in to flip on a light, replace the key, enter, closing the door behind her.

He had to focus on tonight. He could not go back to Hardgrove and tell him May was out. He had to get her to change her mind. He hadn't tried offering her money. She could use it for acting classes. They could put her up in an apartment in New York; sign her up with Richard Boleslawsky. She could immerse herself in all the method crap. He'd known actors who had studied with Boleslawsky. What a pain they'd become. Pretentious self involved artistes. But it was gaining traction. She could study for a year. Maybe two and then come back to Hollywood with some artistic credibility under her belt. Or, even better, she could do a couple of those foreign art films like Louise Brooks did in the early 30's. He thought about May coming out of shimmering pond, naked. All artistic like. The money wasn't going to come out of his pocket, so what did it matter. Roy was rich and he'd consider the bribe an investment.

Davis got out of his car, made sure he was not being observed, and walked quickly and purposely across the street to May's house. On the front porch he thought about knocking but knocking would give her the choice of not answering and he couldn't risk that. He removed the key from under the mat and slipped it into the lock. He turned the key, felt the tumbler disengage and eased the door open, putting the key in his pocket, and closed the door silently behind him. A neighbor reported hearing a scream coming from May's house around 9:30.

• • •

He knew the type. She'd grown up early. You didn't look like she looked and hold on to any illusions of youth or innocence. If he didn't know better, and he did, he would have sworn she was at least in her early twenties. But Amber Dilsner was seventeen. It wasn't just the way she wore her hair, the set of her eyes, the pout of her full lips or a body most often seen in the pages of pin-up magazines, rarely in real life. It was the way she *was*. Confident. A confidence born of years of getting what she wanted the way she wanted it. No woman trusted her. She told him as much. But men trusted her too much. Or, at least they wanted to.

"Men have two brains," she told him, like she just made it up herself. "I got nothing over on the big brain but that little brain belongs to me."

There was a challenge in it. Kind of a dare. See, I know what I got and I know how to use it, and I have no doubt, even though I tell you about it, even warn you about it, you'll be like all the rest. You'll feel angry, foolish and used. Oh, you *will* feel used. But you'll still give me what I want. Big brain might be yelling, but your little brain ain't listening.

They first met a Dixie's Dinner, off Coldwater. Although he'd been watching her for a few weeks. There was that little theater on Melrose and he'd seen her a few times when he got coffee across the street. She was sitting by herself, reading an old copy of Photoplay. There were two guys at the counter who thought a sure fire way to get somewhere with a girl like her was an endless string of fat faced one-liners. The less she reacted the more they pushed. And she was well practiced at not reacting. So, they were pushing hard. After a few minutes, he got up and walked to the two men. The mouthy one was probably in his late forties, thinning brown hair. Everything he wore was too tight. Even his tie seemed a couple of sizes too small and way too tight. Tight Tie tried to ignore the man standing in front of him, but when someone is inches from your face, it's harder than its seems. His friend decided now was a good time to go to the bathroom.

"What say you stop bothering the young lady?"

"What say you go fuck yourself," the guy said, and winked at her as if he were showing her his muscles.

He withdrew a card from his wallet and held it up in front of the guy's face. Held it so he really had no place else to look. It took a few seconds for the guy's eyes to adjust. He read it slowly, as the only way he could make sense of it was to sound it out. When he did, a little of the hot air which had kept him a little too full of himself started to leak out.

"Let's try this again," he said. "What say you stop bothering the young lady. Maybe you and your buddy," who had returned from the men's room and was hovering near the exit, "should call it a day. Maybe head home."

The guy looked over at his buddy and tried, but not very successfully, to look like getting up to leave, was his idea. He got to his feet and had to ease his way around the stranger when he felt a sharp pain at the back of his neck that made his knees buckle. He looked over at the girl as he let Tight Tie guy go. She smiled. He smiled. As he made his way over to her, she got up, put a couple of coins on the table, brushed by him making sure her elbow grazed his stomach and left. And that's when he knew he had her.

They met a week later at Dixie's. He'd seen her at the same table the next day. And the day after that. And the day after that. But he didn't go in. When he did finally show up, she couldn't hide her reaction. She tried. Nothing but her eyes gave her away. And he knew he had her.

"Let's go for a drive," he said. It wasn't s suggestion.

For the following couple of weeks, he *dated* her. They went to movies together, they had dinner together. She was a passionate lover and that gave him even more control over her. The more time they spent together, the more she began to suspect there was more to this guy than he was letting on. Why would a guy like him, in his position, be involved with a girl like her? There was the difference in the ages, to start. She was jail bait. If they got caught out, it would cost him a hell of a lot more than it would ever cost her. Some of his stories didn't add up. But that wasn't that big a deal. Men lied. Men lied to her. He wasn't married, she was pretty sure. She could read a married man a mile away.

She lived with her older sister so she got to come and go as she pleased. He suggested they go away for the weekend a few times, but as much freedom as living with her sister afforded her, she could not be gone over night. So, they had to contend with long afternoons that sometimes stretched into early evenings.

He had a kinky streak which didn't really bother her. It wasn't what they did together. It was the way he behaved when they did. He became a little too serious, too controlling. It was starting not to be fun. And when the fun was gone, so was she.

For him, he was just getting started. He knew how it was going to end up. But he liked having a girlfriend. He'd never really had one. And she was so damn good looking, it gave him a thrill just looking at her and even more so when other men looked at her. But it couldn't last forever. Hell, it couldn't last another week. Pressure was mounting. There were expectations to be met. If it was just him in this thing, he'd let it go for awhile longer. But it wasn't just him and the pressure to do it was pushing hard and heavy.

So, he decided, Friday would be the day. He invited her over to his apartment. A first for both of them. They'd have a couple of drinks, he give her the drug, slip it into a coke or a rum and coke. She liked rum and coke and before she passed out, he'd get her in the car and they'd go to his special place.

"I like your place," she said, walking around the living room, looking at the books on his shelves and the collection of small porcelain elephants he had arranged on a table top.

"Glad you do," he said. "How about something to drink?"

"Sure," she said smiling. She was wearing a sun dress the color of crushed raspberries that fit her like a second skin. She was doing that thing, that tease. Walking around, turning this way and that, making the fabric of her top stretch tight across her breasts. He went into the kitchen to fix their drinks and discovered that he hadn't any coke. He had the rum, but she'd taste the bitterness of the drug and wouldn't drink it and he couldn't make her.

"I'll be right back," he said, gabbing his car keys off the hook by the door. Make yourself at home."

And she did. The first thing she did was go through his closet, then his dresser drawers. She found things that just didn't add up to who he said he was. Why do men hide what they don't want found under their underwear? She thought about writing a book, *The Worst Places to Hide Stuff*. There was a large manila envelope. She sat on the bed and opened it. It was stuffed with newspaper clippings all about the *Scared Pretty* murders. Each article had been heavily underlined. Some of these underlined sentences were linked by a long pen line to a space at the top of the page where he'd added stuff.

"Her favorite movie was the Wizard of Oz. She saw it six times."

"She pooped on the table when I started cutting the bottoms of her feet."

"I wish she hadn't talked about her dogs."

She was shoving the clippings back into the envelope when she heard the front door close. When she looked up, he was standing in the doorway with a brown paper bag in his arms.

"I, uh…"

It was the last thing she ever said.

•••

"Good morning, Mrs. Wallerson."

The phone connection was surprisingly good. They didn't have a phone at the cabin. In fact, nobody did in their immediate area. The only phone available was a pay phone at the market down the hill in town. Marla was armed with a pocket full of dimes and a big cup of coffee so thick you could patch cement with it.

"Good morning, Mr. Wallerson," Marla said. "How are things going?"

"You won't believe it, but May is doing really well. She's actually good."

"May who?" Marla asked as if she'd never heard the name before.

"May *Harrold*," Wallace said playing along. "She's an actress. She's playing Katia. Nice kid. Bright future."

"Oh, *that* May Harrold."

"We did a little script work and it really seemed to help," Wallace reported.

"The four of you?"

"Uh?"

"You, her and the twins?" Marla teased. "Did they *speak* to you?"

"They never said a word, although I think the right one winked at me," Wallace said.

Marla laughed. "Winking is okay. Anything else? Not okay."

"So, how are you and Ethel doing?"

"Our cabin is small, Wally. Too small."

"It's plenty big for two people," he said.

"Ethel and I fit just fine. It's her ego which is crowding me out," she said.

"Sorry to hear that."

"It kind of works out," she said. "She's got some friends in Big Bear and she's gone to see them a couple of times."

"On her own?"

"Yeah," Marla said. "It's a short drive. She leaves early and spends the night. Usually comes back by the afternoon. She went last night and hasn't come back yet but it shouldn't be long."

"So you walked to the store?"

"Yeah. It's really nice up here today and I needed to get out of the cabin before fever set in."

"You think that's a good idea, her going out on her own?"

"Doesn't matter what I think, Wally. The woman has got a mind of her own."

"So, how's it been with her?"

"She's still pretty upset about Moose. If she's scared about someone coming to get her, I don't see it. She's one of the most interesting people I've ever met. Amazing woman. Amazing life. It's okay. The breaks make it easier to handle. But she's okay. I like her."

They made small talk for awhile. Wallace told her how the rehearsals were going and she regaled him stories of camp fire nights with Ethel and the stories she told.

"Someone's at the door, Honey," Wallace said. "Can I call you back?"

"It's okay," Marla said. I've got to get ready for the day anyway. I'll call you tonight if I get a chance. Maybe bring Ethel so you guys can have a chat."

They hung up with *I love you's* and *miss you's*.

Wallace opened the door to find an older, faded, overstuffed version of Kate Harold standing on his porch, wringing her hands. She looked like she hadn't slept in a week.

"Have you seen May?" she asked, worry wrapped in aggravation tighten her voice. "I'm May's ma, by the way."

"I guessed as much," Wallace said. "Want to come in?"

"I want that I should find May, is what I want, Mr. Wallerson. You seen her or not?"

"I saw her yesterday afternoon, at rehearsals. She's doing great, by the way. But I haven't seen her since."

"Well, she's gone missing," the mother said. "I come home from being, you know, being out, and she weren't home. And she didn't come home. I figured she might be with you or that other guy."

"Well, she's not here. I haven't seen her," Wallace said. What other guy?"

"That big shot actor. That Hardgrove guy. They met a couple of times. I guess they're working together on something or other. I don't know. May don't tell me nothing no more."

May and Hardgrove? Wallace let it go for now. "I haven't seen her since yesterday," Wallace said again. "We have another rehearsal this afternoon. I'll be sure to tell her you're looking for her."

"You do that," The mother said as if Wallace had done something to annoy her. "We got some maintenance we got to do. All I do is look out for that girl and this is what I get?" She turned, walked off the porch, down the walkway to a late model Buick and drove away.

"A mother's love," Wallace said to himself and closed the door.

He tried calling May several times throughout the morning but there was no one home. The May and Hardgrove thing bothered him. He'd had to deal with Hardgrove over the years and found the man to be a pompous ass with a mean streak. On the set of *Dark Castle* in which Wallace had a small role, he watched Hardgrove verbally castrate a grip for straying into his sight line. The man, who had been in the business for over twenty years, was reduced to tears and quit later that day. Hardgrove's mistreatment of cast and crew was legendary. The man never did anything that didn't benefit him. So what could he be up to with May Harrold? As he thought about it, May being cast in the role of Katrina, was an odd choice. As it turned out, the right choice, but at first glance and first read, it was a terrible choice. He checked his watch. 10:37. Lois Gibson would have been in the office for an hour and half. He got the phone book Marla kept of all their professional contacts, found Lois's private number and dialed.

"Lois Gibson," Lois answered.

"Hi, Lois, it's Wally Wallerson,"

"Hi, Wally,' she said with real enthusiasm. "I hear things are going really well at rehearsals."

"They are, Lois," Wallace confirmed. "And May, well I have to say she really surprised us all. She's doing great. Who knew?"

"Good to hear, Wally," Lois said. "Very good to hear."

"So, I got to ask you, Lois, what made you cast May in the part? You know, looking at the work she's done, there's just nothing like this role in any of her other pictures. I guess I'm wondering what you saw that we didn't."

Lois launched into a well practiced insight-into-the-artist double speak she'd perfected over the years. Wallace listened and *Uh-Huh'ed* and *I see* his way through it. When she was done, he took a moment.

"You know," he began, "I remember that same speech when you cast Troy Brickman in the *Lady with the Iron Glove*. Turns out, as I recall, you kind of had to cast him in the part. *Pressures to bear* I think you said. We talking about *pressures to bear* here Lois?"

She was silent for a long while. If he hadn't heard her breathing, he might have thought she hung up.

"Lois?"

"What time is rehearsal?" she asked.

"Two o'clock," he said.

"Come to my office at one," she said, and hung up without saying goodbye.

•••

Wallace left Lois's office a little shell shocked. She didn't tell him everything, but she told him enough. He'd been in the business since he was a boy. He knew how things worked, or thought he did. But this? This was something else. There might be a couple of left turns and a few detours, but the destination was the same. Paul Davis got Lois's boyfriend killed so May Harrold could get the part. And once she had the part, she was supposed to compromise the fuck out of him so he'd either back out or be fired. And with him gone, and the movie already in preproduction, they'd have to offer the lead to Roy Hardgrove. He didn't have anything like facts to back it up, but everything added up to it. The big question for

"I haven't seen her. What other guy?"

him now was what was he going to do about it? He'd have to get some kind of confirmation from May. And considering the change in the girl over the last couple of days, he didn't think that was going to be a problem. For the first time, after decades of being in the business he loved, retirement was starting to sound pretty damn sweet. He and Marla up in Arrowhead doing not much but reading, relaxing, taking the dog, maybe two, for a walk and get started on that book he'd been threatening to write for the past twenty years. Maybe *Scared Pretty* would be his last film. He could go out on worse.

Two-thirty came and went and still no May. Calls were made without results. They began rehearsing in earnest at 3:00. At 3:17 the phone rang. Drexler answered it. The color drained from his face. He went kind of limp and collapsed into his chair, the receiver banging hard on the table. He looked at it as if he hadn't a clue what it was or how it got into his hand. Then, mechanically, he slid it into the cradle and slumped back in his chair. His fingers trembled as he brushed his hair away from his forehead.

"What?" Wallace said. Drexler was shaking his head slowly back and forth.

"What?"

Drexler looked up, into the face of each of his actors as tears filled his eyes. His voice sounded as if it came from far away, as if a ventriloquist had thrown it into his voice box.

"May's dead," he said. "May's dead." He covered his face in hands and wept.

•••

When he thought of himself as being of two minds about John Drexler directing *Sacred Pretty*, he laughed out loud. Two minds, he thought, like Jekyll and Hyde. He was in the commissary waiting for his last meeting of the day. A woman dressed as an Indian squaw gave him a look. She was in costume, he thought, just like me. But his costume was so much more subtle, there were moments when he wasn't sure who he was. It was coming together. It wouldn't be long before their work was done. There had been close calls. That girl, what was her name? Amber? The one from Dixie's Diner? She came close. She figured it out. Or she would have if he hadn't, well, if he hadn't done what he had to do. It wouldn't be long now. What kept him going? What helped him get past those times of doubt, through those fleeting shadows of guilt and remorse was the knowledge that *she* was proud of him. That *she* believed in him. That *she* loved him. That he was carrying on *her* work. *Their* work now.

She had been both mother and father to him. And yes, lover too.

Becoming who he was, a man respected for his skill, his insight, his intelligence was due to her. When he was ready to give up, she wouldn't let him. When he complained of being treated like everyone else. She reminded him that people's perception of him as being ordinary, common, one of the every-day, gave him power over them.

When he considered those close calls, dread set into him like a lead weight tied around his heart. Just considering what discovery would mean edged him near panic. For the world to know who she really was? It would be devastating. Everything good she had done, her life's work, would be ridiculed, and worse, dismissed. No one would understand the discipline it took, the planning, the execution. It took genius. True genius. Was she a monster? Were they monsters? In another time, in another place, their work would have been considered noble. Cultures before theirs considered human sacrifice not a marginalization of humanity, but a celebration of it. They lived in a time of a squeamish, morally infantile society. All life was sacred. Really? All life was sacred selectively. Pick up a newspaper.

He was reluctant to admit as they neared the end of their work, he felt apprehensive. Who was he kidding? He was nervous about being able to pull it off. There was a lot at stake. They were no geniuses; that was clear. But they were unpredictable and he'd have to set things up so their choices and subsequent action could be predictable. The next few days would be critical.

He thought about May Harrold. It had to be done. Dealing with her would end up putting the squeeze on Davis, once the cops got their hands on it. Two for the price of one.

She laid it out for him. He was a fringe player. He was the character that reacted to, not acted with action. Hardgrove, Davis, Drexler, Gibson, The Wallersons, even Joe Templeman, he moved them along like pieces on a chess board. He had to cull here and there, but for the most part, things went as planned.

He forced the negative thoughts out of his mind, checked his watch and finished his coffee. He had a half an hour to kill. He got up and walked toward the exit, passing the woman in the Indian outfit and chuckled to himself. She gave him a dirty look. Had she been twenty years younger he would have reached into his pocket and handed her one of his cards.

•••

Electrician, Edward Skoasits, was dispatched to the small rehearsal hall adjacent to the Makeup building to check the wiring of a flickering overhead light. He entered the room at 2:00. He found May sitting at the table, script open in front of her. She was covered in blood but there was none on the floor, table or chair.

At first he thought it was some kind of prank being the Makeup building was right next door. The closer he got, he knew it was no joke. Edward called Studio Security. Security called the cops.

Detective Zander Wilde finished interviewing Drexler and Reggie and the front gate guard by 6:30. The guard, a man in his sixties, who'd been at the post for twenty-three years, told the detective that a "foreign" looking gentleman came to the gate at 1:00 and presented ID. His name was Daniel Pickett, he was a production assistant on a movie currently in production on the lot. And, despite his name not being on the list, the guard let the man through. There's no record of Pickett signing out. Martha Rust was assigned to clean the rehearsal room as part of her schedule. Since the room was very rarely used, she allotted twenty minutes for the job. She arrived at noon and was out and onto the next job at 12:30.

The man posing as Daniel Pickett, it was speculated, was most likely the person to place May's body in its location of discovery. There were no other suspicious entries that day. All sign-ins could be accounted for until their departure.

Wilde saved Wallace as his last interview. They were in an office on the second floor overlooking the iconic Mammoth Pictures gate. They both watched as people slowed to admire the fanciful Gothic style archway they'd seen in movie magazines and in movie shorts.

"Tell me what you know," Zander said.

"What I know," Wallace said not looking at the detective. "I know that May Harrold was murdered. I know that Moose was murdered. That's what I know."

"Tell me what you suspect." Zander said.

Wallace turned to look at the detective. The floodlights that lit up the gate made Zander look like he was in a detective movie. He had the look for it, Wallace thought. Life imitates art.

"What I suspect," Wallace repeated.

"We're just two guys talking," Zander said. "Won't go past this room."

"What I suspect," Wallace said again. He paused, looked at the traffic crawling down Clauson Ave. "I suspect that Moose and May's murder are connected. I suspect that the three *Sacred Pretty* murders are connected to May and Moose. I suspect that all of it is connected to this fucking movie, somehow. Twenty years ago there was a string of *Sacred Pretty* murders. Twenty some years ago. Somehow, it's all connected."

"Movie?" Zander asked.

"*Scared Pretty*," Wallace said. He gave the detective the short version and watched Zander connect the dots at each plot twist.

When he was finished, Zander asked, "Who wrote it?"

"A guy named Leo Chapman is credited with writing it. Been around for years. Long list of credits.

"Credited?" Zander asked.

"His name's on it."

"I need to talk with him."

"That's going to be tough."

"Dead?"

"Dead."

Wallace considered telling him about Lois Gibson and Tom Millerson but didn't want to bring her into it and didn't see how it was relevant, really. If he brought Lois in, he'd have to bring Hardgorve and Davis in. In his gut, he knew they were mixed up in it somehow. He knew, he *knew*, all of it was connected to *Scared Pretty*. He'd look into on his own, if something clicked together, he'd tell Wilde about it and let him run with it.

"You know what suspicions are?" Zander said. "Suspicions are like a skeleton. They're like the framework of a case. Facts are the muscles that make the thing move. If you get to the point where you're adding on some muscle, you need to come to me." Zander handed Wallace a card and wrote his home phone number on the back.

Wallace read the card, "Zander R. Wilde. What's the R for?"

"Family name," Zander said putting his card case away.

"I get muscle on bone, I'll get in touch," Wallace said and shook the detective's hand as he rose to leave.

•••

Wallace took the long way home. He needed time to think and he did his best thinking behind the wheel. Six murders in as many weeks, and all of them linked to *Sacred Pretty*. It came into his life through a little girl named Ethel Rosen who somehow managed to escape the fate of girls not so lucky. That girl kept that terrible secret buried throughout most of her life until she decided to write it all down in the form of a screen play. Rejected and abandoned for a decade or more, it found a champion in the least likely of men, Joe "Blockbuster" Templeman. Him being cast in the lead role brought in Moose. Moose connected him to the rightful author, Ethel Rosen.

Then things got wonky. Lois was pushed hard to cast May in a supporting role. It had Paul Davis's fingerprints all over the push. What happened between her and her live-in Negro boyfriend, she didn't say in any specifics. But she said enough for him to piece it together. His murder was auxiliary. A couple of gun happy cops whose policy was to shoot first and cover up later.

Moose was killed because of his association with Ethel and her screen play. May was murdered because of her association with the screen play. Why? He didn't know enough but that didn't stop it from being true. And those three poor girls. Identical down to the detail of murders committed twenty some years ago. Committed just as the movie had gone into preproduction.

Okay, so he had the skeleton. Now he needed some muscle on them bones. Rather than take the ramp to the 405, he continued on up Sunset to Mulholland, up the hill to Hardgrove's place. He and Marla had been there once, years ago to attend a Christmas party. They arrived late which was a big mistake. Hardgrove was drunk. He was a mean drunk. After watching him humiliate a young girl with more ambition than sense, the Wallersons left.

The lights were on in the Hardgrove mansion. Wallace recognized Paul Davis's car. Two for one. He parked, got out and walked up the twisting cobblestone pathway. He had to force his anger down. He pretty much managed it by the time he rang the bell. He heard footsteps approach, the door opened. Paul Davis's expression dropped from a penthouse of a welcoming smile to the basement of confusion and despair. Wallace saw fear in the little man's eyes and played to it, letting a little of his anger show.

"Wally," Davis said, a little too brightly.

"I want to see Roy," Wallace said.

"He's, uh… he's busy, Wally, now. Busy," Davis tried. "Maybe call tomorrow."

Wallace took a step forward. "I want to see Roy. Now," he said.

Davis retreated a little into the foyer; giving Wallace the impression he was inviting him in. Wallace went with it. Davis didn't have much of a choice, at that point, and turned to lead Wallace down the hallway to the living room. Every element was designed to show power and prestige and it made Wallace sick.

Davis opened the door. Roy stood at the mantle of an enormous fireplace. A young fire had just caught and was crackling to life. Hardgrove wore, what he liked to call, a dressing gown. Everybody else Wallace knew called it a robe. When he heard the door open, he waited a beat and then turned slowly. It was a move Wallace had seen him do in a dozen pictures. To Hardgrove's credit, he didn't break character. His smile stayed where he put it but it drained from his eyes and turned cold. His left hand was in a pocket, fingers deep, thumb exposed. In his right hand, he held a cut crystal cocktail glass. He could have been practicing for an ad for Dewars. Wallace couldn't help but smile.

"Wallerson," Roy said. "What brings you here?"

Wallace fought the urge to reply with a wisecrack. Instead, he went direct. "May Harrold," he said.

"I was so sorry to her about her... her," Hardgrove began.

"Murder?" Wallace said his tone hard as he took a step forward. Out of the corner of his eye, he saw Davis move back a pace.

"Don't," Wallace said. Davis didn't.

Wallace walked over to one of a pair of easy chairs and sat. Hardgrove and Davis exchanged looks and then they each took a seat, Hardgrove in the chair opposite Wallace.

Wallace waited for ether of the men to say something. When nothing came, he began. "What you didn't count on was that she was going to be good," he said looking at Hardgrove. "Hell, she didn't count on it. When she found out that she could act, something changed in her and that kind of fucked up your plan up. Didn't it?"

Hardgrove gave Davis a killing look but still said nothing.

"Here's how I got it figured," Wallace continued. "You tell me if I'm wrong. Your last picture, *Passport to Peril* didn't do all that well. Maybe people are getting tired of watching you walk through the same move over and over again. You needed something to shake things up. *Scared Pretty*. You thought you had it locked up but then, who of all people, Joe Templeman, gets his hands on it and you are SOL. For some dumb ass reason, he casts me. So, now you've got to get me out and you in. *But how?*" Wallace gestured with his hands as if he were telling a story to school children.

"May Harrold. And this is how fucking dumb you are," Wallace continued. "You had it figured that if May gets the part, she'd going to hook me in, make me do something stupid. So stupid, that Joe will have no choice but to fire me, and... offer the part to you."

Davis started to say something but Hardgrove gave him a look that shut him up.

"Let's get something straight. May was a very pretty, very sexy girl with an exquisite body. But, you poor dumb son-of-a-bitch, I'm married. I love my wife. I respect my wife. There was never going to be a way I'd throw that away for a great rack and a nice ass, no matter how great they were. Not all of us are like you, Roy."

Wallace moved to the edge of his chair, putting his hands on his knees. "I worked with her. And you know what? The kid could act, if given half a chance. And she made a choice. And she chose to tell you to go fuck yourself. And that, and I don't know why, but that got her killed."

Wallace turned his hardened look on Davis. "You have no idea what your bullshit blackmail cost Lois. But ever…*ever* try something like that again, and I will *personally* make sure it costs you…big."

Wallace got up and took two steps toward Hardgrove, who despite himself, pressed back into the chair. Wallace turned, gave Davis the stink eye one more time and headed for the door. Davis implored Hardgrove with a desperate expression, not to say anything. To let it go. But Hardgrove was pissed and didn't have the control he needed to keep him mouth shut.

"You've got it all figured out," Roy said. Wallace turned to look at him. "So what? She's dead. Nobody's give shit about some two bit talentless cunt. And nobody is going to give a shit about your lame ass *art* movie. The only hope that picture had was with me in it. Who is going spend good money to see Wallace Wallerson as anything other than some big lumbering second banana? No fucking anybody, Wally. You might as well kiss your career goodbye."

Davis was on the edge of his seat ready to make a break for it if Wallace decided to go for him. Wallace stood there looking at Hargrove, titling his head a little this way and that, as if he were trying to figure something out. Roy looked defiant. His jaw was set hard, his nostrils flared. His left eyebrow raised in condescension. Wallace, and most of the movie going public, had seen that look a thousand times.

Wallace smiled, turned and walked out. As he headed down the hall, he heard Hardgrove and Davis arguing and it made him smile all the more. He opened the door just as a young pretty brunette stepped up on the porch.

"You're Wallace Wallerson," she said in genuine surprise.

"What's your name?" he asked the girl.

"Kitty DeLoral," she said, blushing.

"Do yourself a favor, Kitty:" he said. "Go home. There ain't nothing here but heartache"

"But I want to be…"

"I know what you want to be, Kitty," he said. He reached into his back pocket, took out one of his cards from his wallet, took a pen from his inside jacket pocket and wrote something on the card and handed it to her. "You want to be an actress, call this guy. You want to get screwed, go right on in."

Wallace walked to his car, got in and saw the girl watching him and looking at the card, alternately. As he drove away, he saw the girl head for her car just as Davis came to the door.

•••

Wallace called the store by the cabin as soon as he got home, hoping somebody would pick up and get a message to his wife. He let it ring a dozen times before be hung up. It was heading toward 11:00 p.m. The phone rang minutes later.

"I've been trying to call you."

"You have? Who is this?" Wallace asked.

"Detective Wilde, " Zander said. "Is it too late?"

"I was just trying to call my wife. What's up?"

"I've been doing some digging," Zander said.

"Hold on just a sec," Wallace said, went to the bar and poured himself a brandy, then to his easy chair and settled in. "Okay. What'd you turn up?"

"An Ethel Rosen was born in Boston in 1900. She was an only child. Her father, Isaac Rosen ran a bakery in the Boston's north end for many years. The mother died from cancer when Ethel was five."

Zander paused. "Ethel Rosen was the last victim in the string of *Sacred Pretty* murders."

"What?"

"They found her on a park bench wearing a man's slicker. She was nearly gone. Just like the other's she'd been sliced all over her body and was bleeding to death. In her hand was a note, same penmanship, same paper, read the same, *I'm pretty when I'm sacred.* She died shortly after they got her to the hospital. That was twenty-two years ago. She was the last one until a few weeks ago."

Wallace was silent.

"You there?" Zander asked after Wallace hadn't said anything.

"Whose house was Moose killed in?" Wallace asked.

"Good question," Zander said. "Deed says, Ethel Rosen."

"And Rita North?" Wallace asked.

"Ethel never legally changed her name to Rita North but she did have it set up as a DBA," Zander said.

"I don't know what that is," Wallace admitted.

"DBA," Zander said. "Doing Business As. She set up Rita North as a business which is incredibly smart on so many levels."

'What are the chances of there being two Ethel Rosens?"

"I'm sure there are lots of Ethel Rosens," Zander said. "Both of *these* Ethels were born on October 15th, 1900. Both Ethels had fathers named Isaac. Both Isaacs were widowers and both were bakers. The only difference is that one of them got murdered and the other one showed up in New York City a month later. She appeared as one of the Sugar Plum Fairies in a production of The Nutcracker."

"It doesn't make any sense," Wallace said.

"I talked to one of the detectives who was on the original *Sacred Pretty* case. He's in his eighties but still sharp as a tack. There's something that was never made public at the time and is still buried in the report. At one of the crimes scenes, they found two sets of footprints. A partial of a man's size nine, right. And a full print of a kid's right shoe print. It had them stymied for awhile until one of the detective's wives saw a photograph of the print and identified it as having come from a girl's ballet slipper."

"I don't understand," Wallace said.

"His theory. And *his* only. The *Sacred Pretty* murders were carried out by a man and a girl. Or, carried out by a man with a young girl present."

"That's crazy." Wallace said.

"That's what his chief thought." Zander said. "And had him take it out of the official report."

"Do you know how crazy this sounds?"

"About a week after Ethel Rosen's body was found, the landlord of a house he rented out was contacted by neighbors about a terrible smell coming from the house next-door. He went to check it out. The stench made him wretch. He called police. They found the body of man in the basement with his throat cut. He'd been dead five or six days, according to the ME. The room was setup like a torture chamber; chains bolted to the walls with handcuffs, a couple of wire pens containing animal remains and a surgery table with straps and a blood-drain gutter that emptied into a trough under the table.

"The man was Swedish, born in Stockholm, the landlord thought. He had a daughter, eleven, maybe twelve years old. She was missing and feared kidnapped or dead, or both."

"So, you're telling me that Rita North, a.k.a, Ethel Rosen is the Swedish guy's daughter? She helped her dad kill the real Ethel Rosen, adopted the kid's identify, murdered her own father and skipped to New York to join the New York City Ballet Company? And *then* went on to become one of Hollywood's most famous actresses?" Wallace said. "Is that was you're saying?"

"I'm telling you what I found out, is all," Zander said a little defensively. "That's what I'm telling you."

"No offense, detective, but that's the craziest thing I ever heard," Wallace said. "I know you're under a lot of pressure to solve those murders, but you don't think you're reaching just a little?"

"Let's suppose this stuff checks out," Zander said. "Let's suppose that our Ethel Rosen is a killer. Did she help her dad kill those girls? We'll never know. But it seems likely that she did. She was at the crime scene of his last victims. Okay, so if that's true, then she killed her own father. If that's true, then something made her start up again. She killed three innocent girls in exactly the same way as the first *Sacred Pretty* murders. Exactly. Down to the wound patterns. Nobody knows about those blade patterns except law enforcement. If that's true, then she murdered your friend Moose and May Harrold. Only she knows why. You following me?"

"Yeah," Wallace said.

"So, if you know where she is, it might be a good time for you to tell me," Zander said. "Because she ain't nowhere I've checked. And I've checked everywhere."

"Oh fuck," Wallace said. "Oh fuck!"

"What?"

"Ethel is with Marla up at the cabin." He was starting to panic, Zander could hear it in the man's voice.

"How long she been up there?" Zander asked.

"About a week," Wallace said.

"Your wife's been with her the whole time?"

"Yeah. The whole… No! Not the whole time," Wallace said. "Marla said Ethel went to visit friends she has in Big Bear. Twice. Left in the morning and didn't come back until the next day."

"She could have come to town, done what she planned to do and make it back without your wife suspecting anything. And why would she?"

"Fuck!"

"I'm on my way," Zander said, not giving Wallace to say anything. "Don't go anywhere. I'll be there as fast as I can."

"Fuck."

"You hear me?"

Detective Zander Wilde drove up the Wallerson's driveway forty minutes later. Wallace was pacing the porch. As soon as he saw Zander's headlights, Wallace waved as if the detective might miss the big man on his own porch. Zander pulled the car to a stop and Wallace got in. As they pulled out of the driveway, Zander notice something in Wallace's hand.

"What is that?" Zander asked

"A gun," Wallace said.

"Flintlock?" Zander said smiling.

"What?"

Does it shoot bullets?" Zabder asked.

Wallace was missing the detective sarcasm and looked at him with annoyance.

"Give it to me," Zander said, putting out his hand. Wallace handed the ancient firearm to him and put on a sulk. "Don't worry, I got one that was made this century. I think I got the gun thing covered."

•••

They took the 10 to the 605. Traffic was light and Zander was pushing. They rode in silence, each with his own thoughts.

"I don't understand this," Wallace said. "I've spent time with the woman. There's no way she could be a killer."

"Not to put too fine a point on it," Zander said. "But she *is* an actress."

As they hit the foothills, a light snow began to fall; pearl petals of frozen dust, so fine it looked like they were in a child's snow globe. Whenever Wallace and Marla went to the cabin, Marla always drove the last leg of the journey. All the narrow roads, tight turns and drop offs made Wallace a nervous wreck.

"Ever driven up here?" Wallace asked.

"Nope."

"Oh, good," Wallace said, closing his eyes as they drove into a tight turn, the rear tires fishtailing a little.

"How far?" Zander asked.

"Twenty minutes," Wallace said.

Up a snow slick road, Wallace told the detective to slow down. "That's the driveway," He said, as they stopped at the side of the road. "Goes up about a quarter mile. There's a stand of pines. The driveway goes around them to the left and the cabin is set back behind them."

"Stay here," Zander said getting out of the car.

"The fuck you say," Wallace said, opening the passenger door.

Zander looked across the roof of the car at Wallace. Even through the veil of falling snow, he could see that arguing with the big man was pointless.

"Stay behind me and don't say nothing," Zander said and headed up the driveway with Wallace close behind.

The snow was coming down in heavy wet flakes. Wallace, a North

Dakota boy, barely felt the cold. Zander a native Southern Californian, felt the shiver start in his shoulder and work its way into places never designed for refrigeration.

"What's that sound," Wallace asked, as they sloshed through mounting drifts.

"My teeth," Zander said.

"I thought you might have brought a pair of castanets,"

"You are a laugh riot," Zander said.

They got to the stand of pines and could see the cabin. Lights were on and the car was parked near the front entrance.

"What's the layout?" Zander asked.

"Front porch, front door," Wallace said. "Living room to the left, bathroom off the living room. Kitchen to the right, back door off the kitchen. Storage shed out back maybe fifty feet."

"Front door and back kitchen door the only ways in and out?"

"Yeah."

"Okay," Zander said. "You go in through the front. You called the pay phone, got no answer and was getting worried. Play it easy. Don't tip anything."

"And you?"

"I'm going check out the perimeter and then come in through the back."

"I don't like that plan," Wallace said. "I like the plan where we go into together and you have your gun drawn."

"We don't know what's going on in there," Zander said. "I don't want to push her into a corner if I don't have to."

Wallace thought about it. He still liked plan B better but agreed to do it the detective's way.

They parted at the corner of the cabin. Zander disappeared into the swirling snow. Wallace heard a radio playing as he stepped onto the front porch. The door was open. He let himself in, not knowing what he'd find. Ethel was sitting in one of the two chairs that flanked the fireplace. A small blaze crackled on the grate. She looked up and smiled as if she expected him.

"You must be frigid," she said as he got out of his jacket, shook off the snow and brushed the flakes out of his hair. She motioned for him to take the seat across from her but he opted for a chair at the dining table a few feet away.

"I called the pay phone but there was no answer," he said. "I was worried. I was hoping someone at the store would come up and give you a message to call me."

...a light snow began to fall...

"No one's been here," she said.

"Where's Marla?"

"She went for a walk."

"In the snow?"

"She said she liked to walk in the snow," Ethel said. "I had enough of that when I was a child. I much prefer being indoors by a fire."

"Was that Boston or Stockholm?" Wallace said.

"What was?"

"When you were a child," Wallace said. "Boston or Stockholm?"

Something in her eyes went dark, just of a second, but he saw it and had to force himself not to look in the direction of the kitchen.

"I was born in Boston," she said. "My accent? We lived with my grandparents for some years and they spoke Swedish. Almost no English."

Wallace smiled. "How long ago did she go?"

"Your wife?" Ethel said. "She just left. I'm surprised you didn't see her."

"I came up the front,"

"Oh, well, she started out the back. "She said there was a nice path out the back through the woods."

That was true. There was a well worn path out the back door that looped through the woods for a little over two miles. That Ethel knew that made Wallace worry a little less about his wife. A little less. This game, this, *you don't' know what I know,* was making him anxious. Where was Zander?

"How did you get from Boston to New York? That's quite a journey for a little girl. What? Were you eleven or twelve when you danced in the Nutcracker?"

Her legs had been crossed at the knees, her right foot had been bobbing in a small circular motion. An actor's gesture for *casual.* The bobbing stopped. Her eyes went cold but the smile was still there, but barely holding on.

"I studied ballet when I was a child," she said. "I was good. I auditioned and got the part."

"In Boston?"

"In New York."

"But you were living in Boston, with your dad, in that house on Chambers Street."

She uncrossed her legs and sat up in the chair. The game had been played out. Now would be a good time for Zander to come striding in, gun drawn.

"If this were a movie," Wallace said. "this would be the time when you'd reach behind you, pull out a gun and deliver a line like, I don't know, 'How unfortunate for you to have found me out,' or something like that."

Ethel reached between the cushion and the arm rest and pulled out a gun. It was small and chrome bright. He had no doubt it was loaded.

"I'm not a big fan of guns," she said. "But they do have their uses."

"That's a better line. But then, you're the writer. I'm just an actor."

"She's in the shed," Ethel said in anticipation of Wallace's question.

"Alive?"

"For now."

Wallace heard the back door open and watched Ethel's face. Her expression was neutral. Wallace turned to see Marla walking from the kitchen into the living room with Zander behind her. He started to get up but Ethel moved her gun a little more on target and he froze. Seeing Marla, a smile the size of the Golden gate bridge spread across Wallace's face.

"Thank God," he said with relief.

Their eyes met and she looked to the side and up. He didn't get it. But as she walked into the room and took the chair next to him, he did. Detective Zander R. Wilde stood in the archway holding a gun pointed at Marla's back. Wallace looked at his wife for some kind of explanation but she pressed her lips tight together to indicate he should keep his mouth shut. They both watched Zander cross the room to Ethel. He stopped next to her chair, leaned down and kissed the woman on the cheek.

"I'd like to introduce my mother," Zander said. "Miss Ethel Louise Rosen."

Ethel's face lit up like she swallowed a klieg light.

Zander watched Wallace's face and the penny of realization dropped.

"And this is my son," Ethel said. "Detective Zander Rosen Wilde, of whom I am very proud.

"Oh, for fuck's sake," Marla said.

"You have got to be kidding," Wallace said, as Zander took the chair across from his mother's, keeping his gun trained on Marla.

"We had to get you together," Zander said. "It was the only way."

"How's this going to end?" Wallace said.

"Murder…suicide, I think," Ethel offered.

"No one is going to believe that," Marla said.

"They will after they read your note," Ethel said.

"Write your own fucking note," Marla said.

Ethel leveled the gun at Wallace and pulled the trigger. For such a small gun it made a deafening noise. The bullet sent splinters of hardwood floor into Wallace's pant leg as the bullet embedded itself an inch from his foot.

"But why?" Wallace asked. "Why Moose?"

"He figured it out," Zander said. "Not all of it, but enough. He came by to confront my mother and I took care of him. I had too, you understand."

"And May?"

"She was wrong for the part," Ethel said. "I wrote that part for me."

Wallace laughed. Marla gave him the stink eye, but he couldn't help himself.

"Maybe twenty years ago," Wallace said.

"My mother is a great actress," Zander said defensibly. "Age is nothing when you have talent like hers."

"Talent ain't going to strip twenty years off your mother's face. Don't get me wrong, she's a fine looking woman for her age," Wallace said.

Zander started to get up but Ethel leaned over and put her hand on her son's knee and he sat back in his chair.

"Marla is going to write the note" Ethel said. "Then Zander will shoot her in the head. Quick and painless. And then he will shoot you, Wallace. Put the gun in your hand, fire another shot so they'll find powder burns and then Zander and I will leave in his car parked down the lane. They'll find your car parked by the cabin, just as you always park it. And sooner or later, someone will discover your bodies and that will be that."

"And the three new *Scared Pretty* murders?" Wallace asked.

"Great publicity, don't you think?" Ethel said. "People love that kind of thing."

"You killed three girls for publicity?"

"Business is business, Wallace," Ethel said. "You should know that. "I've been waiting years to have this movie made, and when it is, it will be a blockbuster like no other. I'll be nominated for my screen play and for best supporting actress"

She read him right and added, "No. Roy Hardgrove will not get the lead. I have yet to cast that. You would have been very good in the role but things got complicated."

Zander got up, went to the table, opened the drawer, withdrew a piece of stationery and a pen and placed them both in front of Marla.

"Write just what my mother says," he warned, pointing the gun at her head. "Nothing more, nothing less."

Marla wrote everything Ethel dictated. She took her time complaining about not having her glasses which made writing slow going. The note was a confession of grief, frustration and disillusionment.

"Our bitter disappointment at not being able to have a child of our own is more than we can bear," Ethel dictated. "We cannot love a stranger's cripple. We are sorry."

Marla stopped writing, mid-word and stared at Ethel in shock and disbelief.

"I found the letter from the orphanage," Ethel said. "The child's room, next to your bedroom, so nicely decorated, in greens and yellows. Decorated to welcome a child, not knowing what gender the child will be who occupies that room."

Wallace watched his wife's jaw set hard, her hand tightened into a fist around the pen as a tear spilled down her cheek.

"Write it," Ethel ordered.

Marla wrote the last few words and put the pen down. Wallace's breathing began to sound a little ragged.

"Fuck you, Ethel," Marla said.

"Such language," Ethel scolded.

Wallace's breathing became more labored. Marla looked at him with concern, but he shook his head. *Don't,* he seemed to be saying. *Don't make a big deal of it.* She leaned in, trying to catch his eye, but he kept his gaze locked onto the note. A wet, ragged wheeze tightened each inhale making each breath more shallow.

"Wallace?" Marla said.

Again, he shook his head. His face flushed red in a pattern of white blotches that spread across his cheeks as a sheen of sweat glistened on his broad forehead. His right hand shot up so quickly, Zander bolted from his chair. Wallace, in a panic, patted his shirt pockets, shoving his fingers into them. He twisted his body, wrenched his head over his shoulder to look at his coat hung by the door. He grabbed at his chest with both hands and fell out of his chair to the floor with a dull heavy thud, gasping for air.

"His coat!" Marla yelled. "His pills!"

Ethel, stone faced, nodded to Zander to get Wallace's jacket. He walked to the front door, took the coat off the hook and dug through the pockets.

"Nothing," Zander reported.

"What? No!" Marla screamed. "Wally? Wally? Where's your pills, honey? Where are they?"

Wallace's breathing had become short and shallow, sucking air too fast. He arched his back as if trying to force oxygen into his lungs.

"Do something!" Marla screamed.

Zander looked to his mother. Ethel nodded. If Wallace died of a heart attack in his own cabin, their entire plan would be for nothing. Zander stood by Wallace's side. Looking down on the convulsing man, unsure what to do."

"Chest compressions, for Christ's sake!" Marla ordered. "Give him chest compressions!

Again, Zander looked to his mother who nodded her assent. Zander knelt at Wallace's side, laid the gun down near his knee and began pressing, one hand atop the other, on Wallace's heaving chest in a forceful, regular rhythm.

Wallace coughed, spraying Zander's face with thick globs of saliva. Marla started counting to even out Zander's compressions.

Wallace's eyes rolled back in his head. Only the cusp of an iris was visible under his fluttering lids. His face had gone crimson and spit bubbled up from his gasping mouth to collect in the corners.

"Undo his tie! Undo his tie," Marla screamed. Tears streaked her cheeks.

For a man used to life and death situations, Zander was flustered.

"Undo his fucking tie," Ethel yelled.

A spray of spit erupted from Wallace's mouth, again splattering Zander square in the face. Zander wiped his sleeve over his face and then opened the collar of Wallace's shirt. When Zander felt the cold steel of the muzzle of his own gun pressed firmly against his right temple, he froze. He looked down into Wallace's face to see the actor smiling. A look to Marla to see her stone faced and angry.

"Don't move," Wallace said as he got to his feet with the gun still held to Zander's head. He ordered Zander up and guided him to the chair Wallace had just been sitting in before his heart attack performance. Now behind him with the gun pressed hard enough for the detective to wince, they all three looked at Ethel, who hadn't moved.

"Put down the gun," Wallace said.

"Or what?" Ethel said, defiantly.

"Or I'll shoot him."

"No you won't," she said fisting her hand on her hip while training the gun on Marla. "Do you know how to play chess, Wallace?"

"No."

"If this were a game of chess."

"This is no game."

"If this were a game of chess, Wallace," Ethel continued. "We'd be at, what is known as, a *stalemate*. Neither of us can make a move without giving the advantage to the other." She moved the gun a little to make her point more tangible. "The way I see it, there's really only one resolve. I'm going to take Marla, and together we're going to drive to my house. I'll call the pay phone when I arrive and ask to speak with Zander. When I'm confident he's okay, I'll let your wife leave. Unharmed. If you deviate in any way from my directive, I'll kill her. Where are the keys to your car, Marla?" Ethel asked.

"On the dashboard," Marla said.

Wallace knew Ethel would have no clue how to get herself off the mountain at night, in the snow without Marla's help. He knew Ethel knew it too. The car had trouble starting in the cold. Maybe it wouldn't start at all. He didn't want Zander's car to be a fallback if Marla's car wouldn't turn over.

"Give me the keys to the car," Wallace told Zander.

"I left them in the car," Zander said.

"Bullshit. Give me the keys or I'll shoot off an ear or put a bullet up your ass."

Zander dug into his pocket. Wallace heard the jingle of a key ring.

"Drop them into my hand. And please don't do anything stupid."

Zander did as he was told. Ethel motioned Marla to the door. Marla looked at Wallace who gave her a slight nod and a half smile.

"But mother," Zander said, sounding a little petulant, "What am I supposed to do?"

"You're a big boy, Zander," she said. "You'll figure out something."

Ethel walked up behind Marla, pressing the gun into the small of her back and had her open the door. The snow was coming down in bucket loads. There was half a foot on the front porch and eight to ten inches beyond in the yard. Wallace could just make out Marla's car but couldn't see past it. There was almost no wind and the snow came down in thick vertical sheets.

"Mother," Zander whined as Marla and Ethel walked out on the porch, the door closed behind them.

"A mother's love, eh Zander old boy," Wallace said. He'd bet serious money that the detective had a major pout on.

Wallace was backing away from Zander, around to the other side of the table to take the seat Marla had been sitting in. "I guess we'd better tie you up if I can remember where she put the rope."

The crack of a gunshot made both men jump. Wallace bolted to his feet, grabbed Zander by his jacket collar and pushed him to the door and out into the snow.

"Marla!" Wallace called. "Marla!"

Wallace shoved the detective down the stairs into calf deep snow. Ruts of snow by the side of the car told of a struggle. Wallace pushed Zander ahead of him to the car. Even in the faint half light of a cloud choked sky, Wallace saw several drops of fresh blood in the snow. As he leaned in to see them better, Zander slammed an elbow into Wallace's side and then kicked back hard, sending the actor to his knees. By the time Wallace got a foot under himself, Zander was gone.

"Marla!" Wallace yelled.

The woods were silent except for the creak of branches weighted with new snow. He ran in the direction Zander's footprints led, but stopped and headed for the nearest tree and hid behind it. From his vantage point he had a clear view of the car and driveway. Marla was hurt. If she was smart, and she was, she'd be hiding. She knew these woods. But how badly was she hurt? Maybe too badly injured to think smart, be smart. And there was Ethel. There was no telling what she'd do. He listened hard, tried to calm his breathing and focus on the sounds around him. Something, off to his right, a little behind him, was moving. Deer? Ethel? Zander?

Another sound ahead of him, across the clearing. He thought he saw something move between the trees. The snow made it impossible to see anything clearly and the woods were full of animals that time of year.

Now he was sure. Someone, about twenty-five yards off to his right was crouched at the base of a tree. He heard panting. Short, ragged breaths. Marla? Wallace moved around the tree to his left to give himself more cover, just in case. A full out run would put whoever it was at the driver's side door in less than a minute.

He caught a glimpse of a dark figure as it eased from behind a thick trunked pine to his left. It looked poised for a break to the passenger's side door it. In his mind's eye, they made a triangle with him at the top point and the other two at the opposite ends at the bottom. The snow was lightening. A crack in the clouds sent a wash of silver blue light onto the clearing. A flash of a face to his right. A shape bolted from the shadows, running full out toward the car sending up clouds of white powder into the air.

Four gunshots echoed through the woods, sending an owl into the night sky. The runner, hit, twisted and fell back into a mound of snow. And then silence. It was so quiet you could hear pads of snow falling from branches as they thudded into the snow cover below.

"Mother?" There was so much pain in his voice it made Wallace heartsick.

Wallace watched Ethel run from behind the pine into the clearing, past the car, to her wounded son. She collapsed to her knees, sobbing. She tried to lift him but he kept sliding back through her arms into the blood stained snow. Wallace eased himself from around the tree and took a couple of tentative steps toward the grieving mother. Ethel saw him, righted herself, lifted her right arm, pointed the gun at him and fired. Wallace took two staggering steps and fell heavy, onto his back.

"Wally!" Marla screamed. "Please, oh God. No!"

She dropped from a low branch of a nearby tree and ran to him clutching her left shoulder. She was at his side within seconds.

"Wally. Wally," she cried. "Can you hear me? Wally?"

She heard Ethel coming toward them. Cursing. Angry. Cursing. Striding purposefully.

"That should have been you," she said to Marla, motioning over her shoulder with her free hand to her dead son lying in a ring of blood stained snow. "He was never a very bright boy, but he never deserved this. To be murdered by his own mother. You did that. You made me do that."

Marla felt down Wally's arm, found the gun inches from his outstretched hand. Just as Ethel came into view, standing over them, arm raised, muzzle aimed at Wally's head, Marla shot her three times. Quick. One after the other. The fourth shot made her knees go out from under her. The fifth shot sent her face down into the snow.

•••

The odds of both Marla and Wallace being shot in the same place, left bicep, missing the bone, were incalculable. They shared a room in the hospital under the name Mr. and Mrs. Pennyworth, the name of a character Wallace played in his first talky. Only Joe Templeman, John Drexler, Marla's mother and the detective Philip Stanza, who was now handling the case, knew what happened up on the mountain. The new Chief of Police, Carl Coobie, officially called the case closed based on the information provided by the Wallerson's and some of the evidence secured after the autopsies of Ethel Rosen and Zander Rosen Wilde.

The report was absent the information given to Wallace during the phone call between him and Zander that compelled them to drive to the cabin. Zander knew what he knew because he lived it, lived with it, and both Marla and Wallace decided to keep it to themselves. No good could come from it becoming public knowledge.

"Evil is out there," Marla said. "No sense giving it a poster child."

Scared Pretty was never made. Everyone involved in the project agreed it should be abandoned.

John Drexler and Wallace Wallerson worked together on a movie called *Death Train* in which Wallace played a man with amnesia. As his memory returns he learns that he's a serial killer and has to reconcile the man he was without the memory of his horrible crimes with the man he knows committed them.

Both the actor and director were nominated for an academy award. Neither won.

Drexler and Wallerson worked one last time together on a movie written and directed by Drexler, produced by Joe Templeman for his new company, Starturn Pictures. It was a western called, *The Longest Shadow*. It was a movie about a sheriff of a small town who is forced to kill an Indian in the commission of a robbery. Later, it's learned that the Indian was trying to steal food for his young daughter. Overwhelmed with guilt he adopts the girl and raises her as his own. Years pass and her tribe learns the truth and kidnaps her, brings her back to have her marry the chief's son. In the end, the sheriff frees his adopted daughter only to be lethally shot upon their escape. He dies in her arms.

The critics hated it. The public loved it. Neither Wallerson or Drexler were nominated. The actress who played the daughter was nominated for best supporting actress as was the composer for the score. Drexler went on to write and direct several more pictures until his fatal heart attack at the age of fifty-one. *The Longest Shadow* was Wallace Wallerson's last film. He and Marla sold their house and bought a two story cabin, with a phone, in Arrowhead where they raised their daughter Joy. Wally finished his book which was published posthumously. Marla taught art at the local high school. Joy became a makeup artist and worked for many years at Starturn Pictures. She currently lives in Balsam Lake, Wisconsin with her second husband, Tim. They have three children and two grandchildren.

Several years after the case of the *Scared Pretty* murders was closed, Ethel Rosen's house was sold. The new owners planned to do some major renovations. During preparation for construction of a new sunroom, a secret room was uncovered. It was described as a dungeon, designed, it was believed, for S and M sex games. A diary was also discovered written by a man named Pieter Thorson. In its one hundred and nineteen pages he describes the killing of fifteen young girls between the ages of twelve to seventeen. In detail, he describes the systematic slicing of the girls over their entire bodies, dressing them in raincoats and placing their bleeding bodies at various locations throughout an unnamed city. He outlines how he wrote a note for each one and put it in their hands, confident the notes would be found by the authorities.

"My daughter is a great help to me," he wrote. "She brings the girls to me and encourages me in my work. I have taught her the pattern I use and she has become so expert at the cutting, I'm sure she will, one day, carry on our work with skill and passion after I am gone."

The *Sacred Pretty* diary sold at auction for eighty-five thousand dollars in 1962. Mammoth World Wide Entertainment announced a movie based on the diary and newly discovered police files would soon be in preproduction. The screenplay was written by G. Sanford Rosen, no relation, to be directed by John Drexler Jr. The Hollywood Reporter said veteran actor, Roy Hardgrove, 86 years old, was to have a small supporting role in the film, however, the actor had a massive stroke before principle photography began and died in the apartment of his manager, Paul Davis, with whom he'd been living for the past eighteen years.

THE END

THE MISSING BEAUTY
BY DEREK LANTIN

The 110 degree temperature hit Walters like a wall as he exited the plane door. He had been warned about the heat in this country, but this was more than expected. He hesitated at the doorway but the pretty ground stewardess quickly prompted him,

"This way, please, Sir." she said with a smile, "please mind the steps."

He smiled back at her and followed the other passengers down the steps of the Boeing 747 to the airline transfer bus waiting below. He was sweating by the time he reached the tarmac.

"This way please, Sir" said the stewardess at the base of the steps, indicating that he should get into the bus.

He smiled, hoping that he was looking relaxed and confident, and did as he was told. The air-conditioning in the bus was like a refrigerator and he gave a quick shudder as the doors closed behind him. He fished a handkerchief out of his pocket and mopped his lean face dry, then ran his hands over his short cropped black hair. He hoped he looked like an experienced traveller and not like the novice that he was.

Fortunately the bus journey was a short one. Within minutes he and the other passengers were being directed into the arrivals building.

The graphics and the signage were all in English and Walters followed the signs towards the customs area. The arrivals hall was new, gleaming and spacious, - not at all like the facilities at London's old Heathrow airport. Anxious to get some circulation into his legs, he opted to walk, rather than take the travelator. The flight had been fun and he had enjoyed it, but he now knew that economy class airline seats are not designed for six foot tall men weighing two hundred pounds.

The walk did him good and by the time he reached the immigration checkpoints, he was loping along with his usual athletic gait. More smiling ground-stewardesses directed him to the passport check and he joined a short queue. Less than three minutes later he reached the front of the counter and passed his passport across the desk to the male immigration officer. The officer gave him a relaxed grin,

"Here on holiday? He asked.

"No," laughed Walters, "a short business visit."

"Are you an engineer?" asked the Immigration officer in perfect English.

"No" grinned Walters, "just an accountant."

The officer stamped the passport with a flourish, "Accountants are the ones with the money!" he grinned.

Walters laughed, picked up his passport, said "Thanks" and walked through to the barrier. He proceeded through to the Baggage Area and was directed by yet another stewardess to an electronic console. The console indicated which baggage carousel would be used by which flight. He scanned down the list of flights and saw that bags for his British Airways flight would be delivered to carousel number eight and that the bags would be arriving within three minutes.

Walters liberated a baggage trolley from the rack, and pushed it slowly towards carousel number eight. There was already a crowd of passengers grouped around the carousel, staring at the empty conveyor belt as it circulated. Like everybody else, Walters stood and waited. In all, he reflected, it had been a good flight. Certainly thirteen hours was a long time for a tall man like himself to be cramped into an airline seat, but the staff had been courteous and friendly, the food had been good, and the in-flight entertainment had kept him amused. Nest time, he reflected, he would bring along an e-book reader with some decent books loaded on it.

Surprisingly, Walters was not tired after the long flight from London. He had been warned of jet-lag but so far he felt bright and alert; he reasoned that his high level of fitness should help to keep him alert, at least until he got to the privacy of his hotel room. This was his first overseas assignment for the company and he was determined to look like an experienced and seasoned traveller.

Jolted to attention by the sound of bags arriving, he edged forward towards the carousel. He was in luck, and his bag arrived just a few minutes later. He loaded the bag onto the trolley and followed the directions to the customs check point. He opted for the "Green" channel and walked through without being stopped.

The travel agent in London had confirmed that a taxi would meet him at the airport and take him to the hotel; he had been told to look for someone holding a sign with his name. He spotted it almost immediately. The name "Jack Walters" was displayed on a large brass sign board, held aloft in a pole; a young man in a hotel page-boy uniform was waiting patiently beside it. Walters waved at the bell-boy, who promptly sped towards him and relieved him of the trolley.

"Good Morning Mr. Walters" the bell-boy said in excellent English,

"Welcome to Bangkok. I am the hotel's airport rep. I will escort you to your car."

Walters hardly had time to stammer a "Thank you", before the boy relieved him of his briefcase, and wheeled the trolley towards the exit.

As they emerged into the vehicle reception area Walters was once again hit by the heat, this time made more intense by the smoke and the fumes of the waiting vehicles. The bellboy politely asked Walters to follow him. He did so, and was escorted to a stretch Mercedes limousine. The limo was a pale cream colour and had the name "Four Seasons, Bangkok" discreetly painted on the side, together with the hotel logo.

The bellhop opened the door of the limo, handed the briefcase to him, and politely wished him a pleasant stay. Walters took out a one dollar bill and handed it to the bell-hop. He got a wide and genuine smile in return. He thanked his foresight in putting a wad of one dollar bills in his top pocket for use as tip money and gave himself a grin; at least he had done one thing like a seasoned traveller.

He sat back in the sheer luxury of the limo as the driver closed the door. "This" thought Walters, "is one hell of a taxi."

The driver wished him good morning, explained that the journey to the hotel would take approximately fifty minutes and asked him to please sit back, relax and enjoy the ride. Walters did as he was told, stretched out his long legs, sat back in the seat and watched the scenery go by.

He wondered why he felt so strange. It was not the new surroundings, although they looked exotic enough; it was not the excitement of his first overseas trip for the company, and in fact the first overseas trip of his life. As the limo sped its way along the expressway he realised what made him feel so strange. It was because everybody he had encountered since his arrival had smiled at him. Perhaps it was because the sun was shining and people were happy, perhaps it was because these people were just nice people. He suspected it was the latter.

He noticed that the traffic drove on the left, the same as in the UK; and he wondered why. After all, Thailand was not an ex British colony. Most of the cars were new looking Japanese sedans and the elevated expressway itself was far above the standard of roads in the UK. Thailand might be a third world country, but in many areas it seemed far ahead of the UK.

At first the scenery was flat countryside with waving tropical trees, but the limo was soon immersed in the capital city. The gleaming new skyscrapers gave lie to the notion that this was a "Third World" shanty-town; Bangkok was clearly a developed capital city. Clearly his boss, Archie

Davidson, was trusting him with a serious high-powered assignment, and was throwing his young assistant in the deep end. Maybe, he reasoned, he had a good future ahead of him at Fensons Construction, - assuming he could pull this assignment off and made a name for himself.

Walters was jerked out of his reverie as the limo came to a halt at the entrance to the Four Seasons Hotel. The door of the Mercedes was smoothly opened by a bellboy who smilingly welcomed him to the hotel while relieving him if his briefcase. The boy indicated the way and Walters followed him to the front entrance of the hotel. The front doors were opened for him by two smiling receptionists as he arrived. The receptionists were stunningly beautiful young Thai girls, both wearing long traditional dresses; they beamed welcome smiles at him as he walked in.

He walked across the marbled lobby to the reception desk. A beautiful young receptionist gave him a warm smile.

"Good Morning Sir," she beamed. "Welcome to the hotel."

"Thank you," he stammered. "Err, the name's Walters; Jack Walters."

She glanced at her computer console beside her, and raised one delicate eyebrow. "Mr. Jack Walters of Fensons Construction." she said with a smile. "We have a superior corner room for you."

Without waiting for a reply she smoothly slid from behind her desk and stood at his side, "Please follow me, Mr. Walters, I will show you to your room."

She led the way to the elevators, and pressed the button. The cab arrived in seconds and Walters followed her inside. She pressed the button for the ninth floor and the doors slid to a close.

"You must be tired, Mr. Walters" she said softly. "Your room is very comfortable and you will be able to get a good rest before your work tomorrow."

"Yes," he smiled confidentially, "I'm looking forward to a long shower, then a shave, and then a meal while sitting in a proper restaurant, with real knives and forks."

She laughed. Her laugh was warm and welcoming and her eyes laughed with her. "No problem, Mr. Walters, we have some terrific restaurants in the hotel."

The elevator came smoothly to a halt and the doors opened. Walters followed the receptionist down a wide, lushly carpeted corridor until she stopped at a corner room. She opened the door and went inside, with Walters following her. He put his briefcase down on the floor as she gave him a guided tour of the facilities. The room was huge, the bathroom was wall-to-wall marble, there was a vast king size bed, and the fittings and furniture were exquisite.

The receptionist sat down at the writing desk, produced a Registration Form from her folder and asked Walters for his passport. He gave it to her. She quickly filled in the form, asked him to sign it, and smilingly took her leave.

He sat on the bed and looked at his surroundings. And grinned.

"Jack Walters" he said aloud to himself, "Welcome to Bangkok".

•••

Walters fumbled in his briefcase for the keys to his suitcase. He found them, but only after emptying the entire contents of the briefcase onto the bed. He opened up the suitcase and transferred his clothes to the closet, carefully hanging the jackets and pants onto hangers to ensure they would be neatly pressed for his meetings the next day.

He wandered around the room, opened the television set for some company, and lodged his passport in the room safe. He looked at his watch. It was five o'clock in the evening; time, he thought, for a cool relaxing beer. He took a bottle of beer out of the minibar, poured it into one of the long thin glasses provided and sat down in the easy chair to drink it. .

Walters' instincts told him that he should go out and explore Bangkok, but common sense said that was not a good an idea after a long and tiring flight. It would be better, he reasoned, to have a meal in the hotel, maybe take a walk around the block, and get an early night. What he needed first, he decided, was a long shower, a shave, and another beer, - in that order.

He stripped off his clothes and wandered into the sheer luxury of the black marble bathroom. On the vanity counter he found an array of soaps to choose from, plus body shampoos and hair shampoos. He made a selection and carried them with him into the shower cubicle. The water was pleasantly soft and the pulsating shower-head gave him a gentle massage as he ran the warm water over his neck and shoulders. Feeling the tension begin to evaporate, he treated himself to a long, leisurely shower and shampoo, and then dried himself on one of the large towels provided. He put on the white bathrobe that was hanging on the back of the door and returned to the bedroom. He took a second beer from the fridge and sat down to drink it.

Walters studied the hotel guide and found a bewildering choice of restaurants available within the hotel. The best option, he decided, would be to dine in the hotel's Grill Room and enjoy a good steak. The following day he would be more adventurous and try one of the Thai or Chinese restaurants. Having no idea of the accepted dress code in the Grill Room, he opted to wear a lightweight lounge suit, shirt and tie reasoning that he could always remove the tie and jacket if he was over-dressed.

Ten minutes later Walters was downstairs in the hotel lobby. He asked a bellboy how to get to the Grill Room and was promptly led there in person; he walked inside and admired the heavy-leather club style décor that oozed old money and respectability. He liked it immediately. The restaurant was empty, but a European Maitre d' promptly came to assist him, explained in a French accent that the restaurant would open at eight in the evening, and cheerfully suggested that Walters should relax in the lobby lounge until then.

The lobby lounge was busy with the early evening cocktail crowd. Some groups relaxed in the sumptuous armchairs and sofas, but the majority stood in small groups drinking and talking; the lounge was busy, the hubbub of conversation was loud, and the atmosphere was heady and exciting. The crowd was a mixture of Europeans and Thais, although most of the women were Asian. Everybody seemed to be speaking in English. The women were chic, smartly dressed and full of confidence. New arrivals came in constantly and looked around for the friends. Strikingly beautiful young women chirruped "Oh Chic! It's you" as they exchanged flurries of air kisses with other women they probably had not seen since the same time yesterday.

Walters found a seat at a corner table and sat down. He had been brought up to believe in the cold logic of "work equals money' but now he was in a bar where many of the people had probably never done a day's work in their lives. He gave himself a nervous grin, this was a new and unique experience. A waiter came to take his order and he opted for a double scotch with a bottle of soda on the side. At least he could try to look the part.

The drink arrived in no time, together with a plate of nuts and a copy of the New York Times. Walters drank some of the whisky, opened the newspaper and relaxed. This was an entirely new form of life, and he suspected that he was going to like it.

By six thirty the crowd began to thin out, with most of the guests now sitting comfortably in armchairs; there were mostly couples, several groups of five or six people, and a few solitary businessmen like himself. People continued to blow in and out and Walters realised this was clearly a meeting place for the rich and famous of Bangkok. After two whiskies, Walters switched to beer. The head waiter recommended a local beer and Walters tried it. It tasted good.

"How do you like it, Sir?" the waiter asked with a heavy French accent.

"It's great" replied Walters. "It's more like a German beer."

"Yes" nodded the waiter, "it comes from a German recipe, but the company is Thai owned. I'm glad you like it, Sir." The waiter hesitated for a moment. "May I ask you one thing, please Sir?"

"Yes of course" replied Walters.

"There is a slightly delicate matter I must ask you, Sir." Walters nodded, so he continued, "One of our regular customers is sitting by herself across the room from you. She is a most respectable lady and is a frequent guest at the hotel. She has asked if she may come and sit with you, because she feels uncomfortable to be sitting alone. May she join you sir?"

"Yes of course" said Walters, without even thinking what he was agreeing to, but anxious not to appear gauche.

The waiter looked relieved. "Thank you Sir, I will bring the lady across to you; her name is Senora Gabriella Fabiana."

Walters watched anxiously as the head waiter walked across the room and approach a corner table almost diametrically opposite from him. The man bent low towards a female guest. There was a short conversation, whereupon the waiter pulled back the table to make room for the lady to get up. Walters watched as she stood up and looked directly at him from across the room. His heart stopped more than a beat. Senora Fabiana was a tall, slender and exquisitely poised young woman; somewhere in her late twenties.

She followed the head waiter towards Walters' table and the head of every man in the room turned as she floated across the polished marble floor towards him. Walters stood up to meet her; she put her tiny hand into his and shook it gently.

"I'm so pleased to meet you," she whispered softly. "I hope you don't mind?"

"Of course not," stuttered Walters, "please sit down."

The waiter bowed slowly, placed the Senora's cocktail on the table and raised his eyebrows with a smile. "Is everything all right?" he smiled.

They nodded in unison. The waiter gave each of them a reassuring smile and politely took his leave. Walters envied the man's self confidence.

The Senora smiled coyly, settled into the low armchair next to Walters and crossed her beautiful legs. On most women, legs are simply there to reach the ground, but on this young woman they were an art form. She was lithe and slim, with long auburn hair and flawless bronzed skin. She was wearing "the little black dress" that all rich women seem to have in their wardrobes and as she leant forwards it cleverly revealed the beginnings of a cleavage that promised to be small, but spectacular.

Walters was not sure where to look. He grasped his beer glass for support and wondered what to do next; there was no help in sight and the waiter had long since disappeared. He put his beer glass back on the table and clasped his hands together on the table in front of him. He wanted to give a confident sort of grin, but only managed a lop-sided nervous smirk.

She brushed a few wisps of hair away from her forehead. "Please excuse the intrusion," she said softly in perfect English. "I like to come to this bar, but it's so difficult for a single girl to sit alone here." Walters nodded, so she continued. "As you know, there are so many prostitutes in Bangkok, and I can't tell you how humiliating it is to be mistaken for a hooker."

"A hooker?" echoed Walters blankly.

"Well," she laughed, "even being mistaken for a high-class hooker is embarrassing enough, so it's best for a girl to sit with a man; then she can't be bothered by men on the prowl."

Walters nodded and hoped he was smiling knowingly, but in reality he was out of his depth. High class hookers? In a hotel like this? How could anyone mistake this lady for a prostitute? Where he lived in London there were prostitutes, but they were easy to spot and usually waited around on street corners looking for customers.

Walters raised his beer glass to her in a silent toast. She delicately lifted up her cocktail glass and gave it a small chink against his. There was a kitten softness about her as she sipped her cocktail, yet her voice had a rich and vibrant quality. "My name is Gabriella" she said. "I am from Brazil. What is your name, please?"

"Jack,' he replied, "I'm from London?"

"Mmmm,…" she murmured, "I love London. But I hate the weather."

"So do most Londoners" he laughed, "But I suppose they get used to it."

She laughed with him and when she laughed her eyes softened towards him.

"Do you come here often, Jack?"

He grinned, "This is my first time here."

"Chic!" she said happily. "You must let me show you around if you have some free time. You will have some time off after work, won't you?" she asked with a cheeky pout of her lips.

"Definitely." he said. And he meant it. He looked down at the table and stammered "Is there any chance you could join me for dinner tonight?"

She looked him straight in the eyes. Her eyes were dark and deep and lustrous. "Yes, Jack" she whispered. "I would like that very much."

She leant forward and kissed him chastely on the cheek. He felt wisps of her silky hair brush his face as she did so.

"Is it OK if we go to the Grill Room?" he ventured "I have a table booked for eight o'clock."

"Yes," she murmured, "That would be perfect. I will go to my room and make myself look pretty for you, and I will join you in the Grill room at eight o'clock."

She stood up, waived to the waiter for her check, and walked across to the reception counter to sign it. As she was walking away, she looked over her shoulder at Walters and gave him a little smile. He smiled back, absorbed in her every movement.

•••

Walters looked at his watch. It was seven o' clock and he had an hour to kill. He waved at a waiter for his bill and he signed it. Then he walked out of the bar, into the lobby and across the gleaming marble floor to the front doors. Two bellboys opened the doors and he walked out onto the driveway. The heat wrapped him up like a blanket. He removed his jacket and undid his tie. He put the tie in his jacket pocket and carried the jacket slung over his shoulder. He walked as far as the pavement and felt the thick, hot mixture of humid, tropical air and exhaust fumes. The road outside was in a total gridlock, and the bedlam of angry car horns and drivers was deafening. Walters turned left and walked along the sidewalk. He would walk once around the block for some exercise, and then return to his room.

He was drenched in sweat when he walked back into the hotel lobby. Just a short walk of fifteen minutes had reduced his pants and shirt to a sodden mess. Feeling ridiculous, he made his way directly to the elevator, pushed the button for the ninth floor and went directly to the comfort of his air-conditioned room. He had time for a quick shower and a change of clothes. He opted for a pair of casual slacks and a safari-style long sleeved shirt, and hoped he could pass for an experienced international traveller. He looked in the mirror and decided that he looked all right, but he knew he was way out of his depth. What could he find to talk about with the Senora? This woman was like no other he had met and was certainly from a different planet to the secretaries at the office back home.

Walters walked across to the minibar, took out another beer, and opened it. He poured the beer into a fresh glass and gulped half of it in one go. He wondered what he was getting himself into, and why a woman like the Senora would want to even talk to him? He sat down and stared at the beer glass as if he would find the answer at the bottom of it.

He thought about cancelling the dinner but realised he did not have the Senora's room number. He racked his brains for her surname but it escaped him. In reality he had been so nervous that her name had not even registered when he was introduced. There seemed no escape; he would have to go through with it. Walters looked at his reflection in the mirror once more, then summoned up some courage, straightened his shoulders and took the elevator down to the Lobby level.

The pretty receptionist at the Grill Room gave him a stunning smile as he entered. She was dressed in a demure, Chinese style full length dress that was split up one side to just above the knee. Walters followed her to the table and admired the soft sheen of her beautiful legs and the gentle sway of her lithe little body. He opted to sit facing the entrance so he would see Gabriella when she arrived. He explained to the receptionist that there would be two for dinner, and he ordered a whisky soda. The girl smiled her approval and displayed her white pearly teeth. She had a beautiful smile.

The room was already filling with guests; there were some couples, and several groups of businessmen. Walters was relieved to see that he was neither under-dressed nor over-dressed.; he heaved a sigh of relief that he had got something right. The atmosphere was of quiet elegance and old money; there was a murmur of low and serious conversations, and in one corner of the room a man in a white tuxedo was playing soft music on a grand piano.

His drink arrived promptly and the pretty waitress leant over his table to pour the soda for him. Her eyes met his with a look that was full of promise. Her eyes were deep and brown and soft. "My name is Suchada," she said with a smile. "Please let me know if there is anything I can do for you."

He smiled at her and said 'Thank you'. He was thinking there were many things Suchada could do for him. He jolted himself back to reality with a serious pull at his whisky, and then fastened his gaze on the entrance so he would see Gabriella arrive.

She paused in the entrance, held her head up and looked around the restaurant. She sent a sweet smile flashing around the room, then she saw Walters and walked to his table. She put her little feet on the floor in a way that said she had a lot of poise and confidence; she was wearing a silk dress that swayed as she walked and high heels that showed off the soft curve of her legs.

Walters rose to greet her; she put her cheek against his and kissed him on the cheek. "Do I look all right?" she asked him anxiously.

"Yes," he said, "you look absolutely stunning."

She giggled like a schoolgirl and smiled at him. When she smiled her nose turned up like a rabbit; it was a cute smile. They sat down at the table and a waiter arrived with the menus. Daniella ordered a glass of white wine and Walters ordered a red. As Walters watched her reading the menu, he realized that she was the most poised, sophisticated and stunning woman ever to appear in his life.

She smiled sweetly at the Maitre d' and it was clear that the poor man was captivated. "Carlo", she said, "please bring me a Consommé Julienne and then, if it is possible, a Filet of Sole Bonne Femme."

It certainly was possible; for this creature almost anything would be possible. Walters ordered a chicken liver pate followed by a filet steak medium rare. The two of them were left alone; the soft candle-light kept them company and made her dark auburn hair glisten. Her laugh made sweet music as Walters told her about his plane journey crammed into an economy class seat, and she laughed playfully when he described his disastrous attempt to walk around the block earlier.

The food was excellent and the service was impeccable. They talked of everything and nothing. She asked if his family would miss him while he was away and he told her he lived alone; she told him that she lived with her parents and he registered surprise. "But the Head waiter called you a Senora," he said. "Surely that means you're a married lady?"

She giggled happily, "When I travel, I pretend to be a respectable Senora, so that men will not pester me", she explained. "At home I'm just a simple Senorita and I do as my parents tell me!" She took a sip of her wine, "I'm a banker" she said, "what do you do, Jack?"

"I'm an accountant," he said too quickly. "I work for a construction company in the UK."

She cocked her head to one side and smiled happily. "Chic!" she said, "So we are in the same field. I like being a banker; the work brings me to lots of interesting places like this. I'm here to assist some Brazilian investors who are looking for investments in Thailand. It should be fun." She paused for a while but Jack did not respond. "What is your assignment here, Jack?"

"Well" he said, "my company is doing some modifications to the British Embassy here. I have been sent here to sort out some changes needed to

she was wearing a silk dress that swayed as she walked...

the contract. The work scope has changed so we need to regularise it. It should be fairly straightforward," he said with more confidence than he felt.

She gave a small clap with her hands, "Good" she laughed, "so you will have some time off work and I will be able to show you the sights!"

Walters laughed and she laughed with him. As she laughed, her eyes softened and offered themselves to him. They lingered over coffees and sat with their feet touching under the table. The restaurant crowd was thinning out and Walters called for their bill.

"Jack" Gabriella whispered in a low voice, "I will go the ladies' room. I'll meet you in the lobby."

He rose politely as she got up, and watched her walk elegantly across the room. The bill arrived; Walters signed it without looking and slipped a twenty dollar tip inside the folder. He straightened his jacket, thanked the staff and went directly to the lobby to wait for her.

She joined him moments later and quite naturally slid her arm through his as they strolled across the lobby towards the elevators. The elevator arrived almost immediately; they walked inside and she gave Walter's arm a small squeeze. She pressed the button for the ninth floor, looked up at him and smiled.

They reached the door of Walter's room and he unlocked it. He opened the door for her and she walked in. She turned towards him as the door closed behind them and in the half-darkness he ran a hand softly through her hair. He saw her lips part and he pulled her softly towards him. Her body trembled like a nervous foal as he savoured the lush sweetness of her lips and slowly caressed her long, elegant neck. She put her arms around him and nuzzled his neck.

"Take me Jack," she murmured, "Please take me now."

•••

Walters woke up with the sun shining on his face. He opened his eyes and looked at his watch. It was six o'clock in the morning. He closed his eyes, rolled over onto his side and stretched out his arm, but Gabriella was not there. He was alone in the bed.

He sat up and looked around the room. No Gabriella. He got up and walked to the bathroom. The bathroom door was open and he looked inside; she was not there. Walters tried to fight down a moment of panic. There was no sign of her; she had gone and left nothing behind. He went back to the bed and sat on the side of it; he held his head in his hands and tried to recall everything that had happened. He had arrived in Bangkok; he was tired after the journey; a limo brought him to the Four Seasons hotel and he had been shown to this luxurious room. He remembered going down to the bar and being introduced to Gabriella by the Head Waiter. He had drunk a few whiskies and that had made him bold enough to invite her to dinner, - otherwise he would never have summoned up the courage to ask her.

He thought back to their dinner together, of the way her laugh made soft music to his ears, and of the way her nose wrinkled up whenever she smiled. He remembered how her deep brown eyes looked into his, and how the candle-light at the table made patterns in the soft midnight of her hair. She had walked across the lobby with him, her arm entwined in his and they had taken the elevator to his room. He shook his head to clear his thoughts and remembered how she had melted into his arms as soon as the bedroom door had closed behind them.

He vividly recalled her beautiful, naked body as it shimmered in the moonlight from the bedroom window; her lovemaking had been urgent as her lithe little body entwined with his. Never before had he experienced such heights of ecstasy.

He stood up and walked around the room again. On the bedside table he saw a sheet of notepaper and he rushed to get it. It was a note from Gabriella. It read

"Thanks Jack
Ciao
Gabriella Fabiana."

Walters grinned to himself, grabbed the phone and dialled zero for the hotel operator. The operator gave him a polite "Good morning" and asked how she could be of assistance. Walters asked to be connected to the room of Senora Gabriella Fabiana. He received a polite "Certainly Sir" and the line started ringing straight away. After what seemed like an eternity, the Operator politely told him there was no reply from the Senora's room and asked if Walters wished to leave a message.

"Yes" he stumbled, wondering what to say. "Please leave a note to say Jack Walters called from Room 912."

The Operator assured him she would send a note up to the Senora's room and closed the connection. Walters looked dumbly at the phone for a while and then replaced it on the hook. He looked at his watch again. It was six twenty. He would try to call Gabriella later; perhaps she was still asleep; perhaps she had left for a morning walk. He knew only one thing; he must see her again.

Walters was reluctant to leave the room in case she called. He opened up the room service menu and found a bewildering choice of breakfasts. He dialled the number for Room Service and ordered a pot of tea, cornflakes and toast. The order-taker asked him which brand of tea he required and, sensing his hesitation, she cited a range of options. He opted for "English Breakfast Tea." The girl confirmed the order and assured him a room service waiter would be at his room within ten minutes.

Walters reasoned that he had time for a shave and a shower before breakfast, and went straight to the bathroom. He looked at himself in the mirror. It was not too bad; certainly he did not look like a man who had very little sleep last night. He shaved, had a fast, warm shower and briskly dried himself with one of the large white bath towels provided. His back hurt as he did so and he turned around to look at it in the mirror; there were two lines of scratch marks on his skin. He grinned to himself, remembering how Daniella had raked her nails down his back in one of her moments of ecstasy.

A knock on the door jolted him back to reality. He wrapped himself in a towel and opened it; the room service waiter came in with a tray. The waiter put the tray on the coffee table, politely handed Walters the morning paper, and presented the bill for signature. Walters signed the bill, gave the waiter a one dollar tip and received a warm smile in return. He opened the paper, sat down, and poured himself some tea.

Twenty minutes later, Walters was dressed and ready for work. The phone rang and his heart pounded as he grabbed the receiver off the hook. But it was not her.

"Jack" said a cheerful English voice, "It's John Poulson from the office. I'm downstairs in the lobby."

Walters swallowed his disappointment. "Morning John," he said "I'll be right down."

He picked up the briefcase and his lap top, checked himself in the mirror once more, and went directly down to the lobby. John Poulson was waiting for him, smiling easily and looking every inch like a confident Country Manager. "We can walk to the office from here," he said. "It's in the building next door".

Walters remembered Poulson's easy charm and good manners. "Thanks John" he said brightly. "I'm looking forward to getting to work."

"Then you've come to the right place" grinned Poulson. "I have a whole stack of urgent things for you to sort out. First off, how is your hotel room?"

"Perfect" replied Walters. "Not exactly what I am used to".

Poulson laughed. "Please don't get too used to it. I only have enough budget for three nights at the Four Seasons. From the day after tomorrow we'll transfer you to a serviced apartment. Its just a few minutes from the office and you'll have a bit more privacy there."

The heat outside was intense, although it was still early morning. Walters noticed how Poulson walked slowly in the heat, making a point of staying in the shade wherever possible. The walk to the office took less than five minutes but Walters sighed with relief when they entered the air-conditioned building. The company's open-plan offices were small, compact and cheerfully decorated. Walters was introduced to the rest of the small team, and was immediately made to feel at home. Poulson had a team of just three construction managers, two surveyors and three clerical staff. The atmosphere in the office was friendly and relaxed, and it was clear that Poulson had a close and loyal group around him.

Walters was assigned a desk and Poulson smilingly gave him a mound of files to work through. "Have a look through these" he laughed. "It won't take you long to figure out what to do. We'll go to the construction site after the rush hour, and you can meet the on-site team. They'll give you a tour of the job and get you pointed in the right direction."

Strangely enough, it did not take long to get acclimatised. The files were all properly up-to-date and the task assigned to him was clear. By mid morning Walters knew how he should approach the tasks ahead of him. He called the hotel twice and asked if there were any messages for him. Each time the operator told him there were none. He ate lunch at the construction site with the project's on-site team; Chinese noodles bought from a stall in the street outside were enough to keep him going. He wondered how long it would take to get acclimatised to the heat. He was used to working at a construction site, but the heat combined with the dust was an entirely new challenge. By six in the evening he was exhausted.

The onsite team invited him to join them for a beer after work but he smilingly made his excuses. He was tired and jet-lagged, but most of all he wanted to go to the hotel and look for Gabriella.

The receptionist smilingly gave him his room key and assured him there were no messages. From the privacy of his room, Walters called Gabriella's number. There was no response. The best thing to do, he reasoned, was to have a shower and a change of clothes and to wait at the hotel for her.

An hour later Walters was sitting in the lobby bar, at the same table as before. He sipped his beer, pretended to read the newspaper, and waited. There was no sign of Gabriella. After two beers he switched to scotch; he thought maybe the liquor would cheer him up, but it did not work and he still felt gloomy. The lobby bar was busy, the hubbub of people was the same as last night, the buzz and excitement was the same, but one thing was missing.

At eight o'clock Walters went to the Reception Desk and left a note for Gabriella; he simply wrote that he would be in the Grill Room and would she please join him? Then he went straight to the restaurant. The receptionist smilingly showed him to the same table and he sat down. He ordered a red wine and the little waitress brought it straight away.

"Is Madame joining you tonight, Sir?" she enquired sweetly.

"Er…no" he stuttered. "I'm afraid she's busy."

The waitress smiled again, handed him the menu and left him in peace. Every two minutes Walters looked at his watch and saw that it was two minutes later than before. He waited for thirty minutes, but Gabriella did not arrive. Walters ordered a fillet steak and a salad, plus another glass of wine. The food came quickly and was excellent but he ate mechanically, hardly noticing it at all.

An hour passed. Walters called for his bill, signed it and went to the Reception Desk. There were no messages for him. He went to his room and called Gabriella's number once more. There was no reply. Perhaps she had a business engagement; perhaps she was busy. But why had she not called him? He took a beer from the minibar, switched on the television and watched the news on CNN. Even the news was gloomy. He took another shower, cleaned his teeth and went to bed.

Sleep eluded him. He told himself it was jet lag but in reality he knew it was not that. He tried calling her room again; there was no answer. He tried watching television but there was nothing of interest. He was relieved when the dawn came up at six o'clock. At least he could go to work and keep himself occupied.

•••

The day was hectic. Meetings had to be attended, both at the office and at the site. Quick solutions had to be found, amendments to contracts were quickly drafted and agreed, and minutes of meetings written up. He called the hotel four times, but each time the answer was the same; there were no messages for him.

Walters joined the team for a beer after work, knowing it would look strange if he did not. But he did not linger for long and was back at the hotel by seven-thirty. The receptionist gave him his room key, and smilingly advised him there were no messages. As he turned to go he was approached by one of the hotel's assistant managers, a tall young Swiss with impeccable manners.

"I'm sorry to bother you, Mr. Walters" the young man said quietly. "But there are some policemen here who would like to talk to you."

"Policemen?" echoed Walters blankly.

"Yes" said the manager quietly. "You see, Senora Fabiana has disappeared. The police are waiting for you in my office."

Walters followed the manager to the office behind the reception desk. At the door the manager stood aside and ushered Walters ahead of him. Sitting in the guest chairs beside the desk were two policemen. The two officers were middle aged and both looked confident; they were both armed. They got up as Walters entered and gave him stern looks. Walters looked at the men's perfectly pressed uniforms and highly polished shoes; these were no ordinary cops on the beat.

The Assistant Manager came to the rescue. "Mr. Walters" he said "these two police officers are here to discuss with you the whereabouts of Senora Fabiana."

One of the officers faced Walters and nodded. "Mr. Walters" he said in excellent English, "the Senora has disappeared. According to our enquiries, you were the last person to see her."

The older of the two policemen, pulled over a spare chair and placed it opposite him. Please sit down, Mr. Walters," he said. "We would like to ask you a few questions."

Walters did as he was told, and sat down. "There seems to be some sort of misunderstanding," he said as he looked from one cop to the other.

Neither of the cops spoke; they just sat there, looking at him. The atmosphere was heavy and the looks on the two cops faces spelt just one thing,- "guilty".

After what seemed a long time the older of the two cops broke the silence. "I am Inspector Somchai" he said in slow, but passable English. "This is Captain Prasert." Walters nodded. "The Senora Fabiana has disappeared," the Inspector continued, "We are hoping you can tell us where to find her."

Walters tried his best to look urbane and confident. "I'll be happy to assist," he said.

The Captain turned towards him and fixed him with a heavy stare. "How long have you been in Thailand, Mr. Walters?" he asked.

"Two days" he replied evenly, hoping that his fear was not visible. "This is my third evening here."

"And you have stayed at this hotel the whole time?" asked the Captain.

"Yes" he replied, "Except when I go to work."

"Where do you work?" the Captain asked quietly.

"I work for a British construction company" he said quickly. "Their offices are in Chidlom Road."

The Captain nodded. "Kindly give us the name, address and phone number" he asked politely but firmly.

Walters reached in his pocket for a piece of the company stationery and handed it over. The cop glanced at it, folded the paper over and put it in his shirt pocket. "And how long have you known the Senora?"

"Just since I arrived at the hotel," Walters told him. "We met in the lobby bar on the evening I arrived."

The younger cop looked at his watch. "So that was on the evening of the fourteenth?"

"Yes."

"And what happened after you met?"

"She and I went for dinner in the Grill Room. After that we both retired and went to bed. Look, I've been looking for the Senora since yesterday. Do you know what has happened to her?"

"What time did you retire?" asked the Superintendent.

"I'm not sure, it wasn't late. I was tired from the plane journey and I needed to sleep."

"So you have not seen the lady since the evening of the fourteenth? Is that right?" continued the older cop.

"That's right. I tried to call her room but there was no reply. I left a couple of messages for her, but she did not answer them. Please, has something happened to her?"

"And why were you looking for the lady?" asked the younger cop, ignoring Walters' question completely. "You had only just met, right? So she is not a friend or anything like that."

"Well…" Walters stammered, "She offered to show me around Bangkok and I was hoping she would be free this week."

"Did the lady tell you her schedule for this week? Did she say if she was going out of town?"

"No" replied Walters lamely. "She did not tell me her schedule. She just said she hoped I would have some time off so she could show me around Bangkok."

"So let me summarize" said the Captain slowly. "You met Senora Fabiana on the evening of the fourteenth. You met in the hotel bar. The two of you had dinner together in the hotel's Grill Room. Then you retired and went to sleep. You have tried to call her for the last two days but without success. Is that right, sir?"

Walters nodded. "That's correct. Can you at least tell me what this is all about?"

It was the older Superintendent who replied, "All we know is that the lady has disappeared."

The younger cop handed Walters a name card. "This is my card. Kindly do not leave Bangkok without telling us. Do not check out of this hotel without informing us. Thank you for your co-operation."

Walters nodded and looked blankly at the card. The two cops got up and walked out of the room, leaving the door open behind them.

Walters was alone in the room. He put the cop's card in his shirt pocket, got up, and walked through to the outer office. There was nobody there. He walked out into the lobby, retrieved his key from the reception desk and went straight to his room.

He took a beer out of the mini-bar, poured it into one of the long glasses that were kept on the shelf, then sat down and drank it. He poured another, and sat back to think. Thinking did not help at all. He got up and walked around the room, then he removed his clothes and took a shower. The water was good and hot and he stayed under it for a long time, letting the warm water gently massage his neck and shoulders. He took the bathrobe off the hook and put it on. He felt better.

He went straight across to the mini-bar, poured himself a large scotch and sat down to watch the CNN News. The news was depressing; he picked up the remote and trawled through the stations, hoping for some light relief. There was none and he gave up. He looked at his watch. It was seven o'clock in the evening. He would pull himself together, put on some casual clothes and go to the hotel coffee shop for dinner.

At the coffee shop he opted for the set dinner and a cold beer. The beer arrived quickly and it was good. He had finished his second beer when a pretty young waitress brought his meal. She treated him to a smile that would have melted an iceberg but it did little to improve his dark mood. He ate mechanically, hardly noticing the food.

He had met an incredible girl and the incredible girl had disappeared. He knew he had to find her but was lost for ideas. His two days in Bangkok had already taught him that, outside of the luxury hotels, almost nobody spoke English. How could he possibly find Gabriella if he could not even ask directions from a passer-by in the street? The only option was to remain in the hotel, stay visible, and hope that she was okay and that the authorities would eventually find her. After all he was an accountant, not a detective.

Walters signed his bill, left a one dollar tip, and walked through to the lobby bar. He went directly to the corner seat he occupied when he first met Gabriella, but the seat was already taken. Sitting there was a tall, fit-looking western man; he had the rugged good looks of a movie star; was heavily tanned and wore his jeans and open necked shirt with the smooth confidence of a man who has money,—lots of money. He and Walters exchanged neutral nods and Walters retreated to the far corner seat previously occupied by Gabriella. He ordered a whisky with a soda on the side and pretended to read the newspaper. He drank another scotch, then returned to his room and went to bed.

•••

Walters slept badly, and rose early. Even in his gloomy mood, Walters had to recognize it was a perfect day with a clear blue sky, and some sweet sunshine. By seven in the morning he had shaved, showered and changed, and by eight o'clock he was at the company offices. The boss, John Poulson, was as cheery as ever and laughingly deluged Walters with a mountain of work. The atmosphere in the office was good, positive and "can do" as befits a construction company; Walters worked flat out; twice he called his hotel to check for messages, and twice he was told there were none. He fingered the police Captain's card that was in his shirt pocket; it was time to do something positive. By two in the afternoon he had made up his mind. He walked across to the boss and asked if he could leave early to attend to some personal affairs; Poulson cheerfully agreed; only reminding Walters that he would pick him up in the hotel lobby at six pm and show him the serviced apartment where he would stay for the rest of his visit.

Walters walked to his hotel and went straight to the concierge desk. He showed the Captain's card to the concierge and asked for a taxi to take him there. That, it seemed, was no problem because the police office was in the adjacent block. The taxi was organized immediately and five minutes later it dropped Walters off at a low rise, colonial style government building. He walked up the entry stairs and approached the reception desk. There were two female officers at the desk; neither could speak a word of English. There was much confusion as Walters was asked to sit down and wait. About five minutes another female office approached him and asked what

He drank another scotch.

he wanted; her English was limited, but after three attempts Walters managed to explain that he wanted to talk to Captain Prasert's boss, and that it was about a missing lady.

Walters was shown to a wooden bench by the side of the reception area and was asked to wait. He was given a mug of scalding hot Chinese tea to drink and he waited. Half an hour later a male officer appeared and gestured that Walters should follow him. He was led down a labyrinth of narrow corridors and then asked to sit and wait again. Ten minutes later another officer came and gestured to Walters to follow him. Walters did as he was told and was led to an office and was asked to wait. The office was typical civil service, with metal furniture and filing cabinets and green painted walls. There was one window which gave a view of the mass transit railway at the rear.

The door opened and a male officer came in with a bundle of files in his arms. He beamed a welcome. "Hi" he said, "My name is Likit. Please grab a chair and make yourself comfortable."

Likit was average height, fit looking and close to Walter's age, maybe a few years older, but not by much. He put the files down on the desk with a thump, and shook hands. "Please sit down" he said in perfect English.

"Thanks" grinned Walters "It's a relief to find someone who speaks English."

Likit grinned and laughed. "There's not many like me. My Dad was a big shot in politics here, so when I was a kid I was packed off to boarding school in the UK. Hence the plummy accent. Don't let the accent fool you, I'm just a dumb cop underneath! Now then, you came to see us about your chat with Superintendent Somchai and Captain Prasert, right?"

"Yes" said Walters. "I don't know what's going on. I seem to be in the middle of something and I don't know what it is."

"Sounds like Bangkok," Likit smiled reassuringly. "Tell me what happened...from the beginning and try not leave out even the smallest detail."

Walters gave a sigh of relief at finding someone to talk to. He explained what had happened to him, how he'd had a great dinner with Gabriella, how she had disappeared, and how somehow the cops were also looking for the same girl as he was.

"This woman obviously made a quite an impression on you, Mr. Walters?" The detective observed.

"Yes," grinned Walters, "she did do that."

Likit's eyes were curious. "So much of an impression that you are now concerned for her well being; a total stranger."

"Yes. Well, she's a very charming woman and I'm terribly worried something bad has happened to her."

"Is she pretty?" Likit asked.

"Gorgeous," Walters blurted before thinking. His cheeks reddened instantly.

Likit grinned and picked up the phone. He dialed a number, had a rapid conversation in Thai, and then hung up. "Yesterday," he explained, "I called the Brazillian bank where Senora Garbriella works and was surprised to learn she was available to speak with me."

"What?" Walters wasn't sure he had heard the cop correctly. "You say you spoke with her? That she is …back in Brazil?"

"According to the Senora, she never left. She says she has never been to Bangkok."

Walters ran a hand through his hair totally mystified. "But…I don't understand?"

"Nor I, Mr. Walters, which is why I asked the lady if she would be so gracious as to fax us her picture. She was a bit leery, but I explained we were concerned her identity may have been stolen and her assistance was crucial in our investigation."

"Did she agree?"

"Happily, yes. The phone call I just received was from the clerk outside. The fax photo has just come through and they are now printing it out for us. We should have it in a few minutes."

A couple of minutes later a uniformed clerk knocked on the door and entered, He had an A4 sized photo in his hand. He gave it to Likit and then left. Likit looked at the print with a quizzical expression. "Mr.Walters…"

"Please, call me Jack."

"Thank you. Jack, please describe Miss Fabiana for me, please?"

"Let me see, she had deep auburn hair, looked to be in her mid twenties, a full figure and long…ah…shapely legs."

Likit handed him the photograph in his hand. The picture was of a fattish lady, somewhere in her fifties, with jet black hair and a beak-shaped nose.

"I assume that this isn't her?"

"No, of course not."

"Then our puzzle is getting complicated. That is a picture of the real Senora Fabiana. The lady you met, the one who has gone missing was an impostor posing as Gabriella Fabiana."

Walters looked at Likit in confusion. "But why? Who was…is…she then?'

"That is what we have to learn, Jack. Who is this impostor? What is her game? And why has she now gone missing?"

Walters groaned. "So what should I do now, Likit?"

"You? Nothing, my friend. This is a police matter and not something for you to get involved with. I need you to promise me you will go back to your job and leave this to me and my men."

"Very well, I'll do as you say. Frankly, I'm beginning to wish I'd never met the woman."

"Again, Bagnkok is a city of mystery," Likit repeated. "It can also be extremely dangerous for the unsuspecting. Do I make myself clear?"

"Yes, sir. I understand. I'll stay out of it from now."

Likit stood and gave Walters his business card with his personal phone number on it. "If you remember anything else, do not hesitate to call me."

They walked together out to the front of the building where Likit told the guard to get Walters a taxi, promised to be in touch as soon as there was news, shook hands and then disappeared back into the building.

A taxi arrived moments later. The guard opened the door and ushered Walters inside. Walters sat down and looked out of the window at the crowd opposite. Standing in the pavement was the western man from the hotel bar last night. Their eyes locked and they stared at each other until Walter's taxi disappeared into the traffic.

•••

The taxi stopped at the hotel entrance less than ten minutes later. Walters paid the driver and walked into the lobby, feeling a sense of relief to be back in a safe haven, a place where people spoke English and where he was taken care of. He went directly to the Reception, retrieved his key and was handed a message by the smiling receptionist. He tore the envelope open, his heart beating with excitement; but it was not from Gabriella. It was a note from John Poulson saying he would meet Walters at the lobby bar at six thirty, and take him to see his serviced apartment.

Walters looked at his watch. It was six o'clock. Reasoning that there was not enough time to go to his room and change, he opted to go to the lobby bar. The bar was already humming with people, but he was in luck and the seat he occupied when he met Gabriella was vacant. Walters made a beeline for it. A charming waitress appeared almost immediately and took his order for a beer; it arrived within minutes and Walters began to relax for the first time during the course of the whole day. Poulson arrived twenty minutes later, ordered a beer and sat down to join him. Walters admired the man's calm self confidence and desperately wished he could confide in him. But he knew that mixing personal affairs with business was never a good idea and Walters dared not jeopardize his first overseas assignment.

Fifteen minutes later the two men strolled out of the hotel and walked the short distance to the block where the company had its offices. Poulson then led the way along a side street and they emerged into a busy lane that was lined with restaurants. The lane was already thronged with people and Poulson pushed his way through the crowds. He led Walters to a smart, new residential building that was about ten stories high and set back from the street in an imposing driveway. The sign at the gate read "Somkid Mansions".

Poulson grinned. "Welcome home" he laughed as he pushed the door bell. The gates opened automatically and the two men walked towards the entrance. The lobby was smart and expensively finished, a security guard was in attendance at the doorway and an attractive young receptionist was waiting at the desk. Poulson made the introductions, and within minutes Walters had been registered and escorted to his apartment.

The service apartment was like no apartment he had lived in before. It was new, luxuriously furnished, and with modern fittings and fixtures. Walters smiled wryly to himself; this apartment made his flat in London seem cheap and tawdry. The Receptionist anxiously asked if the apartment was acceptable and Walters assured her it was and that he would move in after dinner. The two of them returned to the lobby where Poulson was waiting patiently.

"All set?" he asked.

"Sure" Walters assured him. "The flat is perfect. Thanks a lot".

Poulson grinned. "Good" he said. "Let's go and eat. Then you can bring your bags and get settled in."

Poulson clearly knew the street well and he described the merits of each of the restaurants that they passed. Stopping at a small Chinese restaurant Poulson explained "This place is a family run restaurant; the food is great and the prices are reasonable. Let's try it."

They walked inside and the place was already busy. A buxom, motherly looking Chinese lady eased her way through the throng to greet them.

"Khun Poulson," she laughed, "Nice to see you again. You want a table for two?"

"Yes" he replied. "Khun Tanaporn, this is Jack. He'll be living at Somkid

Mansions; I want you to take care of him. Make sure he doesn't starve to death."

"Sure" she said, looking Walters up and down as if he was an animal in the market. "He too skinny already. I take care, no worry."

Tanaporn gave Walters an extravagant wink, laughingly showed the two men to a corner table, put two menus in front of them and rapidly brought two beers. Walters opened the menu and was relieved to see that it was in English, with a photograph of each dish alongside the name. Poulson was right; Walters would not starve to death.

The restaurant was full of people, the atmosphere was friendly and relaxed, and the food was excellent. Poulson was an amusing host, regaling Walters with stories about his previous posting in Africa and making sure that his new employee was at ease and comfortable in his new environment. Walters knew he was lucky to have this man as his boss, wished desperately that he could confide in him, but knew he could not do so.

An hour later, the two men returned to the Four Seasons. Poulson settled the bill for Walters stay, wished him a pleasant evening and left him to pack and move into his new home. On returning to his hotel room on the ninth floor, Walters realized that he would no longer have the luxury of English-speaking staff around him. A feeling of dread overwhelmed him as he realized that as soon as he left the hotel he would be immersed in a strange culture and an environment where almost nobody spoke English. The thought scared him. He wondered how he could find Gabriella if he was no longer staying at the hotel, and how she could find him. The best option, he reasoned, would be to stop by the lobby bar every evening, and hope that she appeared.

Walters packed his bags, checked that nothing had been forgotten, and took the elevator down to the hotel lobby. A bell boy immediately took charge of the bags while Walters walked to the Reception, signed the bill and thanked the staff for a wonderful stay. One of the Receptionists escorted him to the front door, and ensured that a bell hop was arranging a taxi.

The evening was dark and humid, with a heavy cloud cover obscuring the moon and stars. The heat wrapped Walters up like a blanket as he stood and stared at the grid-locked traffic on the road in front of him. He saw the bell boy frantically waving for a taxi in the midst of the chaos, and exchanged a grin with the doorman who was taking care of his bags. Walters took two dollar bills out of his pocket, ready to hand to the bell boy and the doorman as soon as the cab arrived, and then saw a disturbance in the traffic in front of him. The doorman saw it at the same time and put the bags down on the pavement, ready to go and investigate. At that moment, four men burst through the traffic and started running towards Walters, each man had a gun and each gun was firing in his direction. The doorman grabbed Walters by the shoulder and pushed him back towards the lobby, but then let out a scream and collapsed on his knees, blood spurting from a gaping wound in his neck.

Walters stood frozen in fear. A man appeared out of nowhere and shoulder-barged Walters out of the way, sending him straight to the ground. Lying on the floor he saw it was the stranger from the bar; the same man who had stared at him in the taxi earlier. Now the man was standing with his legs spread, and shooting at the lead attacker; the attacker fell to the ground without a sound. The other three gunmen hesitated, crouching behind the cars that were stuck in the gridlocked street. It was all the stranger needed; he quickly grabbed Walters by one arm and pulled him upright.

"Quick!" he screamed, pulling Walters by the arm and dragging him along the pavement into a side street. Walters ran and scrambled as fast as he could, following blindly. Fifty yards into the narrow lane, the man came to a halt, desperately pushed Walters behind some garbage bins, and shouted at him to keep down. Walters crouched low and sheltered his head with his hands as bullets began to slam into the garbage bins around him.

The stranger stood behind one of the bins, his arms stretched in front of him and holding his pistol in a both hands. Walters heard him take deep, slow breaths as he fought to control his breathing, and then heard him fire, slowly and methodically as the three remaining attackers rushed along the lane towards them. Walters heard a scream of pain and knew that the stranger had hit one of the gunmen, but the roar of the handguns continued and Walters crouched behind the bins, too terrified to move and too confused to even know what to do.

The sound of the guns became mixed with the howling of police sirens. The sounds were coming closer. Walters ventured a glance around and saw a police car approaching. In the light of the car's headlights Walters saw the remaining two gunmen run back, still firing their guns. Walters heard the stranger let out a cry; then the man's legs slowly crumpled beneath him, he fell backwards and lay on the ground. The firing had stopped, but the sirens were deafening and were now mixed with screams and shouts of the police and the terrified passers by.

Walters stared at the stranger lying on the ground beside him; blood was pumping from the man's chest and his breathing was labored. Walters crouched over him, not sure what to do. "Stay still" he said, "the cops and an ambulance are coming."

The man looked directly into his eyes and shook his head slightly, "Save her" he said.

Then his eyes clouded over and he died.

•••

Walters took a slap at another mosquito and looked at his watch. It was four o'clock in the morning. Six hours since the attack outside the hotel and four hours since the cops had brought him to Likit's office. He absently scratched at the mosquito bites on his arms and legs, then held his head in both hands and tried to remember what had happened. The attack had been too fast for him to feel fear, but the sight of the blood gushing from the doorman's wounded neck burned vividly in his mind. He wondered if the doorman had survived. The chase down the alleyway was a blur, but Walters remembered the sight of the stranger, standing upright with legs apart and carefully taking aim at the pursuing gunmen; he had held the stranger as the man whispered "Save her" and then died.

He shifted once again on the hard bench. He was thirsty, but he did not know who or how to ask for water. Once he had got up and tried to leave the office but the armed cop outside the door had prevented him. He decided to try one more time; he needed to use the bathroom and he needed some water to drink. He got up and started to move to the door when the side door opened. Walters looked up with a start and saw it was Likit.

The relief must have shown in his face.

"Relax" grinned Likit. "Let me get you organised."

Walters tried to grin, but it was a weak grin and he knew it. He was tired and scared and he looked it. "I need to use the toilet" he mumbled almost apologetically.

Likit opened the door to the office and barked some orders in rapid Thai. A cop appeared and politely escorted Walters to the toilets. The cop waited, and when Walters reappeared he handed him a face towel. Walters washed the grime and the dirt out of his face, tidied his hair and did his best to adjust his shirt and trousers. He looked a mess, but he felt better. The cop gave him a grin and a thumbs up and escorted him back to the office.

Likit was sitting at the desk when Walters arrived. He grinned, opened the desk drawer and brought out a bottle of scotch and two glasses. Likit filled both glasses, handed one to Walters, and sank the other in one shot. Walters did the same and felt the liquor burn its way down his throat. He felt better. Likit refilled both glasses. "Cheers Jack" he said with a grin.

Walters sank the second glass. "What's… I mean, look,.. what's happening?" he babbled.

"Not a lot" said Likit. "There was a shooting incident outside your hotel. Somehow you got caught up in it. Fortunately you did not get seriously hurt."

"Likit," Walters said as evenly as he could muster, "that's not the truth and you know it. Those gunmen were shooting at me. They were trying to kill me. That stranger saved my life; he dragged me down the alleyway and he got killed in the process. I'd have been killed too if the police car hadn't turned up in the nick of time."

"True" said Likit with a slow grin. "Fortunately you are all in one piece".

Walters nodded slowly. "How is the hotel doorman who got shot in the throat?"

"Dead" said Likit.

"And the attackers?"

"Two dead. Two escaped. The two dead men were identified as known hoodlums with criminal records a mile long. Hired guns. We don't know who employed them yet."

Walters shook his head. He was too confused. "Likit" he said. "I arrived in this country a few days ago. I met a beautiful girl in the hotel. She disappeared. I got interviewed by the cops and everything was a mystery. Then you told me the girl was not the real Gabriella Fabiana and the real one was a middle aged lady in South America somewhere. You told me that you were looking for the girl that I met and you would keep me informed, but you did not. Then some thugs try to kill me last night; an innocent doorman at the hotel got shot instead of me. I got rescued by a stranger and the stranger got shot and killed. You with me so far?"

Likit nodded, so he continued. "Now after all that you try to tell me I was innocently caught up in a shooting accident. Then you try to fob me off by saying fortunately I'm all in one piece so it doesn't matter."

He paused for breath and tried to regain the courage to continue. "Likit" he said slowly. "Kindly tell me what the hell is going on. I want to know who was the stranger who saved my life and I want to know who is trying to kill me. Can you tell me that?"

"OK Jack" said Likit. "That's fair enough. I know some bits of the story but I haven't put all the pieces together yet, you understand?"

Walters nodded.

"First of all, we identified the stranger through his fingerprints. He was from Belgium and he was an agent working for Interpol." Walters made to interrupt but Likit raised his hand to stop him. "We know that the stranger's name was Dubois and that he was a senior guy. Very experienced."

"Do you know what he was doing here?" asked Walters.

Likit nodded. "We know a little bit. It seems he was here on a mission concerning a drug cartel. One of the cartels operating out of the Golden Triangle at the border with Burma and China. It seems this Dubois was working in Thailand with a partner."

"Who was the partner?" asked Walters.

Likit shook his head. "We don't know, Jack. The guys at Interpol wouldn't tell us. All we know is that a replacement for Dubois will be sent tomorrow. Maybe he can tell us something."

Walters looked blankly at the cop. His mind had reached its limit. He was exhausted. "Likit" he said, "I'm tired and I am scared. A beautiful girl meets me and disappears. You say she was a fraud. Some hoodlums try to kill me and I am rescued by an Interpol agent. I should be dead but I am not. What should I do?"

"Jack" he said. "Just do as I tell you. We collected your bags from the hotel; the bags the doorman had when the attack started. We are now going to put you and your bags in a police car and send you back to your new apartment. Please get some rest. I will call you at about lunch-time if I have any news."

Walters nodded; he knew that made sense. He was exhausted and about ready to collapse. The next few minutes were a haze; he was escorted to a police car where he was handed his bags. He was then driven by two cops to his new apartment. The cops took him to the elevator, and pressed the correct button for his floor. They verified that he had the keys to his apartment, saluted politely and left him alone.

Walters suddenly felt alone and very scared.

He got in the elevator and rode up to his floor. He walked slowly along the corridor, found his front door and inserted his key into the latch. The door opened silently and he went inside. In the gloom of the half dawn he fumbled for the light switch. He found it and turned it on.

He froze. Facing him, at the end of the hall, were two large and menacing

"I should be dead but I am not. What should I do?"

Asian men, Each held a gun and both guns were pointed straight at him.

"Who the hell are you and what are you doing in my..." he started, as a crashing blow caught him on the back of the head and everything went black.

•••

Walters groggily came to. He felt sick. He had a blinding headache; there was pain behind his eyes and his mouth was dry. It was pitch black and he could not see a thing. He was afraid. Trying to fight down the panic he raised his hands to his face and found that his head was wrapped in a bag of some sort.

He realised he was lying on a floor of a van; he could hear typical city noises, car horns and the sounds of traffic. The movement of the van pushed him from side to side and made his splitting headache worse. Walters tried to remember what had happened. A police car had dropped him at his apartment building; he remembered taking the elevator up to his floor and trudging wearily along the corridor. He remembered being confronted by two armed thugs in his apartment, but after that everything was a blank.

It was clear that he had been knocked out from behind; then the thugs had stashed him in this van and were now taking him somewhere. The best thing to do, he reasoned, was to lie still and pretend to be unconscious; that way, he did not risk another beating.

The movement of the van made him feel sick and he rapidly became disorientated by the frequent turns. Sleep or rest was impossible. Walters could not guess how long the van had been travelling. It seemed like a long time, but lying on the floor with his head tied in a bag made him disorientated. After a while the turns became less frequent and the ride became smoother. Walters guessed they must be on a highway. Then the turns started again. Walters could hear no traffic, but the road had become rough and the van lurched from side to side as if the road had a lot of pot holes. There was no way to avoid the movement and Walters was tossed around like a sack of potatoes.

The van stopped a few times, as if the driver was checking the direction to take. Walters could hear two men talking in Thai and occasionally he could hear the sounds of birds and farm animals. Clearly he was being taken to the countryside. For what? Fear gripped him; he assumed he would be killed and his body dumped in the jungle somewhere.

Walters heard the front doors of the van opening, then heard the sound outside of a metal gate opening. The van moved forward again, then it stopped, the engine was turned off and there was silence.

Nothing happened for a long time. He heard no sounds of activity. Fear swept over him, his throat constricted and the sweat poured from his brow and into his eyes. The rear doors of the van suddenly opened and Walters was dragged out of the rear door. He was pulled out feet first and dumped on the ground outside. Walters' head banged onto the ground and he screamed as blinding pains shot to his to his head and neck. Walters heard laughter and feared for the worst. He was pulled to a sitting position and the bag was whipped away from his head. The sunlight was blinding and Walters threw up one arm to shade his eyes. There was more laughter.

Walters used his sleeve to wipe the sweat from his eyes and looked around him. He was sitting in a mud clearing, the van was behind him. To one side of the clearing there were some wooden shacks and a barn; there was dense jungle all around. In front of him stood four Asian men. They were big and tough, and their faces had the blank look of uneducated thugs; they stood grinning at him like a bunch of prize apes.

Two of the thugs grabbed Walters by the shoulders and pulled him upright. Walters' legs almost collapsed as the cramp hit him; he wobbled but just managed to remain upright.

"What…what the hell are you doing?" Walters shouted. He could hear the fear on his voice and so could the thugs; they simply grinned and stared at him.

"I want to know…" he started, but he was shut off by a crushing blow to the kidneys. He fell to his knees and slumped forward, face-first in the mud. Walters heard the thugs laughing as he was pulled half upright and dragged by his arms towards the barn, his feet dragging in the mud behind him.

One of the Thais unlocked the door to the barn and Walters was literally thrown inside. He collapsed, face first, onto the floor and lay still. All he could hear was the rasping sound of his own breath as he struggled to get air into his lungs. He lay still for a long time, he was ready to die.

"Jack, is that you?" It was a female voice calling him. The voice was familiar. "Jack, Jack Walters, is that you?"

Walters shook his head and tried to focus. Images were swimming in front of his eyes. He closed his eyes tightly shut, and then re-opened them. He could see better. He lifted up his head and looked around him. The barn was dark, but there was sunlight coming through cracks in the old woodwork. He peered around him and saw a figure slumped on a hay-bale at the end of the barn, perhaps twenty yards away from him. He closed his eyes again, wiped the sweat away and tried to focus once more. The blurred image began to clear as his eyes focussed in the half light. He looked at the woman. It was Gabriella.

"Jack" she hissed. "Can you make it over here? I need you to untie me."

Walters nodded dumbly. He pushed himself up until he was on his hands and knees, and remained motionless while he recovered his breath. Then he rocked himself back on his heels and used his arms to push himself into an upright position. He wobbled dangerously but, in a half crouch, he made it across to Gabriella and then collapsed at her feet.

"Jack" she said urgently, "try to untie my hands from behind my back."

He nodded dumbly and crawled on all fours around the hay bale until he was behind her. Her wrists were tied with a length of rope. Five minutes later he had loosened the knot sufficiently to untie it; Gabriella let out a sigh of relief and massaged some circulation back into her hands. She turned to Walters as she did so.

Walters stared at her in horror. Her clothes were ripped and torn, her face was covered in scratches, one eye was closed and there was blood caked in her hair from a head wound.

"What happened?" he gasped.

She looked at him steadily. "It's not as bad as it seems" she said firmly. "I'm tougher than I look. It comes with the job".

"It comes with the job?" he echoed blankly.

"Yes" she nodded.

"Are you Dubois' partner?" he asked levelly.

She swivelled round to look at him directly. "How did you know about Dubois?" she asked.

"Some thugs tried to kill me outside the hotel" he told her. "I was rescued by a stranger. The man took on the thugs and helped me to escape. But he got killed in the ensuing fire-fight. He died in my arms and his last words were "Save her". So I reckon the "her" must be you."

"How did you know his name?" she asked.

"The cops told me. They said he was an agent working with Interpol". She nodded, so he continued "That's all I know, really. What I don't know is why these thugs are trying to kill me."

Gabriella looked him straight in the eyes. Her eyes were dark and serious; they were not playing games.

"Dubois and I came to Bangkok to work on a job. One of the big drug cartels uses a bank in Thailand to launder their money. We had to find out how they did it. Then we had to find the names of the people in the bank who are working for the cartel. I posed as a banker from Brazil and Dubois was strictly under cover"

"I understand," he murmured, "but why are these cartel people trying to kill me?"

"Because" she said wryly "they saw us go to bed together at the hotel. So they think you must be Dubois, my partner."

Walters sat and looked at her. He was out of his depth. "Do you think you can get us out of here?"

"Yes" she said firmly. "Listen. What we do is this…." Suddenly there was a deafening roar of automatic weapons outside. "Get down, Jack!" she screamed "Get down!"

•••

Walters crouched behind the hay bale and covered his head with his hands. There was another burst of automatic fire and then a silence. Gabriella shook him by the shoulders, "We're exposed here" she hissed. "We're going to take cover in that cattle stall near the door. Can you see it? The one to your right"

Walters peered over the hay bale and nodded dumbly. He could see the cattle stall.

"I'll try" he said and made to get up.

Gabriella pulled him down by the arm. "I'll help you. When I say "Go" we'll get up and run at a crouch to the stall. You got that?"

He nodded.

Gabriella squeezed his arm in encouragement "Go!" she said

Walters got to his feet and staggered like a drunk. Gabriella pulled him upright, slung his right arm across her shoulders and the two of them lurched as far as the stall. They collapsed on the floor together.

"Sit with your back to the wall" she ordered. "Stay still".

Walters did as he was told. There was sporadic gunfire all around. He could hear men shouting. He watched Gabriella. She had seen a pile of old farm implements at the end of the stall and was crawling towards it. She found what she wanted. It was an old machete; it was rusty but at least it was a weapon.

"Stay here" she snapped, then ran at a crouch towards the barn door and flattened herself against the wall. There was another burst of automatic fire and the barn door began to disintegrate. Then the door was abruptly kicked open and one of the Thai thugs burst inside.

Walters watched as Gabriella swung the old machete down on the back of the man's head. There was a scream and the man fell to the floor, blood gushing from a savage wound to the back of his head. The machete had fallen to the floor and Gabriella threw herself forward to retrieve it. A second man burst through the barn door and unleashed a hail of automatic fire, spraying bullets in every direction. Walters could hear the rounds smack into the wood above his head and he froze with fear.

Gabriella dived, feet first, at the thug and swept his legs from under him. She swung the machete at the fallen man but he was too quick; he rolled to one side; and the blade missed his head by inches. She swung the machete again but the Thai was ready for her; he jumped aside and then and kicked the feet from under her. Walters saw the two of them, grappling on the floor and wrestling for control of the machete.

Walters stood up, just a third man wearing a business suit charged through the door. The man held a pistol in front of him; he loosed off a shot in Walters direction and then turned towards Gabriella and the thug still wrestling on the ground. As the man turned his back, Walters saw red. He staggered to his feet and charged the man from behind, as if in a rugby scrum. Caught behind his knees the gunman slammed forward onto the ground, his head crashing into the concrete floor. Walters dived forward again. Blind with rage and frustration; he grabbed the man's head and slammed it face-first into the concrete floor. There was a sickening crunch. In a fury of frustration Walters grabbed the man's head again and slammed it forward into the floor with all his force. He did it again and the thug lay still. Walters sank to his knees and tried to get his breath. He looked around. Gabriella was crouched on all fours by the doorway, her hands and arms covered in blood. The thug lay alongside her, his throat slit open and blood pumping onto the floor. Walters froze in horror.

He felt someone roughly grasp him by the shoulder and looked up. It was a familiar face. The man was wearing a bullet proof vest and had a gun in his hand

"It's me", he grinned. "Inspector Somchai. You've done well Walters, but I think we'll take it from here."

•••

Walters sat in Likit's office in a daze. Everything had gone so fast, but now there was nothing for him to do. Gabriella sat in a chair along side him; her face was drawn and she looked exhausted. They had been taken by car to the Police Hospital in Bangkok where they had both been examined and admitted for the night. The doctors had told Walters that nothing was broken, but he would have an uncomfortable few weeks until the bump on his head and the bruising to his upper body subsided.

He looked across at Gabriella. Her face was bruised and he could see dressings on her neck and shoulders, but she seemed to have escaped without serious injury. Like Walters, she had been given a police tracksuit to replace her torn clothes. Walters looked sideways at her; she looked terrific.

Likit grinned at them, reached under the desk and produced a bottle of whisky. Three glasses followed. He pushed two full glasses across to them and they took them thankfully. Gabriella sipped her drink slowly, but Walters sank his in one gulp. Likit raised one eyebrow with a grin, promptly refilled Walters glass and then his own.

"So," grinned Likit, "this case is over and done with. We're lucky that you two are okay."

Walters nodded. "How did you know where to find us?" he asked.

"Easy", laughed Likit. "They had already made one attempt on your life, Jack, and it was safe to assume they would try again. So we kept you under surveillance. Our man saw you being snatched at your apartment and he followed the van you were held in. Once you arrived at the farm, he radioed us your location and we immediately put a strike team together."

"And the mobsters?" asked Walters.

"All wrapped up, Jack. Five of them were killed in the raid; the rest were captured. They have been interrogated and have given us the names of their collaborators in the bank, so we can get everything closed up now."

Gabriella nodded, finished her drink and stood up. She stretched out her hand to Likit.

Her voice was neutral and businesslike. "Thanks, Likit." She said "I appreciate everything you have done. I'd better go and see about getting Dubois' body shipped back to Belgium. Then I'd better be leaving myself."

Likit nodded, shook her hand and escorted her to the door. She left without a word.

Walters remained seated in front of the desk. He felt deflated and confused. Likit sat down in front of him and poured both of them another whisky.

"So Jack" he said "you have found the mysterious Gabriella. I agree with you, she is gorgeous." Walters could only give a wry smile. "And," continued Likit, "her real name is Juliana. Her surname is Rossi, and she has a Brazilian passport. She is single, age 27, and she lives in Brussels. Would you like her address and phone number? I have them here on the file."

Walters shook his head. It was clear that the beautiful Juliana wanted nothing more to do with him.

Likit looked sympathetic. "OK" he said. "I'll send you back to your apartment in a police car. Your boss has been briefed and he knows what has happened. You'd better rest for a couple of days before you go back to work."

Likit escorted Walters to the main entrance and opened the door of the police car as it arrived. He shook Walters by the hand, gave him a nod and then slipped a piece of paper into the top pocket of Walters tracksuit, "I think you might need this" he grinned. Then he closed to the car door and walked back inside the building.

The police driver turned on the siren and the flashing lights and then drove out into the driveway. Walters sat back in his seat and looked dumbly out of the window as at the driver sliced expertly through the traffic.

Twenty minutes later the car deposited Walters outside his apartment building. The cute receptionist rushed out to greet him and escorted him upstairs. She opened the door of the apartment for him and followed him inside.

"Somebody from your office came earlier today" she told him. "It was an English man. He said he was your boss."

"Oh right" he told her "Mister John Poulson?"

"Yes" she smiled happily. "He came with his secretary. They stocked the fridge with some ready to cook meals, plus some beers and wine. There is also a bottle of whiskey on the table and some snacks." Walters sat down on the settee. "I'll go now" she murmured, "If you want some help, please call me."

Walters smiled his thanks. The pretty receptionist waved a goodbye and closed the door after her. Walters was alone once more. He got up and went to the fridge. He took out a beer and poured it out into one of the glasses on the side-table. He took a sip; the beer was cold and it tasted good.

Walters sat on the settee and tried to relax. He remembered the note that Likit had put in his pocket, took it out, and unfolded it. Likit had printed Gabriella's real name and had listed her home address, her home telephone number, her mobile number and her work telephone number. He stared at it for a long time, then he screwed the paper into a ball and threw it across the room.

He found the remote, turned on the TV, and sat down to watch it. He surfed through the channels and found an English language channel with the CNN news. He barely paid attention, but at least the channel kept him company. He got up to pour another beer, surfed through some more channels and found himself back at the CNN news.

He felt very lonely, and very sad. He had met a beautiful girl; she had disappeared; he had found her again, and then she had walked out of his life without even a backward glance.

A persistent tapping on the door jolted him out of his reverie. He looked out of the window; it was dark. He looked at his watch, it was six thirty in the evening. He had been staring blankly at the TV for almost an hour.

The tapping on the door persisted and, realising that it must be the receptionist, he moved quickly to open it.

Standing in the doorway, alone, was Gabriella. She stood motionless for what seemed a long time, and then a shy, soft smile played on her lips.

"Hello Jack" she murmured, "I came to apologize. May I please come in?"

"Of course" he stammered, standing to one side to let her enter. "Please sit down. Would you like a glass of wine?"

"Mmmm…" she whispered, "I'd like that very much."

Walters gathered his wits sufficiently to walk to the kitchen, take a bottle of white wine from the fridge and open it. He poured two glasses and carried them to the salon. Gabriella was sitting on the sofa, She wore a high neck blouse that hid the marks on her neck and a simple grey skirt showed her figure to perfection. She had kicked off her shoes and her legs were demurely tucked up under her. He handed her a glass of wine and she took it from him.

"Gabriella…" he started, "Oh, I mean Juliana…"

She laughed a soft, warm smile. "It's okay, Jack, I like it when you call me Gabriella"

Walters laughed shyly. He felt gauche and as awkward as a teenager.

"I came to thank you for saving my life in the barn yesterday. I also came to apologize" she said quietly. "First of all I'm sorry that I was offhand with you this afternoon at Likit's office. I was scared. Likit is a senior man in intelligence in Thailand. I didn't want him to report me for being intimate with a stranger, like you."

"It's okay. It was not important," he said.

"It was important to me" she said urgently. "I wanted to hug and kiss you, but I didn't dare. Also I want to apologize for seducing you at the hotel that night. Because of that, you have been beaten up, shot at, captured and I don't know what else. It's all my fault".

Walters began to relax a little. He sat on the sofa alongside her.

"Jack," she said earnestly, "I have never, ever, behaved in that way with a man before. Do you believe me?"

"Yes" he whispered.

"I don't know what happened. I saw you in the lobby, and I wanted you."

"Please don't apologize" he laughed. "I have never had so much adventure in my life. But," he added with mock severity, "there's no need to repeat it".

She giggled like a schoolgirl. "I don't leave for Brussels until tomorrow night" she said. "Can we repeat part of it?"

Walters moved closer to her. His face was almost touching hers. She slowly licked her lips. He kissed her and she responded eagerly. She ran her fingers through his hair and pulled him closer to her.

"Which part shall we repeat?" he whispered

She laced her arms around his neck and snuggled her face against his.

"Which part, Jack? The part where you take me to bed, of course. Please take me now."

THE END

ABOUT OUR CREATORS

WRITER

TIM BRUCKNER - is best known as a sculptor. Over the past forty-five years he has produced hundreds of action figures and collectible statues for companies like DC Direct (now DC Entertainment), Side Show, Gentle Giant, Dark Horse and many more. Early in his career he created art for several album covers. Most notably the art for Ringo's *Ringo* cover. Around that same time he worked as an illustrator and designer. In his late twenties he wrote, performed and produced three children's albums for Casablanca Records. Sandwiched in there were a couple of special effects projects, sculpting and art directing work on the alligator suit for the movie *Alligator*. These days Tim has semi-retired from commercial work, exploring his own creative projects and writing. Tim has been writing shorts stories since he was a kid. A couple of years ago he co-wrote *Pop Sculpture: how to create action figures and collectible statues*, published by Watson-Guptill. Last year he published by first book of fiction, *Sensible Redhorn*, a collection of four pulp driven stories centered around a hardnosed crime reporter. Most recently, Tim has had the great fortune of being able to work with Ron Frotier and Airship 27. Of that Tim says "Hold onto your seats, it's going to be a pulpy ride!" Visit his site at www. timbruckner.com and visit his Facebook page for the latest news.

WRITER

DEREK LANTIN - was born in London and was educated in the UK and France. He graduated with an economics degree from London University and embarked on a career in real estate. He started writing as a hobby ten years ago, initially doing a weekly humor column. He then graduated to writing novels and has completed four adventure novels to-date. Derek now lives and works in Thailand and travels extensively in Southeast Asia

ARTIST- COVER & INTERIOR ILLUSTRATIONS

ROB MORAN - is a comic book artist/writer based in the UK: as a writer he has created; comic book series and wrote a nationally syndicated American newspaper comic strip. As an artist he has been a magazine illustrator, newspaper cartoonist, computer game designer and created posters for Scottish Opera. As a comic book artist he has worked for publishers in the UK, Europe and the USA such as Marvel, Dark Horse, Image Comics, Silver Phoenix Entertainment, Classical Comics, 2000 AD and many others. His comic book mini-series *BLOOD NATION* is currently being made into a major motion picture. You can see more of his work at http://robmorancomicart.blogspot.co.uk/

ARTIST-COVER COLORIST

WARREN MONTGOMERY – has been in the comic book industry since 1988. He has produced comic book lettering for such publishers as Boneyard Press, London Night Studios, Bluewater Comics, Simon & Schuster, and BOOM! Studios, and has colored for many small press publishers. He currently self-publish under the Will Lill Comics banner. Born in Chicago, he currently lives in Portland, Oregon. (twm1962@yahoo.com) (www.wlcomics.com)

DO YOU HAVE ANY MYSTERIES?

Would you believe that is the one question most repeated to us every single time we go to a Pulp convention, whether it be Windy City in Chicago or PulpFest in Columbus. Every single show, a new reader will stop by our tables and as they start looking through our dozens of pulp titles spread out before them, one will invariably look up at me or my partner, Art Director Rob Davis, and ask, "Do you have any mysteries?"

And for the longest time all we could was point them to our one and only, genuine mystery title, *The Ruby Files,* Volume One, which features a 1930s New York private eye created by wordsmiths Bobby Nash and Sean Taylor. The book contains four great Rick Ruby tales, two by the creators and two others by Andrew Salmon and William Patrick Maynard respectively. It's really a great book and we do have a sequel in production, though it has taken far longer to complete and get out than any of us are happy about.

But I digress.

As I said, that was pretty much it, our one and only straight up mystery title. Rob and I quickly realized we needed to correct that and in the past two years I've been working on filling our catalog with other, legitimate, traditional pulp mysteries. And I'm happy to say I've had some successes and some set-backs.

Some of the set-backs include another new private eye series based on a classic pulp character from the 30s named Marty Quade. We have the four stories assembled for his first volume but regrettably an art team has yet to be recruited. This was the same issue with a grand novel by Fred Adams Jr. called *Dead Man's Melody* which is one of the best books I've read in quite a while. We did finally manage to land a very talented young artist named Richard Jun. He is now half-way through drawing the nine interior illustrations each of our novels requires. Look for this book to be out by the end of this year.

The major success was releasing another solid mystery suspense thriller, *Motor City Manhunt*, by authors Michael Vance and R.A. Jones. Again, this was produced back in Jan. of this year and is truly a gripping, powerful tale that I have no hesitation recommending to all our pulp mystery lovers.

And now here we have *Pulp Confidential Vol One,* to add to our steadily growing list of mystery titles.

Short story writer Derek Lantin is a retired construction engineer residing in Bangkok, Thailand. He approached several years ago with a private eye tale he'd written and asked me to look at it. Although that particular piece had lots of flaws in it, they were all typical first-time-writer mistakes. Despite all that, I could see a real talent hidden beneath those missteps and suggested to Lantin that if he were willing to work with me guiding him along, we might be able to coax out of him something worthy of publication. To my delight he agreed to accept my challenge and the result of that effort was, "The Missing Beauty," which is a terrific little gem of foreign intrigue highly reminiscent of the old British thrillers of the 40s and 50s. Hopefully this will only be the first of many more stories from this gifted fellow.

Of course, at the time we were getting "The Missing Beauty" put together, I'd warned Lantin it might be a while before we could get it published as we had no place to put it.

The idea of doing an actual mystery anthology was the furthest thing from my mind at that time. But I thought, what the hell, if Lantin finished the project then I'd file away and see what the future might bring.

The answer to that thought came a year later when Tim Bruckner, a well established sculptor, came knocking on my door with a novella he'd done about a serial killer on the loose in old Hollywood. After reading it, I very much wanted to publish it but the problem existed that it wasn't long enough for our usual novel length requirements. Then I remembered Derek Lantin's short and suddenly like a bolt out of the blue, I realized we not only between them we had enough wordage to fill a book, but we also had the makings of a real mystery anthology in our hands, finally.

Thus was born *Pulp Confidential.*

In reading Bruckner's novella and its Hollywood setting, it was easy for me to recall all those old great sensation crime and police magazines that filled the drugstore racks in the 50s, titles like *True Detective,* or *Detective Confidential,* etc. etc. For whatever reason, the word confidential immediately evoked images of those great old mags and that was exactly the feeling we wanted to capture with this new series.

The last piece of the puzzle was, of course, Scottish artist Rob Moran. His love of old Hollywood movies made him the perfect choice to both illustrate these stories and produce a dynamic cover that would jump off convention tables. And as ever Rob delivered beyond our wildest dreams.

Now it is up to you, our loyal readers, to let us know if we've succeeded and are delivering the quality mysteries you've asked us to bring you. We think titles like *Motor City Manhunt* and now *Pulp Confidential Vol One*, are steps in the right direction and hope you'll agree. Thanks as ever for your support.

Ron Fortier
Managing Editor
Airship 27 Productions
6/15/2016

THE WAYS OF MAGIC

During World War II, C.O. Jones, under a different name, was recruited into a special unit of the OSS (Office of Strategic Services). Special in that all the members had some kind of extrasensory abilities bordering on magic. Their main mission was to seek out and combat the Nazis' top secret Occult Practioners.

But the war is now over and C.O. is just another veteran looking for a fresh start. He hopes the quiet little town of Brownsville, Pennsylvania is the perfect place to do so. That is, until he gets involved with the local criminal element and discovers, through his own unique gifts, that someone is using dark magic to further their own illegal agenda. For C.O. Jones, it seems the ways of magic are to be found in the most unlikely places.

Popular new pulp writer Fred Adams, Jr. delivers another scorching thriller that races across the pages with fresh, original characters, suspense and ever-exploding action. Hold on to your seatbelts as you meet the C.O. Jones, one of the toughest new pulp heroes of them all.

C.O. JONES

MOBSTERS & MONSTERS
FRED ADAMS JR.

AN AIRSHIP 27 PRODUCTION
AIRSHIP27HANGAR.COM
NEW PULP

PULP FICTION FOR A NEW GENERATION!